SAVAGE HELIX

JONAH BUCK

SEVERED**PRESS**

SAVAGE HELIX

For Brittani

Now this is the Law of the Jungle — as old and as true as the sky;
And the Wolf that shall keep it may prosper, but the Wolf that shall break it must
die.

...

The Jackal may follow the Tiger, but, Cub, when thy whiskers are grown,
Remember the Wolf is a Hunter — go forth and get food of thine own.
Keep peace with the Lords of the Jungle — the Tiger, the Panther, and Bear.
And trouble not Hathi the Silent, and mock not the Boar in his lair.

...

If ye plunder his Kill from a weaker, devour not all in thy pride;
Pack-Right is the right of the meanest; so leave him the head and the hide.
The Kill of the Pack is the meat of the Pack. Ye must eat where it lies;
And no one may carry away of that meat to his lair, or he dies.
The Kill of the Wolf is the meat of the Wolf. He may do what he will;
But, till he has given permission, the Pack may not eat of that Kill.
Cub-Right is the right of the Yearling. From all of his Pack he may claim
Full-gorge when the killer has eaten; and none may refuse him the same.
Lair-Right is the right of the Mother. From all of her year she may claim
One haunch of each kill for her litter, and none may deny her the same.
Cave-Right is the right of the Father — to hunt by himself for his own:
He is freed of all calls to the Pack; he is judged by the Council alone.
Because of his age and his cunning, because of his gripe and his paw,
In all that the Law leaveth open, the word of your Head Wolf is Law.
Now these are the Laws of the Jungle, and many and mighty are they;
But the head and the hoof of the Law and the haunch and the hump is — *Obey!*

-Rudyard Kipling, *The Jungle Book*

ONE

INTELLECTUAL PROPERTY AND YOU: A NEW LAWYER'S GUIDE TO THE FIELD

Cora Sundararajan stood on the beach of the dinosaur-infested island, sweating through her cream-colored pantsuit. The buggy, tropical heat clung to her with the tenacity of a frightened child. A fat, iridescent fly buzzed around her head, and she waved it away with her tablet.

The tablet in her hands displayed the blueprints for an elaborate power supply system, complete with a bank of sixteen refrigerator-sized batteries, roof-mounted solar panels, diesel generators, and a networked series of transformers and backup relays. It was everything that a large theme park needed to weather a major disaster without losing critical systems. And it would have worked brilliantly if hackers hadn't remotely circumvented Primeval's security protocols shortly before the dinosaur park opened its doors to the public.

Cora hadn't designed the park's power system. She was an intellectual property lawyer, not an engineer. But she had shepherded the blueprints through the Patent Office, locking up their sophisticated operating systems and innovative equipment for Richard Drake and RexNetics. They would have been the beating heart of Primeval, allowing the park to showcase all the company's prehistoric creations in perfect safety.

Even though she hadn't invented the power system, it was still partly her baby. Securing the patent had been her first project when she was hired by the RexNetics legal division. After she managed to guide the power system through the Patent Office, she had all but begged to be placed on the project to copyright the dinosaur DNA sequences that RexNetics was working on.

But her boss, Arthur Bainbridge, oversaw the legal aspects of the DNA project. And he didn't allow just anyone on that team.

Securing the intellectual property rights on the dinosaur DNA was a big lift, even before things went wrong at Primeval. However, with the park's collapse, all work in that department had ground to a halt.

The genome sequences were now inaccessible, since they were kept under digital lock and key at the park's science center. The sole copy of the DNA sequences existed on a hard drive right here on the island. A single, master copy. Bainbridge and his team didn't have access to the genomes to secure the necessary patents and copyrights.

There were benefits and drawbacks to keeping a single digital copy of the genomes isolated here on the island, not connected to any network. The obvious drawback was that if something went wrong, that data was gone. There were no backups. There was no backdoor into the system. RexNetics employees needed an actual, physical key to access the DNA data computer, like it was a rare book in a library vault.

The advantages were also plain, though. That data was worth an absolutely preposterous amount of money. A metric buttload of money, to use the legal term. And since it was worth several small fortunes, there would be the temptation by bad actors to either steal or corrupt it. Ransomware this. Malware that. Isolating the data meant that even when the park's systems went down, the hackers never got to the genome data. It was like a safe full of gold at the bottom of a lake. Very difficult to get to, but completely secure.

Regaining access to that data required an on-site crew.

That was why Cora was here. That was why Richard Drake and RexNetics had assembled a whole team. The island, leased from the government of Papua New Guinea at great expense, was the company's chief asset, and the genome data locked away here was its crown jewel. Today, the company was taking the island back, starting with securing that data.

The beach Cora now found herself on looked like a little corner of paradise. Blue water lapped at the white sand. Clouds sat low in the late afternoon sky. Dense green jungle rimmed the beach, broken only by a path leading toward the center of the island and the core of the park. The scene looked like a postcard Cora might send to someone back home if she secretly hated them and wanted to make them jealous of her vacation.

Eventually, this southern quarter of the island would be built up into a bigger tourist hub, with rides, jet ski tours, and branded shopping. The eastern quarter of the island was for employee quarters and logistics. The western quarter was where the initial dinosaur enclosures were located, and the northern quarter was planned as an expansion opportunity once RexNetics had developed a larger stable of dinosaur species.

At roughly the center of the island, there was the main pavilion. That was home to the science and learning center, which also contained corporate office space and Cora's beloved auxiliary power system. Plus, a luxury hotel and some other amenities.

Most of the infrastructure, including a network of interconnected shelter tunnels in the event of a catastrophic emergency, were tucked away so as to be hidden by the tropical jungle. Richard Drake's vision for the island was to transport people back in time to the age of dinosaurs as seamlessly as possible. And to charge exorbitant sums for doing so.

As assistant corporate counsel, Cora was getting the paradise tour for free. It would have been marvelous. Except the island was as warm and humid as Satan's armpit and it was populated by loose dinosaurs and Arthur Bainbridge was here.

Cora had been thrilled when Bainbridge asked her to accompany him to the island to help retrieve the DNA data. It was her big chance to prove herself. When he told her that he wanted to show her the ropes first-hand, it was the most exciting thing a new legal associate could possibly hear. The head of the department had seen promise in her and wanted to bring her on board the project that would save the company.

At the time she agreed, she hadn't thought about the roaming dinosaurs. Or the damp, sweaty heat. Or about Bainbridge's other potential plans.

"Cora, there you are," Bainbridge said, sidling up to her and putting an arm over her shoulders. Unlike Cora, he was dressed in a Hawaiian shirt, obnoxiously patterned swim trunks, and an ill-advised hat. And, incongruously with the rest of his outfit, he had a huge cowboy revolver holstered on his hip. Bainbridge gave her a big, toothy grin.

Cora saw her reflection in his mirrored sunglasses and gave him a polite but professional smile. She could smell the alcohol on his breath.

"Do you like my gun? Strapped it on as soon as we landed. Important to be prepared in a place like this. You shouldn't wander off from the group. For a second there, I thought the lizards had gotten you," Bainbridge said. His smile widened.

"I just wanted to review a couple of things before we head for the science center, Mr. Bainbridge," Cora said, holding up her tablet and the blueprints for the reserve power system.

"Bah," Bainbridge said. "C'mon, you've got to learn to have a little fun. I take you to a tropical island, and all you can think about is work? We're not at the office."

"There's just a few things I want to check on, Mr. Bainbridge," Cora said.

"Call me Arthur. Come over to the dock with me. I want to show you off to the investors."

"Oh, I will," Cora said, wondering if maybe she could artfully arrange to have the cargo tug take her back to Drake's giant yacht.

The boat lay anchored off the shore, its staff keeping champagne chilled for the group's return with the dinosaur genome data. The docks had suffered some minor damage during the last storm that rolled through the region, so Drake's mega-yacht had ferried everyone and their equipment to the island via a cargo tug, itself the size of a lesser multi-zillionaire's yacht.

3

"Do you have anything... different to wear? This is bathing suit weather, believe me. I don't know how you're surviving in that pantsuit."

"Silly me. Didn't do a very good job of packing, I'm afraid," Cora said.

Cora had brought more clothes than her pantsuit. She almost didn't bring the pantsuit at all, since it was deeply impractical for the climate. In the end, it only came along because she was worried about not having something appropriate to wear in case Richard Drake called a meeting and maybe, just maybe, she would be invited to sit in.

But she'd found herself almost living in the pantsuit. She'd had to lie and say she hadn't brought enough clothes. However, she'd found that wearing anything that even implied cleavage was like dangling a porkchop in front of one of the island's dinosaurs when Bainbridge was around.

"I'll see you over there. I'm mixing my signature drink for whenever I find myself on an island full of flesh-eating prehistoric beasties. I call it Rex on the Beach. Stick close. I'll whip one up for you."

"Sounds great," Cora lied. "I just want to triple-check one more thing." She looked around to find something she could plausibly triple-check.

Her eyes slid over the heavily-armed security team establishing a perimeter at the docks, the three equally heavily-armed investors Drake had invited along for a safari-style tour of the park, and then her eyes landed on Burt Westfield.

Burt was standing near the edge of the jungle by himself. He had his arms crossed and he was staring into the foliage as if he could see something far away. Cora had spoken to almost everyone on the boat on the way to the island in an attempt to avoid Bainbridge, including Drake's personal assistant, Nella, and the expedition's head of security, TK Ryder. Burt Westfield had avoided her the whole trip over, though. Cora knew he was some sort of scientist who had worked here at Primeval, but he seemed to be something of a black sheep. No one mentioned him much, and he kept to himself.

"Mr. Westfield was on the island when the park went down, right? I want to ask him a couple of things and compare notes," Cora said.

Bainbridge's smile curdled. "Burt, yeah he was here. Head of the genetics division. You don't want to talk to him, though. He's an asshole. Trust me. Had to work with him all the time when it came to copyrighting the DNA sequences. If we didn't need him to retrieve the genomes, we never would have brought him. Absolutely not a team player."

4

"Yeah. Those geneticists. Real jerks, am I right? Still, duty calls. I just need to check with somebody who was on-site about this stuff. You know how it is."

Bainbridge sighed. "Always the little worker bee, Cora. You've got to learn that this job isn't about the details. Don't sweat the little stuff. That's why we have people like Nella. And Ryder. And however many men Ryder brought along for security. Leave the details to the little guys. People like us, we've got to go for the jug." Bainbridge wasn't quite drunk, but his speech was a little mushy.

"The... jug?"

"The jugular. You're an intellectual property lawyer. You don't need to know how the thing works. You don't even need to know what it's for. You just need to know who's in the way and how to either take them out or make them your best friend. RexNetics needs attorneys who fight, not sit in study hall all day. That's what Drake hires nerds like Burt for. C'mon. Let me show you a thing or two. We have the three biggest investors in RexNetics here. I'll show you how to woo them. You need to make friends and influence people. Maybe get influenced, too. You know what I'm saying?"

"This will just take a minute," Cora said. "Then you can show me how you charm the pants off those investors." She batted her eyes, as much because she had sweat rolling down her eyelids as because she wanted to be charming.

Bainbridge's smile returned and he made a pair of finger guns before he wandered off back toward the trio of investors. At least he hadn't used the actual gun strapped to his hip. But as beefy as Bainbridge's Dirty Harry gun was, it was a peashooter compared to the huge rifles the investors and Ryder's security team were all carrying.

Cora was becoming increasingly aware that she was the only one on the expedition who hadn't brought a weapon. Part of her was relieved, since she'd never fired a gun in her life and didn't want to learn just for this. Part of her was pissed because it only seemed to confirm that her presence was an afterthought, that Bainbridge only brought her along so he could valiantly offer to protect her and she would melt with trembling, feminine gratitude.

Cora had interacted with Bainbridge in the office plenty. She wasn't even above admitting that she had tried to play teacher's pet, since she wanted on the genome copyright project. Had he misinterpreted her attention? Or was he just being an ass? Scratch that thought. He was definitely being an ass. Cora took a moment and beat back the urge to second guess herself and wonder if she was really the problem.

Bainbridge was fully capable of putting on his big boy boxers and acting like an adult.

In the office, he was professional, shrewd, and maybe a little cocky. But he and Richard Drake had been college roommates, and Bainbridge had been Drake's attorney when Drake was still just a cowboy financier riding the wave of small tech companies he'd founded and grown into a minor business empire.

Richard Drake was well-known for his impulsive, shoot-from-the-hip investments and off-the-cuff and unsolicited political opinions. Normally, Bainbridge was the voice of reason for the company.

But when Bainbridge was in the same room with Drake, it was like he was a college frat boy again. They fed off each other's energy in a way that was neither professional nor healthy.

Cora watched Bainbridge weave back across the sand toward the trio of investors. Giving an internal sigh of relief, Cora trudged across the beach. She gritted her teeth at the feeling of sand kicking into her hiking boots. The boots were the one part of her outfit that wasn't ready for a board meeting. She was not wearing heels or flats to a jungle island, but the boots weren't ideal in the sand.

She looked at Burt Westfield's back, committing to the lie she'd told Bainbridge. Cora would need to chat up the geneticist now that she'd used him as an excuse to escape Bainbridge's sweaty-palmed clutches.

She had no idea what she was going to talk about with Burt. She hadn't realized he was the *head* of the genetics division. She figured he was just some junior scientist looking for a means to worm his way into the company's good graces, not so different from her.

He looked to be about the same age as Cora, which had surprised her on the yacht. She pictured some gray-haired professorial type when they told her that a Primeval scientist would be on the expedition. He was in his early thirties or so and built like he used to run track in college but had been weened down to suburban jogging sessions in recent years. Gangly but not scrawny.

He still had his back to her as Cora approached. She cleared her throat and stepped up next to him.

"Hi, I'm Cora. Cora Sundararajan. You're Burt Westridge, right?" She offered her hand.

Burt turned slowly, as if reluctant to let go of whatever he'd been thinking about while he stared into the jungle.

"That's right." He didn't extend his own hand to shake.

Cora glanced back at Bainbridge. He had a drink in his hand. The drink had a tiny paper umbrella sticking out of it. Where the hell had he gotten a drink umbrella? Had he brought a supply along with him? Cora figured she probably had until Bainbridge finished his drink before he started to wonder when she'd come join him.

He caught her looking at him and slugged back half his drink in a giant gulp. There went half of Cora's timer. Great. She turned back to Burt.

"You were here when Primeval was evacuated, right?"

"I was," he said. He paused and looked at her for a moment. Something complicated went on behind his eyes. "You're one of Drake's lawyers." It was a statement, not a question.

"Well, I work for RexNetics, not Mr. Drake directly, but yes. I'm one of the company's intellectual property lawyers."

Burt looked at her as if she'd just told him that she could fart the entire alphabet song. "I already told Drake I was on board. After this, I'm done."

Cora wasn't sure exactly what she'd stepped into the middle of, but she was about to explain that she just wanted to ask him about... Damn, she still didn't know exactly what to ask him while she delayed joining Bainbridge.

But then there was a shout from one of the armed crew members on the dock. Cora recognized Ryder, the man in charge of security for this expedition.

"Spectrovenator!" Ryder set down his binoculars and pointed further down the beach. Instantly, a dozen big rifles, plus Bainbridge's six-shooter, were pointed in Cora's general direction, and she felt a cold sensation deep in her stomach.

She looked down the beach and saw a shape scramble free of the jungle. The creature walked on two legs, its head came up to about Cora's waist, and it was colored mostly black with a scattering of tan patches all over its body. The creature saw the assembled people and stopped dead in its tracks, as if it had just walked in on its dinosaur wife in bed with its dinosaur best friend. For the first time in months, it was seeing people on the island.

Bainbridge fired the first shot at it, and the creature took off running down the beach. A moment later, it vaulted a driftwood log and disappeared back into the jungle.

Cora and Burt both ducked as Bainbridge fired again. The three investors, each armed with rifles, also took a few potshots at the fleeing creature. The gunshots reverberated down the beach. Cora could have sworn she felt the snapping breeze of one bullet passing uncomfortably close.

"Hold! Hold your fire, goddammit!" Ryder shouted at Bainbridge and the investors.

"We almost got him!" Suzanne Fischer yelled right back at Ryder. Suzanne owned a huge stake in Primeval, along with a number of other ventures in biotech. She was also, so far as Cora could tell, a psychopath.

Suzanne fired another desultory round into the jungle. Cora and Burt had just stood back up and had to duck back down into a crouch.

Ryder turned to Cora and Burt, raising his deep voice to a commanding shout. "You two. Come back closer to the docks. We can't guarantee your safety over there."

Cora looked at Bainbridge and the investors, who were now chattering excitedly about their first dinosaur encounter. Again, she wondered if it hadn't been a mistake to come here. Her heart beat hard in her chest.

Bainbridge had sworn it was safe. Or as safe as an island full of loose dinosaurs could be. Drake had hired a small army of well-armed professionals to keep a beachhead near the docks secure and protect his coterie of VIP investors.

For the first time, Cora noticed that Burt was the only other person who had come to shore without a weapon. Maybe that was reassuring? He was one of the dinosaur experts, and he wasn't armed to the teeth. If he felt like he could wander around the beach without a machine gun, that surely meant that the island was reasonably safe, right?

"The Spectrovenator. Is that, uh, one of the dangerous ones?" Cora asked as she scurried across the sand, Burt a few steps behind.

"I thought you were one of the intellectual property lawyers. You seriously don't know anything about these animals?"

"Well..." Cora felt her cheeks flush. She knew a little bit about them. Well, she recognized the name. She grew up near the site of the original dinosaur theme park in Florida. Global Fossil Fund's park was still the most successful dinosaur adventure destination, despite increasing competition from Paleo-Genomics and RexNetics. Global Fossil Fund put some previously obscure dinosaurs on the map for the public, including Spectrovenator, which was why RexNetics had bred a population of their own Spectrovenators. The once obscure dinosaur now had a certain amount of star power, but Cora knew very little about them.

She prided herself on always being prepared. But now she felt called out, like when her mother used to pore over her report card and question her about every test and missed exam question.

Cora bristled. The dinosaurs weren't her area of expertise. It wasn't her job to know anything about them other than how to get the secret mix of genetic herbs and spices RexNetics used protected under intellectual property laws. She started to sputter something about working on the reserve power system patents and not the dinosaurs themselves, but Burt interrupted her.

"Christ. Fine. I take pity on you and your ignorance," Burt muttered. "Spectrovenator is the smallest predator bred at Primeval. One Spectrovenator on its own probably won't attack a person. Probably. But they're real bastards in a group. The first thing we told the handlers who worked with them was, do *not* get separated from your team. They can pull an arm right out of its socket, if they're feeling motivated. So, yes, they're dangerous. Just keep to the group and you'll be fine, though."

"Ah," Cora said. She had been hoping for more of a *they're more afraid of us than we are of them* speech and less of a *arms pulled out of the socket* speech. You don't have a gun? In case a Spectrovenator attacks?"

"I'm a scientist, not one of Drake's hired commandos. If something big manages to surprise us, the odds that I land a perfect kill-shot and save us all is approximately zero percent. No, if a Suchomimus or Carcharodontosaurus comes at us, I'm running like hell."

"Ah," Cora said again. "But the island is pretty safe overall, right? It's over forty thousand acres, and there aren't actually all that many predatory dinosaurs loose in the park. Most of the big ones have probably eaten each other by now. That's what my boss said."

Burt looked in Bainbridge's direction. "Did your boss make you sign a liability agreement before coming here to hold RexNetics blameless if you were injured here?"

"Yeah. Everyone did. Part of the cost of doing business."

"Did it make you promise to hold RexNetics blameless if you were mauled to death by my menagerie of genetic abominations?" The geneticist's words were bitter, and he didn't bother to look at Cora as he spoke.

"Something like that." Cora had not in fact bothered to read the liability agreement. She'd simply signed it when Bainbridge handed her a copy.

"The fact that they made all of us sign that liability waiver means that the island is not perfectly safe. The fact that you're on this island at all proves that you are a fool, actually. That's just logic, at this point."

"You're also on this island," Cora said, just barely managing to pinch *"dumbass"* off the end of her statement.

Burt stiffened for a second. Then he gave an ugly, bitter laugh. "Yes. Yes, I am. I'm here because I owe Richard Drake. And that probably makes me the bigger fool. Listen. Corinne, was it?"

"Cora."

"Cora, we are not friends. You leave me alone, and I'll leave you alone. Deal?"

"Sounds splendid," Cora said. She regretted coming over to talk to the scientist. Bainbridge had been right about this one. Burt Westfield was a certified, Grade-A asshole.

She walked off in a huff, still seriously considering whether she could beg for a trip on the cargo barge back to the yacht.

But then there was a deep, ugly growl from the jungle. The noise grew louder, and everyone on the beach turned to face the pathway leading to the heart of the island. Bainbridge swallowed the remainder of his drink in a gulp. Cora squinted, and she despaired when she saw what was rumbling down the path toward them.

TWO

CROSS EXAMINATION: TIPS & PITFALLS WHEN DEALING WITH HOSTILE WITNESSES

Burt Westfield tensed. The noise from the jungle grew louder. He saw Ryder and the security team exchange glances, their rifles in their hands.

Burt had been on the island when the park's systems collapsed and the dinosaurs escaped. No matter how much Drake hailed the evacuation as "largely successful" in board meetings, Burt knew all too well that a handful of lives had been lost. He knew better than anyone else here what the animals here were capable of.

That Suchomimus, its eyes glowing in the dusk like a cat's...

He shook his head, as if that would clear the memory away. A shiver ran up his spine, despite the sweltering temperature. Why had he allowed himself to be dragged back to this hell hole?

Because Richard Drake owned him. That was why. Drake had asked for Burt's help in this, and Burt knew perfectly well that, no matter how politely the request was phrased, it was not actually a request.

The fact that one of Drake's pet lawyers had come over here to spy on him was only proof of that fact. Burt had dealt with Bainbridge before and never found the experience particularly pleasant. Burt wasn't sure if it was better or worse that he only ranked high enough on Drake's interests to warrant one of Bainbridge's minions instead of the head of the legal department himself.

The noise from the jungle grew into a roar, and then the BMP-3 armored personnel carrier crawled out, its engine snarling. Its metal treads made a jackhammering noise on the paved path.

The BMP had all-terrain backhoe-style treads. It had armor that could deflect small arms fire and shrug off small explosions. It even had a mighty big gun sticking out of the top. The Soviet-designed vehicle was meant to ferry Spetsnaz troops around Western Europe as they spread the peoples' revolution to the oppressed proletarian masses via extreme violence and atomic devastation. It was more than capable of standing up to even a pissed off dinosaur.

Burt had been told the vehicle was not technically a tank, but Burt didn't have the military background to know why. It looked like a duck, it walked like a duck, it quacked like a duck, and it could spit large caliber machine gun fire and high-explosive shells like a heavy-duty armored assault duck.

The BMP rolled onto the beach, kicking up rooster tails of sand before it ground to a halt. The not-tank then laboriously pivoted in place, spinning around until its angled rump faced the docks and the assembled group.

A hatch on the rear of the vehicle swung open and out stepped Richard Drake, in an outfit clearly curated to convey a combination of "suave jungle explorer" and "savvy but casual business professional." He had a long-brimmed hat on his head, a satellite phone to his hip, designer jeans, and the biggest rifle Burt had ever seen strapped over his shoulder. He also had a leather jacket that was meant to look vintage and careworn, but Burt knew it was brand new and had a hidden cooling pump gadget to stay comfortable even in the tropical heat. Drake was the only person on the beach not dripping with sweat.

Nella Graves stepped out behind Drake. She was wearing teeny-tiny shorts, a crop top that probably required a hoist and winch for her to fit into, and a police-style pistol in a holster on her hip. Burt was surprised that Drake had let his personal assistant have a gun, since Burt had always been under the assumption Nella was almost entirely ornamental.

Behind her, the BMP's Russian driver and gunner piled out and stretched their legs. The man and woman wore sweat-darkened combat fatigues and looked absolutely miserable.

Drake stepped forward as the huge vehicle's engine cut off. He spread his arms wide. "Ladies and gentlemen, welcome to Primeval," he said with a showman's flair.

"Wooooo!" Bainbridge shouted, pumping his arms in the air like his team had just scored a touchdown.

Drake tipped his hat like he thought he was the suavest man in the world. It was entirely possible he thought exactly that.

"I'm pleased to announce," Drake continued, "that my little reconnaissance trip has been a success. The way to the center of the park is mostly clear, so we'll be able to proceed directly to Primeval's science and learning center and collect the genome data."

Suzanne Fischer stepped forward and gestured with her rifle. "When do we get to hunt some of the dinosaurs?"

Drake chuckled. "Always straight to the point, Suzanne. As soon as I have my DNA sequences, we'll turn you loose. First, I'm going to give you a proper tour, though."

Suzanne scowled, but she stepped back with the other two investors. Burt had met all three of them, at least briefly.

There was Suzanne, who was the big fish Drake had on the line. She'd sunk a lot of money into Primeval. Burt was pretty sure she'd be fine walking away from the park, but Drake knew how to keep her attention. Operations couldn't resume here until the dinosaurs were cleared out. Drake could have simply hired his private army to sweep the island and shoot everything that moved. But if Suzanne Fischer was allowed to hunt some of the creatures her funding had helped create, she'd put more money on the table to replace them.

The other two, Perry Crocker and Oleg Prasolov, probably couldn't afford to just walk away from the huge sums they'd invested into Primeval. They were here to take the tour and reassure themselves they hadn't flushed their money down the toilet, that Primeval could be salvaged with minimal additional investment, and the funds would start rolling in after this minor speed bump. Drake knew they wanted assurances and was happy to pat them on the head and take them on a stage-managed tour of the abandoned park.

Once upon a time, Burt had the utmost respect for Richard Drake. But like so many other idols, Drake had feet of clay.

"Please join me for the very first tour of Primeval. I will be your humble guide as we explore this prehistoric world together." Drake actually gave a little bow.

Nella clapped her hands like a child excited about the start of a show and jumped back in the BMP. The Russian crew members piled back into the armored personnel carrier as the engine snorted back to life, burping out plumes of blue smoke. Suzanne, Perry, and Oleg shuffled in after them. Ryder was next. He had a book under his arm like he'd been waiting for a train.

Burt liked Ryder from the little they had interacted. The man was large, dark, and bald. Burt knew he was the one who convinced Drake to acquire the BMP.

"Arthur," Drake said as Bainbridge came up to the vehicle. "Ladies first."

Bainbridge gave Drake the finger and then grabbed his assistant lawyer's wrist. Cora made a face as Bainbridge guided her into the vehicle like a gentleman trying too hard to impress a date. Bainbridge then proceeded to high-five Drake before hopping into the BMP himself.

Drake turned to Burt.

"I need you to verify the hard drive with the genome data. Everything is riding on that. Ready to save the day, Burt?"

"Sure. I guess." The words came out as flat as Burt meant them to be. Burt would rather not be in charge of saving Primeval. He'd rather be cleaning a bus station bathroom or working as a test subject for bear spray, actually.

"Good. That's the spirit. Use that enthusiasm," Drake said, his tone teasing. But there was something hard hidden under the joviality. Something sharp.

Burt sighed as he climbed into the armored personnel carrier's cramped body. It felt like he was shimmying his way into a can of extremely sweaty sardines. The vehicle had room for three crew, which consisted of the two Russians serving as the driver and gunner, and Ryder as the vehicle commander. In addition, there were bench seats lining the sides of the BMP with room for about ten people. Drake had modified the BMP slightly to increase the seating space because he wanted it to serve as a heavily armored party bus.

Burt sat in the nearest empty space, close to the vehicle's rear hatch. He could feel the rumble of the engine through his seat, like some sort of massage chair designed by the Spanish Inquisition. A second later, Drake climbed in and shut the door behind him, sealing them all in together. Ryder and the crew proceeded to examine a variety of gauges and dials, readying the vehicle for its journey toward the island's science and learning center.

"Mr. Westfield is the chief geneticist for Primeval, the man responsible for bringing our attractions to life," Drake said, speaking loudly to be heard over the sound of the engine.

All eyes turned to Burt. He gave a little nod and wave. He did not want any more attention drawn to himself than strictly necessary.

"Once Primeval is up and running properly, we'll have a scripted tour to answer some of the frequently asked questions," Drake said. "But since I have our three biggest investors here, I think it makes sense to give a more intimate explanation for what we've accomplished here, because I think it's something really special. That's one of the reasons that I wanted to bring Burt Westfield along."

Oh no. Burt smiled gamely. This was his punishment for his lack of enthusiasm a minute ago. Drake was going to make him dance like a sideshow clown. Burt could always refuse. He could gather himself into a ball of righteous fury and tell the truth about what happened the night the park went down.

He could do that, but he had no doubt that he'd simply be kicked out of the BMP, and Drake would have the whole group eating out of the palm of his hand again in a few hours, after apologizing for not realizing the degree of trauma Burt had been through. Then, Drake's legal goons would make his life a living hell.

"You see," Drake continued, "when I first found Burt, he was just a junior geneticist with Global Fossil Fund. But I saw that he was a man with more potential. A lot more. One of the things that I pride myself on is spotting talent and snapping it up early. Burt was one of their best and brightest, but his talents were almost completely wasted there. When I was evaluating whether or not it made sense to jump into the dinosaur entertainment market, I knew that there would be competition from the big players who had already established themselves. But there's also a number of other businesses trying to muscle their way into the market. SaurCorp. Epoch Studios. The First Creationist Church Genesis Research Center. Hell, even Martin and Wong Labs and their plan to introduce lab-grown dinosaur nuggets, bronto-burgers, and dino jerky to the market had to be factored in. But I knew there was a path. If I was quick and nimble, recruited the best people, and harnessed the newest technologies, I could create the world's premier dinosaur attraction."

"The numbers, Mr. Drake. I would like the numbers," Oleg said. "Forgive me, but I have no patience for the sales pitch."

Yes, ask about the accounting. Forget about the science. Burt sat perfectly still as the armored personnel carrier began to trundle forward at a sedate cruising pace, not much more than a leisurely walk. Let Drake put down an investor rebellion, no matter how minor, with profit projections and licensing opportunities. Burt would be useless in that conversation, and he could slip quietly into the background.

"Hold on, let him finish," Perry said with his Texas drawl. "My background is the entertainment industry, and I want the full razzle-dazzle before we get down to brass tacks. Give me the vision for this place. Why should I park my money here when Global Fossil Fund is up and running? What can you do that they can't deliver? Sell me the sizzle. If you get that right, the numbers will come."

"But the accounting," Oleg said.

"Sod the accounting," Suzanne interrupted. "What sort of results do you have? I paid good money to breed some prehistoric monsters on this damn island, and I want to see them."

Drake kept standing, one hand on a safety rail. "All three of you will get what you want, but let's focus on the attractions while we're here on the island. There will be time for the numbers when we're back on the boat. I want you to really experience Primeval. I want you to see it the way our legions of crowds will. And that all comes down to our attractions. Burt, why don't you explain how we make the magic happen here?"

And there it was. The handoff was complete, whether Burt wanted it or not. He just had to tread very, very carefully with what he said. He choked back the urge to self-immolate himself with the unvarnished truth. Instead, he put on a big grin.

Drake smiled because he knew exactly what Burt was thinking.

Bainbridge grimaced because he knew exactly what Drake was doing.

The investors looked at him expectantly because they wanted to know exactly where their money had gone.

Cora looked at him like she was getting ready to take notes from a snooty professor.

Ryder, the BMP crew, and Nella just looked bored.

"Thanks for that introduction, Mr. Drake," Burt said, talking over the vehicle's growling mechanical noises. Sweat rolled down his forehead. "As you know, there are two market leaders in the dinosaur business. I used to work for the original and, until recently, only major prehistoric genetics company, Global Fossil Fund. Their theme park in Florida revolutionized the fields of both science and entertainment by fusing them together like never before."

So far, so good. Burt had heard Drake give variations of this speech at various luncheons and conference calls a dozen times, and he was fine stealing big chunks of it, even if it made him sound like a smarmy version of Drake.

"The science, Burt," Drake said. "Tell them more about the expertise you bring from Global Fossil Fund."

"Of course, of course. I was just getting to that. Obviously." Burt licked his lips and tasted sweat. "When Global Fossil Fund opened their park, they had three major attractions. They had seven species of dinosaurs overall, but there were three that really caught the public's attention. Those were, of course, Spectrovenator, Suchomimus, and Carcharodontosaurus. I believe you've already met a Primeval-brand Spectrovenator, at least from a distance." Burt chuckled awkwardly.

"Would have seen it a lot closer up if you hadn't gotten in the way," Suzanne grumbled.

Burt pretended not to hear. "Spectrovenator, whose name means 'ghost hunter' because it surprised the paleontologists who discovered it when they found the first bones under a different fossil they had been excavating. Suchomimus, whose name means 'crocodile mimic' for, uh, for its long snout and, uh, its…"

Those eyes, glowing in the darkness from the tree line. High above Burt's head. Reflective, eerie, silent. Then, the chuff of air through enormous nostrils. The pounding of huge, scaly feet as it charged. Florence's scream.

The scream. Oh, God. Her scream. He could still hear her, if he just listened.

"And Carcharodontosaurus, whose name means 'shark-toothed lizard,'" Burt said, recovering his composure.

16

He took a deep breath of the oily, sticky air trapped in the military vehicle with them. Everyone rocked briefly as the huge machine rolled over a dip in the path.

"Of course, everyone always asks, why did Global Fossil Fund make *those* dinosaurs? Why not produce some of the dinosaurs that have captured the public imagination for generations? Tyrannosaurus. Triceratops. Stegosaurus. The dinosaurs every child can name and that have appeared in every dinosaur movie since filmmakers were using iguanas with papier-mâché horns glued to their heads as special effects.

"Since Mr. Drake hired me and my non-disclosure agreement with Global Fossil Fund was voided thanks to some clever legal wrangling by Mr. Bainbridge, I can tell you exactly why they don't produce those more famous dinosaurs. Their dirty little secret is twofold. First of all, the technology they use is extremely dependent on the fossils they can dig up out of the ground. There are a lot of limitations to that approach. Can't make a Tyrannosaurus if you can't get your hands on Tyrannosaurus genetic material."

Burt was starting to find his footing in the little presentation. Stick to the facts. Don't get sidetracked. Just a basic overview of the technologies. Like he was back in his grad school days, running an Intro to Biology lab group full of bored undergrads.

Oleg raised his hand. He did not wait to be called on, though. "But Global Fossil Fund does not use actual genetic material, *da*? It is the whole mosquito in amber problem. Blood in the mosquito is like soup in the can. It lasts a long time, but not sixty-five million years. It has an expiration date."

"Yes," Burt said. "Exactly correct. No one has ever recovered actual, usable genetic material from the Mesozoic era. Anything that has been preserved, either as a fossil or in amber, is unusable. It's either turned to stone or decayed to sludge. However, that doesn't mean you can't still reconstruct the genetic material. When Global Fossil Fund went looking for dinosaur genomes, they weren't looking for actual dinosaur DNA. They were looking for biomineralization patterns."

"This part isn't going to be on the tour, right Drake?" Perry asked. "People are going to come here to be amazed. Not sit through a lecture."

"Hush. This is interesting," Oleg said. He and Cora seemed to be the only ones interested.

Suzanne rolled her eyes.

"Just a little context to let you know why we're doing this better than everyone else, Perry. The devil is in the details, right? Burt, please continue to explain why my prospective business rivals are scientifically backwards imbeciles and how I rescued you from their idiot clutches."

"Well, it's actually a pretty clever process. There's just a lot of flaws to the system compared to what we do," Burt said.

"Give us the version with more flaws and less clever."

"Right. So, biomineralization. It's, uh, well think of it this way. When paleontologists are digging up dinosaur fossils, they aren't digging up actual dinosaur bones. The actual bones crumbled away millions of years ago. They're digging up rock that has replaced the bone through a complex chemical process. So when you're looking at a fossil, there's no DNA there. But there are chemical signatures that correspond with an animal's genetic code. DNA only really has four components: Guanine, Adenine, Thymine, and Cytosine. Rearrange those a tiny bit, and you have a unique individual's genetic code. Rearrange them a little bit more, and you have an entirely different species. But all the millions and millions and millions of genetic lines that make up an individual or a species are still just those four chemical elements. Well, the same way that a fossil is chemically different than the rock around it, those four DNA building blocks all mineralize differently. We don't go looking for Guanine, Adenine, Thymine and Cytosine. We look for what those molecules mineralize into when the material fossilizes. It's like geological Morse code. Dots and dashes instead of letters, but if you know how to read it, it says the same thing. Even if it's no longer biological material, we can see, oh, here's a string of DNA that used to read G-A-T-C and another that used to read C-T-A-G."

Burt saw Oleg nodding along. Perry looked like a college undergrad who had just discovered that the class he was excited about was taught by the oldest, most doddering professor on campus. Suzanne was cleaning her gun.

For her part, Cora actually was taking notes on her tablet now. Was the RexNetics legal department planning to use this against him somehow? He craned his head and tried to see if she'd doodled a big skull and crossbones under his name or something, but it looked like she had simply arranged what he'd said into a simple outline. She noticed him looking and gave him a vaguely dirty look. He'd be just fine if Bainbridge's lieutenant didn't like him. She surely knew she had the whip hand here. He still would have appreciated the courtesy of not being so obviously monitored.

"That means that the fossils don't have any actual genetic material, but on the microscopic level, you have the essential instructions written down in the rock itself. It's not exactly carved stone tablets for how to make a dinosaur, but it's pretty close. Of course, there are plenty of gaps due to the fact that it's impossible to get perfect preservation down to the cellular level. You can grind up a whole fossil and only find a few usable fragments of genetic code, so Global Fossil has an AI system that examines the fossils at a granular level and then fills in the gaps as best it can. You have to powderize *a lot* of fossil material, but eventually, the AI hoovers up enough data to give you a fairly complete picture of the genome. The AI recognizes which chemicals and mineralogical signatures correspond to what DNA element and extrapolates as needed."

"You use AI to fill the gaps? Not just borrowing DNA strands from another living organism?" Oleg asked.

"No need to. The entire genome is digital. Just a blueprint. There's no DNA involved until we start building it from scratch, using the digital genome as a guide. Like how a cake recipe isn't made out of cake," Burt said.

"No messy dinosaur goop needed," Drake added. "Now, tell them the dirty little secret Global Fossil Fund doesn't like people to know about."

"Right. That gets back to why they didn't try to grow a Tyrannosaurus straight away. They would need a Tyrannosaurus fossil to put together that blueprint. Probably a lot of Tyrannosaur fossils, honestly. And the process destroys the fossils. Most of the best-known dinosaurs, like Tyrannosaurus, are from the United States. Or sometimes Europe. Most of the early paleontologists were American or British. Othniel Charles Marsh. Edward Drinker Cope. Gideon Mantell. So obviously the early big discoveries happened in their proverbial backyards."

"Hmmph." Suzanne Fischer made a frustrated noise, and Burt realized he was losing his audience. She sat like a child who had been told to finish her peas if she wanted ice cream.

He talked faster. "North America and Europe have some very strict laws against digging up and then grinding up their fossils so you can make fat bags of money running a dinosaur zoo. Politicians tend to get a bit upset when you plunder the nation's geological history to make a cheap buck. But back in the Mesozoic, dinosaurs were spread across the globe. Sure, certain species mainly lived in what are now separate countries, but there were a lot of dinosaurs in places that currently have little to no legal infrastructure about preserving their fossil history. Spectrovenator fossils are found in South America. Suchomimus and Carcharodontosaurus are both most easily found in certain remote African fossil beds. Where there are laws about preserving geological finds, Global Fossil Fund found legal loopholes, smuggled fossils out, or just paid some generous bribes. I won't say that absolutely wouldn't work in the United States, where Tyrannosaurs fossils are found, but it would be harder to do systematically and at scale. The governments that are the most amenable to selling their fossil riches aren't the places where the best-known dinosaurs come from."

Maybe it was just Burt's imagination, but it seemed like Suzanne perked up a little at the word 'bribes.'

"But Paleo-Genomics has a T. rex at their park," Perry said. "Velociraptor. Spinosaurus. All the classics."

"And that brings me to Paleo-Genomics, Primeval's other big competitor. Yes, they do have a Tyrannosaurus. Well, technically, they don't, actually. They have the same problem as Global Fossil Fund. They can't get their hands on any genuine Tyrannosaur DNA. Biomineralized DNA, that is. They can't dig any specimens up, and museums aren't willing to sell them fossils that will be destroyed. So Paleo-Genomics came up with a solution. They use CRISPR to make their dinosaurs."

"They use what now?" Perry asked.

"The DNA splice-y thingy," Oleg said, clearly pleased that he had a leg up on Perry.

"Exactly. The DNA splice-y thingy. CRISPR stands for Clustered Regularly Interspaced Short Palindromic Repeats. Scientists studying the immune systems of bacteria discovered it. CRISPR is basically an enzyme that bacteria use to identify foreign DNA sequences, like say, from a virus trying to hijack the cell. The enzyme detects the viral DNA, springs into action, and chops up the invader's genetic material. But it's surprisingly easy to train CRISPR to target any DNA sequence you want. If you convince CRISPR to go after a particular gene, it will go and chop that gene out of a cell's genetic code. But you can also swap out the gene for one of your choosing. It's a relatively easy matter to take lab mice embryos, lop off the gene that gives them their pigmentation, and *voila*, you have a litter of albino lab mice. Paleo-Genomics starts with an entirely different, modern-day animal DNA sequence. Then they add their various bells and whistles until they have a different organism from their starting one. Global Fossil Fund is using a photocopier on genuine DNA sequences. Paleo-Genomics is using modeling clay and smooshing it into a new shape."

"What starting point organism does Paleo-Genomics use?" Oleg asked.

"Chickens," Burt said.

"Chickens? Like, the Kentucky-fried kind?"

"Yes. Birds are the closest living relatives to dinosaurs. Chicken genetic code is pretty well understood, and it's very, very easy to get more chickens if you screw up your do-it-yourself dinosaur genes the first few thousand times. But you can see why Paleo-Genomics doesn't like to publicize the science behind their dinosaurs. Their T. rex is actually just a very, very large, custom-made Rhode Island Red."

"And since Primeval has Spectrovenator and Carcharodontosaurus instead of Velociraptor and Tyrannosaurus, then you must use the Global Fossil technique of grinding up real fossils, yes?" Oleg asked.

Burt glanced at Drake for a second. Drake nodded almost imperceptibly.

"Actually, no. We use the CRISPR method," Burt said. The answer was practiced and smooth and even partially true.

All three investors looked annoyed by this information.

"If you're using CRISPR, why not make the A-list dinosaurs, then? Sure, Carcharodontosaurus is a big deal now, but it'll never have the same cultural cache as a Tyrannosaurus," Perry said.

"Drake, please don't tell me you've screwed the pooch on this," Suzanne said. "People like their classic dinosaurs. That's the whole reason that Paleo-Genomics has been able to eat into Global Fossil Fund's market share so handily."

"Fear not," Drake said, raising a placating hand. "It's all part of the plan. Primeval was always meant to be a multi-phase project. We're taking advantage of the fact that our competitors have exclusive dinosaur creation tools and combining their respective strengths. Step One was to basically copy off Global Fossil's notes because Global Fossil has authenticity on its side. By creating more or less exact duplicates of Global Fossil Fund's creatures, we can establish that we also have 'real' dinosaurs. So when we move on to Phase Two and make a Tyrannosaurus, it will benefit from the perceived authenticity of our first batch of dinosaurs. If we make a Tyrannosaurus now, the public will just say it's another big chicken, and what's worse, a copy of our competitor's big chicken. But if we show we *perfected* CRISPR dinosaurs, and then we make a Tyrannosaurus, it will be more 'real' than the Paleo-Genomics Tyrannosaurus. Not because we used real DNA, but because our dinosaurs are perceived as having that authenticity. We'll bridge the gap and have an all-star lineup that pulls from the stables of both Global Fossil and Paleo-Genomics. We'll copy both their rosters, plus come up with a few surprises of our own that I'm *very* excited about. That will put us in a good position to become the market leader in just a few years."

Nella, Drake's personal assistant, spoke up, her California accent a bubbly counterpoint to the grumble of the BMP's engine. "You're so smart, Mr. Drake."

"Hold up a second. Wait," the junior attorney said. Cora looked around, realizing that the attention of her boss and her boss's boss was suddenly upon her. "Can we just avoid saying we copied anybody's dinosaurs? I don't know what Global Fossil's legal team is up to, but let's not give them an opportunity to take anything out of context."

"Don't worry about it, Cora. We have a plan," Bainbridge said.

Suzanne spoke up for the first time in a while. "Do you have a plan, Drake? Because if I were Global Fossil Fund and I heard about this conversation, I think I'd have your ass on a magnet on my refrigerator."

Burt wasn't sure what that meant exactly, but the gist was clear enough. He was more interested in Cora, though. How had she not known about the legal maneuverings on the genomes? That was her job. Was she just an incompetent plaything for Bainbridge? Or was she simply teeing up a pitch for her boss?

If anybody noticed the expression on Burt's face, they didn't comment on it.

"That's been accounted for," Drake said, throwing a quick glance toward Burt. "And my legal team actually raises a good point. Arthur, do you want to explain this part?"

"Sure," Bainbridge said. "Cora, stay out of this. It's beyond your expertise. At a glance, it looks like Global Fossil Fund delivers a very similar product to what we produce. But from a legal perspective, that's not actually true. Again, Global Fossil is making, for lack of a better term, 'real' dinosaurs from real, naturally occurring genetic instructions. They've simply used a very roundabout way to acquire their animals. But really, they're just a fancy zoo. And at the end of the day, you can't patent a lion. Even if you have a lion breeding program, the cubs aren't your intellectual property. You don't get to tell every other zoo in the world to take down their lion exhibits just because you already have a lion. But if you *build* a lion? From scratch? That's something else from a legal perspective. You can take your lion blueprint and make it your intellectual property. That's what Paleo-Genomics did, and it's what we're doing, too. The dinosaurs on this island look essentially identical to what you can see at the Global Fossil Fund park, but our animals are very different under the hood. We *own* these animals, right down to their genetic code. That's part of the reason it's so important for us to get that genetic information off the island. It's like Coke and Pepsi. Pour them in an unlabeled glass, and you can't tell which is which just by looking. But their lawyers will come knock your teeth out if you infringe on their trademarks and licensing deals."

This answer seemed to satisfy Suzanne.

"Once we have that genetic code back, we can patent it. We can license it. We can sue startups that look like they might be infringing on our intellectual property rights. We can shove our weight around to better control the market."

"All the benefits of real prehistoric monsters. None of the downsides," Drake said.

But there were downsides.

Burt thought of those glowing eyes in the darkness again. Florence's scream. The mad dash through the jungle as Primeval's systems started to fail one-by-one. The very same jungle the BMP was currently carrying them deeper into.

There were definitely downsides.

THREE

PROTECTING SENSITIVE DATA: YOUR LEGAL GUIDE TO KEEPING PRIVILEGED INFORMATION SECURE IN A DIGITAL ERA

Cora sat in the rumbling BMP, trying not to look as annoyed as she felt that Bainbridge had undercut her in front of everyone. *Cora, stay out of this. It's beyond your expertise.*

What a burlap sack of horse shit.

She was the one who had been pushing to get onto the genome patenting project after her work on the power system. She was the one who had been telling Bainbridge how excited she was to go to this island to get first-hand experience with the DNA, since she'd been studying up on the case law surrounding bioengineering. She knew as much about the topic as anybody.

Cora was increasingly aware that she wasn't here for any particular job. Almost everyone but her had a gun. And now she was noticing that almost everyone but her had a satellite phone, too. Burt was the only other person who hadn't received one for some reason. But she'd been left out of the loop entirely.

Goddammit.

She sat and stewed, trying to look unperturbed by the insult and probably failing. She caught Burt looking at her. She shot him a look that could curdle milk from ten paces and then forced herself to ignore him.

She'd come here to learn the ins and outs of RexNetics, and she wasn't going to let Bainbridge's antics spoil that for her. It was still a major opportunity to listen to Richard Drake wine and dine his investors.

Perry, Oleg, and Suzanne were here specifically because they wanted Drake to financially seduce them. Getting to watch the man in action was a golden opportunity for Cora, too. It would be a major feather in her cap to say that she was on the expedition where Drake convinced his backers to bankroll Primeval to its successful opening. Just being in the room, or the crowded, smelly armored personnel carrier, was something of an honor. Not even Bainbridge could take the shine off that part of the experience.

Cora sat and listened as Drake continued to lay it on smooth for the benefit of his audience. The BMP was crawling along, barely faster than a walk, so as not to rush Drake and force him to wrap up his spiel too early.

One thing Cora did notice was that Drake effectively glossed over the reason that Primeval wasn't already operational and ready for visitors. Leasing the island from the government of Papua New Guinea was a done deal. The park had nearly all the infrastructure it needed, including a mostly furnished luxury hotel, emergency shelters and tunnels, a state-of-the-art paleo-veterinary center, utilities, and all the other facilities a zoo and theme park could need. Plus, the island had a prime global position to attract visitors from Australia, New Zealand, China, Japan, and the west coast of America. Cruise ships should have been disgorging visitors hourly months ago.

If not for the hackers, Primeval would have completed Phase One of the business plan, the park would be awash in tourist money, and Drake would be barreling toward Phase Two.

No one was exactly sure who had brought down Primeval's entire computer network. Every interconnected system was affected. A rather obscure group of animal rights activists had claimed credit, but no one really believed they had the capability. Internal security audits had been circulated, but the only thing they made clear was that whoever accessed the system had stolen the keys to the whole prehistoric kingdom.

The power hadn't gone out at Primeval. The auxiliary power system and backup batteries Cora was so familiar with had ensured that. But it might have been better if the power had failed altogether.

Instead, incubators cooked the giant eggs they were meant to hatch as their temperature settings went haywire. The fire control system in one of the science labs went berserk and nearly killed a technician when it started to fill the room with suppressant gas. The "smart" vending machines charged every single employee on the island for forty-one thousand cans of grape soda and tried to automatically deduct the amount from their paychecks.

And the dinosaur enclosure gates opened all across the island.

The power was shut down when the last employees evacuated the island, but the damage had been done. Cora had seen some redacted error logs, sections of which were blacked out like CIA classified documents to protect Primeval's secret projects. Not even Cora knew exactly how much the hackers had disrupted the park's systems. Maybe only Drake had the full picture.

The hackers were good. Due to the island's remote location, there were limited avenues to get into the park's systems. Most of the crucial networks operated on a semi-closed loop, with only a few, closely monitored ways to connect to any mainland networks. But somehow, the hackers found a backdoor.

But strangely, the individual or group responsible didn't seem to want anything. There'd been no demand for money that Cora was aware of. No rambling manifestos about how Richard Drake was a pig. No warnings that hellfire and brimstone would rain down on Primeval if the scientists didn't forgo their plans to tamper with God's will. So far as anyone could tell, none of the employee data or company emails had been stolen to sell on the dark web, which was extremely low-hanging fruit.

It looked more like straightforward sabotage. Just plain, good ol' fashioned malware, barfed directly into the central computing system and allowed to wreak havoc. Somebody had effectively taken a digital monkey wrench to the whole network and then simply walked away. Cora had never been a prosecutor or defense attorney, but she had to take criminal law classes to get her degree and pass the bar exam. Criminals typically *wanted* something.

Maybe it was the work of dumbass teenagers who got scared when they heard that a handful of people died on the island. The leading theory seemed to be that it was a disgruntled employee, though no one had found a way to substantiate that idea. The real fear was that it was corporate espionage. Paleo-Genomics hired some black hat hackers to wreck the park or something. But Cora didn't think that was likely. People died. If word ever got out it was an intentional attack, it would evaporate any goodwill a brand had and get a bunch of people arrested. And ruthless as the business world could be, most of its big players were also quite risk averse.

The only thing anyone agreed on was that it absolutely *wasn't* the rinky-dink animal rights group that had claimed credit. Someone had brought Primeval to its knees, but they didn't seem to have any sort of plan beyond simply kicking over Richard Drake's sandcastle.

Drake had already brushed past that whole incident like it was a tiny little speedbump and was explaining to the three investors why it was a great idea to pour more funds into Primeval.

Despite working for RexNetics, Cora wasn't a part of the Richard Drake fan club. She could see why some people did admire him. His ascent from a twenty-something pizza cart owner, to a cryptocurrency guru, to the world's most prominent bioengineering executive by the age of forty-five was the stuff of legends. Cora could appreciate the mythos that surrounded him.

Her parents owned a convenience store in what had once been just another pitstop in Florida gator country. Then, when she was just a toddler, Global Fossil Fund opened their dinosaur park nearby and brought in twenty times more business. Global Fossil Fund had inadvertently given her parents the funds to help send Cora to law school and probably helped put her on the path to specializing in biotech intellectual property.

No, Cora didn't necessarily like Drake. He was loud. He had *a lot* of opinions that he liked to blast out on social media. He was mercurial, thin-skinned, and a consummate egomaniac. And his band of groupies only served to rev him up. There was talk, and more than a little dread, that Drake would enter politics someday.

But still, Cora had to admire how he had Suzanne, Perry, and Oleg wrapped around his finger.

"With all the infrastructure already in place, Primeval is essentially operational as an all-inclusive resort already. The place will need to be spruced up, and we'll need to bring staff back in, but we have the centerpiece hotel fully constructed. We have the amenities. We have the security systems. We have a state-of-the-art operations center that can coordinate everything. I could open this place up in a month, and it would be a world-class resort destination even without the dinosaurs. Once we secure the genome data from the operations center, we can begin making the star-attractions again. Suzanne, you do realize that by hunting my attractions, you are in fact slowing down your return on investment?"

"It's the price for my continued patronage, Richard. When will anyone get another opportunity like this?"

Drake smiled.

Cora suppressed a smile of her own.

Suzanne Fischer thought she'd extracted a major concession from Drake in exchange for a considerable influx of liquidity. But Cora knew perfectly well that Drake wanted this batch of dinosaurs hunted back to extinction.

It was impossible to safely corral the dinosaurs that escaped when Primeval went down. Tranquilizing a Carcharodontosaurus wasn't an easy task if the animal was safely secured in a paddock. When the beast was loose on a forty thousand acre jungle island, people would die in the attempt. And that was just one of the monstrous things. Primeval had several.

Carcharodontosaurus was a Tyrannosaurus-sized apex predator. It was the big bad boogeyman of Cretaceous Africa. The species had been moderately obscure until Global Fossil Fund hatched one and transformed it into their star attraction. Global Fossil Fund's Carcharodontosaurus was affectionately known as Mayor Carl the Carcharodontosaurus because he was indisputably in charge of their park's dinosaur community. Calling him "Mayor Carl" was simply a marketing coup that sounded a lot better than "the thing that would eat all our other dinosaurs and most of the guests if ever given a chance." Mayor Carl was something of an international celebrity now. He was currently the sponsored mascot for a Japanese beer company. Cora had a stuffed Mayor Carl plushie in her room growing up after someone accidentally left one at the convenience store. There had even been a short-lived Mayor Carl cartoon.

Mayor Carl also killed two of his handlers, their bodies hopelessly irrecoverable, when an enclosure lock failed several years ago. Global Fossil Fund had spent an enormous sum of money on public relations after that, but it had mostly only served to make Mayor Carl more famous. The cartoon was even briefly revived before being canceled again.

Having loose dinosaurs on the island was an enormous liability.

If some unsuspecting fishermen came to the island and got themselves eaten, that was a very expensive lawsuit. Cora didn't necessarily like it, but she agreed with Bainbridge's recommendation that the dinosaurs needed to be hunted down and destroyed rather than rounded up like some prehistoric cattle drive. Even if the dinosaurs could be herded back to their enclosures, the park wasn't operational, so they didn't have the staff and experts on hand to keep the dinosaurs secured and fed. Drake had agreed surprisingly quickly about the need to cull the dinosaurs.

Now, he was letting Suzanne help with the dirty work and making her pay exorbitant sums for the privilege.

Drake wrapped up his planned spiel and delved into small talk with the three investors, continuing to work his charms. Burt, the geneticist, looked relieved to disappear into the background, an impressive feat in the cramped military vehicle.

"Some trip, eh?" Bainbridge said, placing a hand on Cora's knee. His booze breath wafted in her direction.

"Sure is," Cora said. "I just need to, uh…" Her brain raced for some excuse to avoid her boss. She needed to shanghai someone else into a conversation. Burt? No. Absolutely not. Drake and his coterie? No, butting in now might get her fired. Nella? Drake's assistant was near the front of the vehicle with the machine's two Russian operators, Nikolai and Maryna. Nikolai, the BMP's gunner, was chatting her up in slightly broken English and trying to steal occasional glances down her top. Not a big improvement.

TK Ryder, Drake's head of security for the expedition, sat quietly, scowling as he watched Nikolai. The big man was cramped in his seat. He had a somewhat battered book in his lap titled *Carrion Safari: The Memoir of Denise DeMarco, Big Game Hunter*. Something that looked to

Cora like a pair of grenades dangled from his belt, occasionally clinking together as the vehicle shifted. He also had a compact submachine gun fitted snugly on a loop over his shoulder.

Cora pivoted in her seat so Bainbridge's hand fell off her knee and turned her full attention to Ryder.

"Were you part of the staff at Primeval?" Cora asked, knowing full well that he wasn't.

He glanced at her, seemingly surprised that anyone from the business side of things was paying attention to him. Despite the unpleasantly swampy atmosphere in the BMP, Ryder had only a faint sheen of sweat on his bald head.

"I wasn't," he said. "I recruited a few folks from the former security team here though, when I was told what the job was." He made a vague gesture back in the direction of the docks, where his men were establishing a beachhead for their future base of operations. "When Drake told me what he wanted to hire me for, well, I thought he was a little nuts. I told him the logistics of what he wanted were going to be hard to pull off. Lots of manpower. Lots of big guns. I told him I wanted an armored personnel carrier, thinking that would be the end of it. But no, he just gets on the phone, and then asks me if a BMP-3 is good enough. So here I am. Maybe I'm the one who's a little nuts."

"Cora, let's put business aside and enjoy the tropical paradise for a minute," Bainbridge said.

Cora pretended she hadn't heard him over the machine's grumbling engine. She kept her attention on TK. "You're a big game hunter, then?" She pointed at the memoir in his hands. She actually didn't know where Drake had dug up Ryder.

"Not exactly. I was in the military for about ten years. Supported some special operations-types in a few different environments. I wasn't the tip of the spear or anything. Helped with logistics, local intel, and extraction, mostly. Nothing glamorous. Retired from that and ended up with the California Department of Fish and Wildlife. Sort of became a specialist in dangerous animal control."

"Like rabid dogs?"

Ryder smiled at that. "Big cats, mostly. Cougars that had attacked people sometimes. Lions and tigers other times."

"California doesn't have lions and tigers."

"Not naturally. But you get these rich doofuses who smuggle in a tiger cub from the black market because they think it'll be cool as hell, and then, in a shocking twist no one could have possibly foreseen, they can't take care of a five hundred pound carnivore, and it either escapes or they release it into the mountains. Then, you have a huge, out-of-place predator prowling around the hills outside of LA. Doesn't happen every day, but it happens more often than you would think. We usually had to destroy the animal, since we couldn't guarantee anyone's safety if we tried to tranquilize it. Turns out big cats get mad when you shoot them with a dart gun, and then they either run into the brush or try to claw your face off. It was bad news no matter what. I assume that's why Drake hired me instead of a big game hunter. I'm used to working with a large team, and I'm from a background that prioritizes public safety. No cowboy shit."

"Ryder, are we there yet?" Drake shouted over the vehicle's engine noise.

"First stop on the tour is about two hundred yards ahead, Mr. Drake," Ryder said after a quick glance out the BMP's command turret.

"Bring us to a stop fifty yards out."

"Yessir." Ryder relayed the message to the Russian duo. They nodded. Maryna slowed the BMP from its already leisurely pace down to a crawl. Nikolai stopped trying to peer down Nella's shirt and manned the vehicle's cannon. A moment later, the lumbering machine came to a halt.

Drake opened the armored vehicle's rear doors, allowing sunlight to flood in. Cora felt like a moleman as she stepped out and squinted. The first thing Cora noticed was a gift shop backdropped by jungle. The gift shop's glass door lay in a shattered pile of fragments along the entryway, and something had torn the display shelves down inside the structure.

The second thing Cora noticed as she ducked through the BMP's doorway was the dead Atacamatitan.

The third thing she noticed was the smell, which hit her like a bag of ham and egg sandwiches that had been left out in the sun for a month and then dropped on her head from a blimp. A fly buzzed past her face as if to investigate if she was worth its time and then lazily continued on to the dead dinosaur.

The Atacamatitan was a titanosaurian sauropod, which was a fancy way to say it was a big, long-necked herbivore. The Atacamatitan was another creature lifted from Global Fossil Fund's bestiary.

The dinosaur had been some forty feet long before it died. The island's carnivores had scavenged the corpse, carrying away individual tail and neck vertebrae and other small bones. Hunks of rotting flesh and leathery skin clung to the bigger bones, and the suppurating flesh was alive with maggots. The beast lay half on the main path, its back end partially engulfed by the jungle.

"The Atacamatitan," Drake said, gesturing like a child showing off a beloved action figure ensconced in its Malibu Dream Dungeon. "This is the largest dinosaur we've bred. So far. When the park opens, we'll have a herd of about seven of them on three thousand acres in the western exhibit area. They're one of the four herbivore species we'll have on display when Primeval is open to the public. In conjunction with our three predatory species, we'll have all the Global Fossil Fund exhibits. Plus, a few secret projects that I've had up my sleeve. Like the Piltdowns."

What the hell is a Piltdown? Cora wondered.

"What killed it?" Suzanne asked, gesturing toward the huge, dead sauropod.

"Carcharodontosaurus, probably," Ryder said.

Drake continued talking, making occasional grandiose hand gestures. Most everyone kept their eyes on him, but Cora couldn't help but stare at the dead dinosaur.

Despite the smell, Cora took a step closer to the slain giant. This was the closest she'd been to any of the dinosaurs, alive or dead. She'd seen promotional photos of the animals, but photos just didn't convey the sheer scale of the creatures. Even dead, it was impressive. It was like something from a different planet.

And in a way, it was. The dinosaurs had roamed the earth before grass evolved. If the Atacamatitan could have retained any of its ancestral memories, it would have found itself on an alien world controlled by skittering mammals. Nearly every leaf on the tree of life had fallen and been replaced since the last of the original dinosaurs perished.

But something had caught Cora's attention. A lot of the Atacamatitan's bones were snapped and shattered. That wasn't surprising. If the giant beast had been hunted down by another huge creature, it met a violent end, and hungry predators had likely returned to the corpse over and over again to scavenge.

Some of the bones looked like the flesh hadn't just been chewed off, though. It looked like it had been hacked and scraped off the bones. There were marks and etches all over the broken ribs that didn't look like they'd been made by teeth. They almost looked like someone had been at the corpse with an axe.

Cora took another step closer. There was a big wooden stake jammed through the creature's guts. The stake was meant to hold up a young tree, but it looked a little bit like vampire hunters had decided to make sure the dinosaur didn't rise again. The Atacamatitan must have collapsed onto the stake as it died, crushing some of the landscaping as it fell.

Squinting, Cora tried to figure out the angle. Maybe if it toppled over just right…?

A warm puff of air brought an even stronger carrion scent. Cora scrunched up her nose. How was the air near the sauropod's body becoming even more putrid? Another humid gust stirred up more of that sickening offal odor. And then another rotten little breeze.

Why was the smell almost rhythmic?

Cora froze in place at the same time there was a shout behind her. Drake's speech to the investors cut off abruptly.

The puffs of air. They weren't a breeze. Something nearby was breathing. Something with breath like spoiled meat.

Cora looked up into the nearby jungle. Up further. And then further still.

The Carcharodontosaurus looked down directly at her, its many, many teeth gleaming in the sun as it opened its mouth wide and prepared to devour her.

FOUR

INTERMEDIATE BANKRUPTCY LAW: LIQUIDATING LARGE ASSETS

Burt saw the Carcharodontosaurus as it took its first step onto the path, towering over Cora. Carcharodontosaurus, the shark-toothed lizard. The insatiable demon-god of an extinct world. Hunger made manifest.

Nearly forty feet of prehistoric death lumbered out of the jungle, led by a gaping mouth full of knife-sized serrated teeth. The creature's body was mostly dark emerald with a patchwork of black stripes, almost like a tiger. Despite its size, it could move like a shadow in the jungle. The dinosaur's head was colorful, crimson markings on its throat and snout faded to a burnt violet around its eyes. The bright colors were both a threat display and a show of virility to potential mates.

Saliva dribbled from the predator's jaws as it focused its gaze on Cora.

A memory Burt had done everything in his power to suppress these last six months lashed out and cinched itself around his brain. Even as shouts and yells filled the air around him, his mind went elsewhere, dragged back to that horrible night.

He'd been out in the northern sector of the park with his fiancé, Florence Bellfountain. The northern slice of Primeval was essentially the experimental zone. When RexNetics cracked the formula to create a Tyrannosaurus or Velociraptor, those creatures would eventually be enclosed in new exhibits in the northern sector, completing Drake's much vaunted Phase Two. Until then, Burt was allowed to field test some of his more promising projects out there. The less promising subjects would be relegated to the Biological Containment vault for study and disposal.

Florence was the chief paleo-veterinarian on the island. Burt still remembered seeing her for the first time, waist-deep in a dinosaur autopsy. He'd been dispatched to take notes regarding the death of one of the dinosaurs. Recreating an extinct species had proven to be more complicated than expected. Much more complicated, though he hadn't yet figured out why at the time. Many of his first draft dinosaurs were sickly and prone to any number of diseases, cancers, and catastrophic medical incidents.

Burt had been introduced to Dr. Bellfountain, gotten into a heated argument about RNA transfer sequences, and was immediately smitten. There were a lot of sordid little affairs and love triangles and hookups on the island due to the cheek-to-jowl housing, stressful work, and intense pressure. Most work relationships at Primeval failed almost immediately and sometimes spectacularly, so the Human Resources department had tried to stamp out most island romances. But he and Florence stuck together. She even moved into Burt's comparatively spacious quarters in the employee lodging.

The way she smiled right before she told one of her terrible jokes. The way she cursed under her breath when she had to scribble something out on one of her crossword puzzles. The way she compulsively twirled her dark hair when she was working a problem over in her head. He'd loved all of her.

She'd been twirling her hair that evening as she examined the herd of miniature dinosaurs in the northern enclosure. He'd been taking notes as she caught and checked each Massospondylus.

They'd almost finished examining the entire herd, and the day was growing long. The sun had crept lower in the sky, spearing the island with brilliant hues of red and orange that filtered through the jungle's tree cover. The two of them would need to work fast to round up the last few dinos in the enclosure before it grew dark.

"I don't think it's a problem with the enclosure. They have plenty of shade available. I think there's an error with the DNA somewhere," she said.

Burt gritted his teeth. He loved Florence, but there were things he couldn't tell her about his work. And Drake had just flown down to the island, taking his private helicopter and landing it on the roof of the nearly finished grand hotel. Drake had been pushing Burt on the Massospondylus project.

Once upon a time, Massospondylus had been a sauropodomorph native to what was now Southern Africa. They were very distantly related to the Atacamatitan. They were much smaller, a little less than half the size at roughly fifteen feet long, and it walked on two legs instead of four. Most of that length came from its extremely long neck and tail. In the Jurassic Period, they would have been something like a moose, a large, roaming herbivore that could still fall prey to sufficiently determined predators.

But Drake wanted Primeval to be more than just a copycat of Global Fossil Fund and Paleo-Genomics. He wanted something that nobody else was doing. He wanted dinosaurs that didn't just have to be put on display behind fences. He wanted dinosaurs that could be sold as pets.

A natural Massospondylus was far too large for nearly any buyer, so Drake had ordered Burt to create a population of tiny counterparts to the creatures on display, like Miniature Pinschers compared to full-size Dobermans.

And Burt had succeeded. Sort of.

He'd tinkered with the dinosaurs' genetic code until he had a Micro-Massospondylus that was roughly German Shepherd-sized. The creatures looked a little like a collection of land-lubbing juvenile Loch Ness Monsters.

There was one problem Burt couldn't seem to solve, though. Altering the dinosaurs' growth genes had also affected their tolerance for sunlight. The little creatures became terribly sunburnt very easily. Florence constantly had to apply ointments to the dinosaurs. One of the animals had died after falling asleep in the sun on a hot day, its skin as red as a boiled lobster.

What was more, the little bastards were feisty. The full-size version could certainly do considerable harm to a human being. They were big, not terribly bright, and they had an oversized claw on their hands that could do just as much damage as a butcher's knife. But the big ones were mostly docile, so long as it wasn't mating season.

The little ones bit. And clawed. And *aggressively* urinated, if sufficiently provoked. They often felt provoked when someone was trying to chase them down and apply medicated sunscreen to them. They were like those tiny, vicious rat-dogs that hated everyone.

Drake wanted forceful innovation. He wanted to implement attractions that would thrill audiences, but he also wanted to make RexNetics a household brand. Disney wasn't just a theme park. Drake had something similar in mind. Drake wanted to dynamite the current dinosaur entertainment industry and build it up again as an entire lifestyle brand with RexNetics at the core. Having some dinosaurs on display was easy money, sure, but Drake was pushing for something else. Drake wanted an honest-to-goodness business empire spanning across dozens or hundreds of revenue streams.

People would buy miniature Massospondylus pups from RexNetics, feed them RexNetics-brand food, buy their pet a RexNetics-brand leash and harness, take it to the RexNetics-owned dinosaur daycare center while they were at work, and turn on the RexNetics streaming service to watch a Carcharodontosaurus battle Piltdowns when they got home.

Burt was supposed to be working on the Piltdown project right then, but the science center had been experiencing some technical glitches that made it impossible to work. Besides, Burt did not like working on the Piltdowns, even if they were important to Drake's vision of Primeval. The things gave him the creeps, and he'd designed them. Burt didn't necessarily feel like a mad scientist when he was tinkering with dinosaur genomes and trying to twist them to Drake's will. But he felt like he was starring in some black and white monster movie whenever he worked with the Piltdowns. Even though they were probably his greatest success since leaving Global Fossil Fund for RexNetics, the creatures made his skin crawl.

So instead of spending all day in the lab watching his gene-editing program boot up, encounter a critical error, shut down, and repeat the process over and over again, Burt had ridden out to the northern end of the island to check on the Micro-Massospondylus herd with Florence.

He hadn't known that the computer issues had begun to spread and cascade. He hadn't known that communications were down across the island. When he saw Drake's helicopter zoom past overhead, he had no idea that Drake was on board, evacuating at the behest of security staff. He had no idea all the security gates on Primeval's enclosures were gaping wide open.

He was just enjoying working with Florence.

"What about something in their diet? Could that affect their tolerance for daylight?" Burt asked.

"We've tried upping their intake on a few different vitamins and nutrients. No dice. They still end up looking like wieners on a grill after a couple of hours in the sun," Florence said, slathering the last glob of medicated ointment down the back of another Massospondylus. The dinosaur whipped its neck around and tried to bite her, but she had expertly positioned herself out of reach. The Massospondylus began peeing furiously in response.

"Allergies, maybe?" Burt suggested.

"Not so far as the veterinary team can tell. And that sounds like a problem for the genetics team to iron out, anyway."

"Immune response from a modern day infection their prehistoric immune systems can't handle?"

"Yeah, I hate it when I catch a cold and it turns me into a vampire so I can't go out in the sun anymore."

Florence released the Massospondylus, and the creature squealed and scampered away to join the rest of the herd, which was running toward the far end of their enclosure. Several of the little dinosaurs stood more upright, wielding their thumb claws in a threat display. Burt ignored them. Three more of the little punks needed their sunscreen applied, whether they liked it or not.

Burt wondered if this was what it would be like to have kids. He and Florence agreed they wanted at least one child. But later. Much later. They needed to get out of their RexNetics contracts so they could have a normal life somewhere. Oddly enough, the experimental dinosaur island they worked at didn't have the best school districts. It would just be harder for Burt to leave RexNetics.

Drake wouldn't like it if Burt tried to leave. There would be complications. Complications that not even Florence knew all the details of. Burt knew that it was probably a bad idea to sell his soul to someone like Richard Drake. But it had brought him to Florence. He'd make it work in the end somehow.

"Some sort of adverse reaction to parasites, maybe? There was that outbreak of mites a few months ago," Burt tried.

Florence grabbed another bottle of formulated lotion in preparation for her next patient. "We checked all the dinosaurs last week. No parasites to be found. Inside or out. You remember all those stool samples I had to collect?"

"How could I forget? I just don't get it, though. None of the genes I replaced on these guys should have anything to do with their tolerance for sunlight. I'm mostly just denying their ability to produce certain growth hormones."

Every member of the herd of tiny dinosaurs was displaying their claws now in a sort of thumbs-up imitation of The Fonz. Some of them swayed side-to-side like angry owls, gazing in Burt and Florence's general direction. These things would make awful pets. Burt would need to make the next generation more docile somehow.

Dusk had begun to settle in over Primeval, and the sky had faded from the brilliant dazzle of sunset toward a humid twilight. That was when Burt noticed how quiet the island had become. No stirring tropical birds. No insects humming their nighttime symphony. Not even the constant clatter of far-off construction equipment that worked at all hours to put the finishing touches on the theme park before opening.

One of the miniature dinosaurs in the group hissed like an angry goose. And it was at that moment that Burt realized that the cantankerous little animals weren't looking at him and Florence. The creatures were looking at something behind their human handlers.

Slowly, slowly, Burt turned around.

Those eyes, glowing in the darkness from the tree line. High above Burt's head. Reflective, eerie, silent. Then, the chuff of air through enormous nostrils. The pounding of huge, scaly feet as it charged.

The Suchomimus was on top of them before he even had a chance to react. The massive, crocodilian snout snapped down. Florence screamed. There was a sound like someone biting into a particularly crisp apple, both crunchy and juicy, and the scream cut out.

Burt was left there, standing alone. He felt the wind from the creature's passing, as if a semi-truck had just driven right past him. The

Suchomimus raised its head toward the darkening sky and swallowed the broken, limp shape caught in its jaws.

Burt didn't remember much beyond that. He must have run for the nearest emergency shelter and taken one of the tunnels back to the science center, where he learned that the park's communications had gone down and the series of odd glitches affecting his computer programs had metastasized into a full system crash. Malware had brought nearly every aspect of the park down, crippling every automated system and computer in Primeval.

He didn't really remember being evacuated from the island with the rest of the staff. Honestly, he didn't remember a whole lot from the last few months. Not until Richard Drake walked through Burt's door and said that they were going to retrieve Primeval's dinosaur genome data. Richard Drake didn't beg for Burt's assistance. He didn't ask politely. He didn't frame it as an adventure or a chance to get back on the proverbial multi-ton, extremely carnivorous horse.

Drake simply informed Burt that he would be on the expedition because he knew exactly what Drake needed. It was a command.

And Burt had followed, because Richard Drake and his minions owned him.

But seeing the Carcharodontosaurus zero in on the attorney brought it all back in a flash. The glowing eyes. The scream. The sickening wet crunch.

The Carcharodontosaurus stretched its jaws wide as Cora turned to run, its long teeth glinting in the late afternoon light. Burt's gut twisted as he waited for the crunch he knew was coming. Crisp. Yet juicy.

Instead, the thunderous boom of a 30mm 2A72 Soviet autocannon filled the air. The belt-fed, recoil-operated cannon began lobbing 300 rounds per minute at a velocity of nearly a kilometer per second. The roar of the BMP's main armament turned into one, long tearing sound, as if the whole world was wrenching itself apart a short distance behind Burt's head.

Burt found himself on the ground as if a giant hand had pressed him flat. He could feel the boom of the autocannon in his chest cavity as it spewed rounds.

The Carcharodontosaurus lurched as huge, gaping wounds appeared across its chest. One of the giant dinosaur's arms flew off and spun into the jungle. Each impact sent a ripple across the creature's flesh, like someone had dropped a huge stone in a still lake, bone and muscle pulverizing under each new shockwave.

The beast's legs went out from under it, and it stumbled. A gout of blood erupted from its throat as it tried to roar in shock and surprise. The anti-material rounds continued to stitch across its frame, found the monster's head, and blew its skull apart like a party balloon. There was a crash even louder than the roar of the autocannon as the Carcharodontosaurus smashed into the earth.

For another second, the BMP continued to spit shells into the dinosaur's crumpled form, and then it fell silent. The Carcharodontosaurus twitched its tail once, and then it went completely still.

Burt's ears rang. He looked at the pile of wet dog food chunks that used to be a massive apex predator. He felt vaguely disoriented, not only from the surprise of the attack but the sudden, heart-wrenching memory of losing Florence.

It was also shocking to see Cora alive. As soon as he saw the Carcharodontosaurus, Burt had written her off as dead.

Cora stood in front of the fallen giant, her entire body trembling. Blood pooled across the pathway and beaded toward her boots. Burt stood the closest to her, having distanced himself from Drake's entourage.

"Are you okay?" Burt asked, not sure if he was yelling or not over the ringing in his ears.

She made a visible effort to compose herself. "I'm fine," she said, though she didn't sound entirely convinced herself. She scurried back to the group, almost like she was embarrassed.

Burt realized his fists were clenched so tight that his fingernails were digging into his palms. He forced his hands to unclaw themselves. Despite himself, he was glad that the lawyer hadn't been eaten. He didn't want to think about witnessing that again.

Burt looked around. Ryder and Suzanne lowered their heavy-duty weapons. Apparently they too had been firing at the Carcharodontosaurus, and Burt simply hadn't been able to hear them blasting away over the sound of the BMP's autocannon. Drake jerked his giant gun around from where the strap had gotten caught on his designer adventuring jacket, noticed Burt watching him, and then posed like he had personally and single handedly brought down the Carcharodontosaurus.

Drake stepped forward in front of the group and held his gun up. "The T-Gewehr 1918. German anti-tank gun. Just the tool for the job, but she kicks like a mother," he said. Not the first time Richard Drake had claimed sole credit for a group project.

Bainbridge gave Drake a high-five. "God damn! Cora, you should have seen your face."

"That was *awesome*," Suzanne said. She cracked open her double-barreled elephant gun and loaded two more gigantic bullets before snapping the weapon shut again. "Is that her?"

Drake stepped past Cora and checked the dead Carcharodontosaurus. "Nope. Looks like this was Bitey."

Primeval had three Carcharodontosaurs. Two adults and a juvenile. The two adults had been named on Drake's podcast, Mister Future Perfect. He'd allowed his audience to name the male in an online poll. The name "Bitey McBiteface" narrowly beat out "Shaquille" and more distant contenders like "Jumbo Chonkosaurus" and "RoboCop." Naturally all the names that made it to the final ballot had been approved by Mister Future Perfect's Council of Bros, consisting of the show's most frequent guests. Mister Future Perfect attracted a very particular audience, which so far as Burt could tell, mostly consisted of business majors who were into soft drugs.

Suzanne Fischer had been Drake's guest of honor for that episode as an honorary member of the Council of Bros in order to discuss the financing of Primeval, which mostly just served as an hour-long advertisement for the park.

Suzanne had won some sort of drinking bet with Drake, and her prize was that she got to name the adult female Carcharodontosaurus. Thus, the two largest predators on the island were named Bitey McBiteface and Big Suzanne.

"Poor Bitey," Drake said. At least, that's what Burt thought Drake said. It was difficult to tell over the ringing in his ears.

Burt looked around at the others in the group. Oleg and Perry both had their rifles up, but it didn't look like either one of them had fired. They looked like a pair of green Confederate soldiers who had just made first contact with the Union troops at Gettysburg and discovered that all their bluster and imagined glory didn't hold up in the light of day. Nella had her pistol out of its holster, a determined look on her face. She had stood her ground and adopted a surprisingly good firing stance. She popped a fresh magazine into the weapon quickly and professionally. That was... odd. She noticed him looking and quickly holstered the pistol.

Meanwhile, Arthur Bainbridge was waving his enormous revolver around like a child with a garden hose. Burt winced as the gun was briefly pointed in his direction.

Something shifted in the bushes, and several sets of weapons all shifted to focus on the noise. A dinosaur burst out of the jungle.

At first, Burt thought it was a Spectrovenator. It was about the right size, coming up to his midsection, but then he realized it was the juvenile

Carcharodontosaurus, Bitey Jr. Bitey Jr. didn't have his adult coloration yet. He was almost entirely dull green, without the bright red neck and violet eye mask.

Bitey Jr. rushed up and inspected the fallen adult Carcharodontosaurus. He nuzzled the still form once and then turned and hissed at the group of hunters.

"Mr. Drake, he's so cute. Can't we keep him?" Nella asked. There was no sign of the woman Burt had just seen a moment ago, practiced and deadly. Burt almost wondered if he'd imagined that version of Drake's assistant. Or maybe she had just struck a pose she'd seen in movies and fired randomly at the adult dinosaur.

Ryder stood nearby, lugging a can of gasoline, awaiting Drake's response.

"Well..." Drake said, apparently considering the idea.

Bitey Jr. launched himself at Drake, teeth flashing. He made it about two steps before he blew apart in a shower of red goop and a hail of bone fragments. Drake leapt back, too late to avoid a mist of gore wafting over his expensive jacket. He sputtered.

Suzanne loaded two more bullets into her elephant gun. The elephant gun really wasn't meant to be used on such a small creature. It was like dropping a bunker buster missile on a cow.

Ryder picked the gasoline can back up and began to dump liquid on the adult Carcharodontosaurus and the juvenile without saying anything.

"It's for the best," Bainbridge said, putting a hand on Drake's shoulder.

Since it had been decided that this batch of dinosaurs would be eliminated, it was essential to destroy the bodies. Their DNA had to be systematically cleaned away, even if it meant pouring bleach over half the island. Their genomes were the intellectual property undergirding the entire park. If someone took an ampule of blood or a shard of bone from one of the bodies, it could potentially ruin Primeval. Burt understood perfectly well why Drake and his legal team were taking such drastic measures to protect the park's trade secrets.

Ryder struck a match and lit the bodies. The smell of burnt barbeque chicken soon wafted through the jungle.

"I call dibs on the remaining Carcharodontosaurus," Suzanne said.

"You had a juvenile? You were breeding these things?" Oleg asked.

"Holy shit, Drake. Please tell me that letting people hunt these things is Phase Three of your big plan. That was amazing," Perry said.

Drake chose to answer Oleg's question. "As a matter of fact, we do allow the animals here to breed. It proves the quality of their genomes that they're able to reproduce. And also, it distinguishes Primeval from our competitors and will eventually get us an enormous amount of free press. Think of the coverage every time the nearest zoo has a newborn rhino or panda. The reporters go absolutely apeshit because they know people love seeing cute baby animals, and it's an easy way to get clicks on their articles. Imagine the publicity down the road when we announce the very first naturally born Tyrannosaurus in sixty-five million years right here at Primeval."

"Is it safe to let the animals breed on their own?" Oleg asked.

Burt noticed that Cora was still collecting herself. She looked like her life had just flashed before her eyes on VHS and she was trying to rewind to where she'd left off. She leaned against the side of the BMP and quietly threw up into some tall grass lining the edge of the path.

Drake continued to talk about all the reasons it was a genius plan to breed the dinosaurs. A proven lineage. Good press. Easier to open another park in the future, populated by naturally born dinosaurs. On and on it went.

Burt leaned against the BMP a respectful distance from Cora. "You sure you're okay?" Burt asked.

Burt wished he'd had an armored personnel carrier watching over him that night.

He wished he'd never come to work here. No, that wasn't quite true, because then he never would have met Florence.

He wished the Suchomimus had taken him instead.

Cora made a groaning noise. "Just nerves. Leave me alone," she said.

Burt nodded. He looked around, double-checking nothing was about to lunge out at him, and he ducked through the shattered door of the ruined gift shop. Everything near the entrance had been ruined by rain and the elements, but he grabbed a clean and neatly folded beach towel with the Primeval logo from deeper in the store and brought it outside. He laid the towel on the BMP's sloped armor where Cora could grab it and wipe the vomit off her lips. She gave him a little nod, and Burt turned around and pretended he couldn't hear her retch.

But before he could go back to pretending Drake's speech was interesting, a terrible noise rang through the jungle. He and Cora both jumped.

There was a booming roar from the other side of the path. Everyone spun on their heels as one. The third and final Carcharodontosaurus, Big Suzanne, poked her head through the foliage and stared at the burning remains of Bitey McBiteface and Bitey Jr. Big Suzanne's coloring was more subtle than her mate's, with only a thin streak of red on her throat and almost no violet around her hate-filled eyes. She was also noticeably bigger than the male Carcharodontosaurus.

Several sets of rifles came up. The BMP's autocannon swiveled around.

But Big Suzanne had already sized up the situation and turned and disappeared back into the jungle. The BMP fired a burst after her, mowing down the plants where she had been a moment ago, but there was no shriek of pain or the crash of a massive body.

"Damn," Regular Suzanne said.

"You'll have another shot at her," Drake said, as if this was all part of the tour plan and they hadn't just been attacked by one of evolution's attempts at a war crime. "C'mon. We're almost to the main plaza. I'd like to show you all where the magic happens."

Ryder splashed a bit more gas on the adult Carcharodontosaurus and spread the flames onto the remains of the rotting Atacamatitan. Bones crackled and marrow bubbled in the growing heat, and clouds of flies burst into the sky with the rising smoke.

Suzanne seemed mollified that she would have another chance with the Carcharodontosaurus. Burt was not. Because he knew that that meant the huge dinosaur would also have another chance at them.

They'd just killed her social group, her family. She was a rogue now. And she would hunt them. Not for food. But for revenge.

In the distance, Big Suzanne roared her pain and outrage, the jungle muffling and distorting the sound so it seemed to be coming from everywhere.

"Let's just get the genome data and go," Burt said to no one in particular. Only Cora heard him.

FIVE

CLAUSE AND FANGS: THE PERSONAL INJURY ATTORNEY'S GUIDE TO WILDLIFE LAW AND LIABILITY

Cora stared at her hands, trying to force them to stop shaking. They weren't listening to her, so she stuffed them into her pantsuit pockets.

She could hear her mother's voice in her mind. "Stupid girl. How are you going to get into a good school when you do stupid things like this? Dumb. Very dumb."

She looked over to where Burt and the others were staring into the jungle where the Carcharodontosaurus had disappeared. He had his back to her. Bainbridge had his hands on his hips like he'd just realized that the lumber he'd bought wasn't going to fit in his car after all. An intractable problem with no immediate solution.

Cora glanced at the smoking pile of meat that used to be the first Carcharodontosaurus. Whatever Drake was paying the BMP crew, Cora was going to request that he double it.

She grabbed the towel from where Burt left it and cleaned herself up as best she could. She felt embarrassed throwing up in front of everyone. But she also felt painfully stupid. Her mother's voice continued to berate her in her head.

She should have been paying better attention.

She shouldn't have strayed from the group.

She shouldn't have made such a fuss over herself.

Her mother, who viewed being the center of attention as the ultimate sin, would fuss and cluck and chide about something like this forever if she were to find out. Cora was supposed to be demure. Cora was supposed to be composed. Cora was supposed to always deflect attention away from herself with the utmost humility. Cora was supposed to be a damn sphinx, wise and imperturbable and knowing all the answers. Anything else was unseemly.

Her parents had always pushed her, but Cora's mother was always the one who wanted more. Nothing was ever good enough. Cora needed to take more extracurriculars. She needed to study more. She needed to take life more seriously. Stupid girl.

When Cora was a child and she said that she wanted to drive garbage trucks when she was older, her mother smacked her upside the head. When she was applying to universities and said that she was thinking about majoring in art history, her mother cried. When she was in law school and told her mother that she was trying to decide between focusing on criminal law and going into corporate law, her mother smacked her upside the head again.

Cora's mother was a force of nature who had grown up desperately poor, and she wanted more than anything for her daughter to make absolutely *disgusting* amounts of money. She wasn't a bad parent necessarily, but she was extremely single-minded, and she wasn't good with boundaries. She loved that Cora worked for Richard Drake because Richard Drake had about the same net worth as a small Baltic nation, and Cora's mom thought that was the same thing as respectability. In a pinch, it was better than respectability.

But as a consequence of her upbringing, Cora now lived with a drill sergeant in her head who had the voice of a cantankerous little Indian woman.

Cora did not feel smart or tough right now. She was dressed in a pantsuit on an island full of dinosaurs with her boss who wanted to snog her. She wanted to go home. She wanted to sit on her couch and watch her favorite show with her cat.

She wanted to do the smart thing. She wasn't sure what the smart thing was right now, but she sure as hell knew it didn't involve tromping around on this island anymore. She balled her hands into fists in her pockets and tucked her arms tight against her sides.

"You look like someone who's never been hunted by prehistoric monsters before," a voice said.

Cora looked up, surprised. It was Burt. He leaned against the side of the BMP a respectful distance away.

"Zero out of five stars. Island sucked. Drinks were expensive and dinosaurs tried to eat me," Cora said.

Burt smiled a little at that, and that made Cora feel slightly better. Talking was flushing the adrenaline out of her system a little faster.

"Two out of five stars," Burt said. "Park completely non-functional, but dinosaurs tried to eat the lawyers, so there's that."

Cora, gathering all her poise and rhetorical talent as a trained legal professional, gave Burt the finger. But she did feel slightly better.

"Don't worry, folks. Perfectly safe," Ryder said, addressing the group. "We're running this like the old Jim Corbett tiger hunts. My men and the BMP will beat the proverbial bushes and provide covering fire, and your clients can bag anything that comes scurrying out. Time-tested and proven strategy. Basically a science at this point. Once my men are done setting up camp on the beach, we'll have even more firepower available. Nothing to worry about."

But Ryder did *not* look happy. Cora had a suspicion Drake or Bainbridge had elbowed the man into giving a reassuring speech of some kind.

Not far ahead, the pathway opened up. The jungle fell away to either side, and Cora could see a vast open area. She could see structures up ahead. That would be the main plaza at the island's center.

Cora straightened out, no longer leaning against the side of the BMP. She looked around. The jungle to either side of the path felt claustrophobically close now. The shadows among the branches and leaves seemed too dark. It was entirely too easy to imagine more creatures and beasties hiding behind the foliage.

Drake started forward, leading the investors toward the park's main plaza just ahead. Ryder gestured and the BMP started following behind, nineteen tons of steel and aluminum trundling forward on heavy treads. Cora kept pace with the vehicle as it inched forward.

Bainbridge, who had trotted up to stay close to Drake, turned around. "Cora, hurry up," he shouted.

"Let's catch up to the group," Burt said. "Best not to be separated."

"Yeah, alright." Cora forced her legs to shuffle forward. Her knees were a little rubbery at first, but she found her stride shortly. After a few moments, she looked back at the burning remains of Bitey McBiteface and his son.

"You made those things?" Cora asked. She had understood that intellectually before. Growing up in the shadow of Global Fossil Funds's park made it simple enough to accept that people could create dinosaurs. But her brain had to struggle to connect the horrifying creature she'd just seen with the reams and reams of projected profits, bio-copyright case law, and numberless emails she'd skimmed through in her office.

Even growing up so close, Cora had never been to the Global Fossil Fund park. She'd never seen a dinosaur in person. Even seeing pictures and videos of the RexNetics attractions had been abstract enough that she could file them away in her head.

But now, she knew she could never look at the creatures the same again. Something had clicked in her brain in a way it hadn't before. These creatures absolutely would kill her if given the opportunity. She wasn't sure how many other people on the expedition understood that. Ryder seemed to understand, though he had to keep Drake happy by acting as a hunting guide. Burt was the only other one who seemed to actually understand just how dangerous this place was.

"Well, it's not like I personally sat on the eggs and hatched them, but I led the genetics division here. The whole process is just reading a script of genome data and then assembling it. Gene assemblers made the creatures, but I got to press a big red button to turn the assemblers on sometimes."

Cora trudged down the park's main thoroughfare, the smell of burnt chicken slowly fading. Up ahead, she caught her first glimpse of the park's ten-story hotel. Something troubled her.

"Does it bother you? Seeing your creations gunned down like that?"

Burt didn't answer her right away. "No," he finally said. "I was here when Primeval went down. I've seen what these things can do. I... I spent a lot of time blaming myself for some of the things that happened. I made mistakes here. Big mistakes. I think it might be better if the slate was just wiped clean. Personally, I'd hoped to be done with the dinosaur business. I never would have come back to this damn island again if I had any real say in the matter."

"So why did you come back?" Cora asked.

"Really? You need to ask?" Burt shot her a dirty look, like she'd just asked something that was both dumb and offensive. She considered prying deeper, but no. This wasn't the time to act like a lawyer and dig up new facts. Not while she was on this island. She didn't need to cross-examine him like a hostile witness.

"Sorry," Cora said, not wanting conflict right now. Her mother's voice was still echoing in her head, and she forced herself to focus on taking slow, deep breaths.

They walked together for a few more moments, the snarl of the BMP filling the silence. Cora normally didn't mind a few moments of quiet time. She'd never been one to fill every minute with conversation. But her brain was still popping and ticking like a hot engine cooling down in a cold driveway after she saw those massive teeth bearing down on her.

"Will you come back to Primeval when it's time to reopen?"

Burt looked around as if to see who all might be watching. No one was paying the least attention as Drake continued to give his tour speech to the investors, and the sound of the BMP was loud enough to make sure Burt's next words didn't carry. "You really think the park's going to reopen?" He gave a dismissive chortle, like Cora was another rube looking to buy the Brooklyn Bridge.

"But that's the whole reason we're here," Cora blurted. *So much for not cross-examining him, but this was insane. Of course Drake was going to reopen the park.*

"The reason we're here is to grab that genome data and to show Drake's investors that the place is safe. If Drake just wanted to reopen the park, he could send a private army in here, comb the island for a couple of weeks, and shoot everything that moves. He doesn't need to bring the investors here, give them the whole dog and pony show, and let them live out some dinosaur hunting fantasy. This is the least practical way to secure the island and get operations up and running again. It's all a sham."

"But he's investing a huge amount of money back into reopening Primeval," Cora said.

"Sure. And if he convinces his little fan club to twist his arm and buy him out, he makes most of that money right back. It's a different business environment than it was even a few years ago. More competitors moving into the market. More risks. Drake has a reputation as this high-flying visionary. Writing off the park now would make him look like a chump. If he hangs onto it just long enough to offload the assets, it doesn't matter if Primeval goes belly-up. Someone else will be holding the bag then, so he comes out smelling like roses. Besides, you're on the legal team. You know the troubles we've been having. None of the genomes are patentable as is."

That was news to Cora. Bainbridge had been assuring everyone that RexNetics would have its intellectual property rights in the bag just as soon as the final kinks were ironed out. Burt must misunderstand. She'd found that scientists and engineers rarely fully appreciated what went on in the legal departments of the companies they worked for. Different specializations. Common logical fallacy. Very smart people sometimes made the mistake of thinking they understood the whole process because they understood one part exceptionally well.

Just because the genomes were designed to mimic the Global Fossil Fund dinosaurs didn't mean they couldn't be patented. A fashion designer with a new line of blue jeans couldn't prevent other designers from making their own lines of blue jeans, even if they looked similar.

"The dinosaur genomes are already patentable, though," Cora protested.

Burt gave her another strange look, as if she'd just sat next to him on the bus and informed him her cat was the president.

Then, Ryder signaled for the group to halt. The BMP rumbled forward another few feet and then came to a rest. For a terrifying instant, Cora thought the Carcharodontosaurus was back.

"What the hell is that?" Ryder asked in a stage whisper loud enough to be heard over the BMP's engine. He pointed at something in the main plaza.

Cora shaded her eyes and squinted. At first, she didn't see anything, but then she caught a flicker of movement.

There was someone standing in the central plaza's giant lagoon fountain, half-hidden behind the enormous sculpture of Drake holding a baby dinosaur that stood in the middle of the water.

The figure was muscular, making even Ryder look like a pipsqueak. The figure was also extremely hairy, dense brown fur covering nearly every inch of its body. Arms. Legs. Stomach. Chest. The only part of its body that wasn't thick with hair was its face, particularly the jutting brow and mouth. The figure was also butt-naked, not that it mattered very much when his body was so thick with hair. The figure squatted down and scooped some water into his palm and then slurped it up.

Cora rubbed her eyes. She was going insane. That was the only possible explanation. Because she was fairly certain that she was looking at Bigfoot.

"Is that a caveman?" Perry asked, also sounding as if he wasn't sure if he was losing his mind.

Cora wanted to scoff at the question. Primeval was a theme park, not a time machine. But that massive Neanderthal brow line. The stooped, half-upright posture. The limbs that were a bit too gangly to be quite human.

That couldn't be right. It had to be a park employee that was somehow left behind. But all the employees were accounted for, either rescued or deceased.

Maybe a castaway from a boat wreck who got marooned on the island somehow? And who had slightly inhuman body proportions?

The figure had spotted the approaching entourage, probably from the sound of the BMP. He sucked down another cautious palmful of water and then he straightened up. He stood semi-upright behind the leg of the Drake statue, watching the group with yellow-golden eyes. He stood there like a shy child hiding behind his father's legs at a party.

The figure was roughly man-sized, if a head shorter than average, but he was broad in the shoulders and chest. His arms were too long, like a cartoon character who had been pulled in two different directions, but they were thick with knotted muscle. His legs were also disproportionate but powerful looking. And he was football player-wide, too. The figure was almost built like someone had taken the blueprints for a squat, hairy spider and then done their best to build a man with them.

Even through the matted hair, Cora could see the figure had several injuries. There were a handful of puckered scars, leaving shiny bald patches. There were also a dozen swatches of crusted blood from fresher wounds up and down the figure's long, bulky arms. They ranged in size from nasty scratches to long, gashing claw marks. And those were just the injuries Cora could see from a distance.

"Well, I'll be damned," Drake said.

"Is that a person? What the hell is that?" Ryder asked.

"It's a Piltdown," Drake said. "I figured they were almost certainly all dead. This must be one of the last survivors. Maybe *the* last survivor."

"What is this… Piltdown?" Oleg said.

The figure kept wary eyes on the group. It reached down again, and Cora thought that it was about to scoop up more water. Instead, it picked something up off the mounted support holding the statue upright and bit a chunk off of it with large, yellow teeth. It was the severed arm of a Spectrovenator. The Piltdown chewed thoughtfully on the meat, watching them in agitated silence.

"We bred them here," Burt said.

Drake pulled something out of his pocket. It was a protein bar. He peeled back the shiny foil and took a few steps forward.

"Hey there, buddy. You want some of this?" He gestured with the protein bar.

The creature squatted behind the statue, adopting a defensive posture. The Piltdown looked from side-to-side, as if deciding which direction to run.

"Mr. Drake, I really don't advise…" Ryder said, hefting his submachine gun. He glanced back at the BMP, as if to make sure the crew were also seeing this.

"Should we…?" Suzanne also lifted her gun in the figure's general direction.

"No," Drake said, creeping forward a little bit more. He was still a good distance from the fountain and the statue, maybe a hundred feet, but Cora saw the Piltdown becoming more upset. It stared at Drake, its eyes laser-focused on him as he approached. It bared its long, yellow teeth and made a surprisingly high-pitched chattering noise.

Drake jiggled the protein bar in his outstretched hand enticingly and took another step forward. He made a noise like he was trying to befriend a skittish cat. "*Pspspsps.*"

The Piltdown turned and fled with a loping gait, heading for the park's science center. The thing threw a look over its bulky shoulders to make sure it wasn't being followed and then disappeared through the building's shattered glass doors and into the darkness within.

Cora looked at the entrance to the science center, where they were all going.

She looked at Drake, who now wore a big grin.

She looked at Burt and noticed that all the color had drained from his face.

SIX

THE ZEALOUS ADVOCATE: LEGAL ETHICS FOR DIFFICULT CLIENTS

Burt watched the Piltdown disappear into the science center. He was about as surprised to see the hairy creature as it was to see him. He never dreamed any of the Piltdowns would have survived this long after the park went down.

"Well, damn," Drake said, taking a bite out of the protein bar in his hand and chewing thoughtfully.

Ryder pulled his satellite phone out of his pocket and punched in a number. "Watts? Uh, yeah. There's something else on this island. Something they didn't brief us about. It's like a, well, it'll sound weird if I try to explain it over the phone... Dangerous? I don't think so. It ran from us. Just keep your eyes peeled on the beach, alright?"

"Drake, why is there a caveman at your dinosaur park?" Perry asked.

Drake turned slowly around and raised his arms in an expansive gesture, like a prophet about to explain the divine plan to a wayward follower. Burt recognized it as Drake's default stance when he was about to launch into a full sales pitch. This was Drake the park founder. This was Drake the technological wizard here to wow the world with another dazzling proposal. This was Drake at his most dangerous.

"Well, I guess the cat's out of the bag. When I said that I didn't want Primeval to be just a rip-off of other dinosaur attractions, I meant it. That 'caveman,' as you called him, is part of the greatest live entertainment show ever conceived. That caveman is how Primeval is going to blow our competition out of the water from Day One. That caveman is what our science team lovingly calls a Piltdown."

He gestured in the direction the Piltdown had vanished. The investors looked perplexed but intrigued. Bainbridge looked annoyed. Nella looked on with practiced adoration at Drake. Ryder and Cora just looked confused.

"Is it... human?" Oleg asked.

"It's a macaque," Burt said, squashing Drake's pitch before it could really ramp up. He didn't want to stand out here in the sun for another hour while Drake worked the trio of investors into a lather. Drake looked annoyed to be cut short but he didn't try to wrestle attention back to himself. He would have forced Burt to explain eventually anyway.

The day was growing late. This was taking longer than Burt had hoped. As the shadows grew incrementally longer, that fateful twilight weighed heavier on his mind.

Those reflective, iridescent eyes in the darkness. That crunch. To suddenly be alone with only the echoes of a scream in his ears.

"Like the monkeys?" Suzanne asked.

"Like the monkeys," Burt confirmed.

"But macaques are little scrawny things. I've seen a gang of them steal food from tourists in Asia. Or Africa. Wherever it was. One of them grabbed some guy's phone. Funny video," Perry said.

"They are modified macaques. Like how the Paleo-Genomics Tyrannosaurus is a heavily modified chicken. These CRISPR gene edits are admittedly a lot less extreme. Pretty easy too, since we have a good understanding of macaque genomes. They're used for medical testing sometimes, so they're cheap and easy to get. We simply took some macaque embryos and edited them into what you just saw there, a Piltdown. Something meant to roughly approximate a Neanderthal or caveman. We just bulked up their muscle mass, adjusted their limb proportions to encourage a more upright posture, edited off the tail, and greatly increased their pain tolerance."

"But... why?" Oleg asked.

"Come. Follow me. I'll explain," Drake said, wrenching the conversation back from Burt. He started forward, walking at a casual pace toward the operations center. Burt and everyone else followed. "The entertainment industry is a cutthroat business, my friends. Back in the vaudeville days, entertainment was small beans. No budget. No stakes. If you bomb, maybe the crowd throws rotten tomatoes at you, but you just move onto the next town. Now, entertainment is the hardest industry to break into. Film. Video games. Sports. Muscling your way into that space takes a huge sum of money and a lot of talent to play with the big boys. And what happens to most of the companies that try to force their way into the party? They get the door slammed in their faces. Audiences write angry reviews online and form a big, disgruntled mob. Or worse yet, shrug and ignore you completely because there's so many competitors for their time. No, you can't just knock at opportunity's door anymore in this business. You need to kick that door in with something people can't look away from. The Piltdowns are Primeval's great trump card in that arena. My personal guarantee that the park will be successful, because no one will be able to tear their eyes off the spectacle. People will talk about this place a thousand years from now, and it's because of the Piltdowns."

"You're going to have some oversized baboons on display and turn that into your key selling point when you also have dinosaurs?" Suzanne snorted. "Jesus, you can throw peanuts at the monkeys at just about any zoo in the world. Nobody is going to come to the ass-end of Papua New Guinea to see a chimp on steroids."

"We're not going to put the Piltdowns on display, though. We're going to feed them to the dinosaurs," Drake responded.

"You're going to *what*?" Cora asked.

Burt looked at the junior attorney. Had she not read some of the memos that had been circulated around about the Piltdown project? Or had she simply not been provided with them?

Burt looked around. He, Drake, Nella, and Bainbridge were apparently the only four that knew about the Piltdowns and the plans for them. Burt was surprised Drake had been able to keep his big mouth shut this long.

"Picture it," Drake said. "It's one of the most enduring images in media. A group of cavemen fending off a Tyrannosaurus with nothing but a crude spear. Just like sixty-five million years ago. We herd a group of Piltdowns into the carnivore pit each day. Primeval Premium members get to vote on which predator is brought out, and the event is live streamed to our subscribers. We'll have a special viewing booth for Primeval Premium Platinum members who visit the park in-person, too. The greatest struggle in history, brought to you live."

"I changed my mind. I like it," Suzanne said.

"There's no way that's ethical," Cora said, looking completely flabbergasted. She looked at Bainbridge with a *you knew about this?* expression on her face, and Burt's respect increased another notch. She was still a RexNetics lawyer, so she was basically a human shark, but she had some heart.

Then Cora looked at him with that same expression, and he had to glance away. Despite Drake's enthusiasm, Burt had always felt uneasy about his role in creating the Piltdowns and worse yet about their purpose at Primeval. But he couldn't say no to Drake.

"It's just as ethical as any zoo," Drake retorted. "If you look at the tigers on display, are they eating a salad with a raspberry vinaigrette? Perhaps a quinoa bowl? A tofu platter? No, they're eating rabbit or mutton or a cow haunch." Drake had clearly known that this argument was coming and prepared for it, though he looked a little surprised that he needed to give the lecture to one of his own employees.

"But those animals were killed humanely. They don't just throw a live chicken into the tiger pit and let the bigger animals rip it to shreds," Cora continued.

"We've also taken measures to make sure this process is as humane as possible, right Burt?"

"Sure," Burt said, reluctant to be drawn into this conversation.

Cora looked at him again, and he resisted the urge to cringe. Her gaze bored into him. He stayed quiet, forcing Drake to do the explaining.

"We've intentionally tweaked their genetics to deaden their ability to feel pain. You could throw one into a stump grinder, and it would probably just tickle them. In the wild, our predators would inflict much worse agony on any prey animal they came across. I can't say the Piltdowns would necessarily enjoy the process of being eaten; I imagine it's still rather unpleasant. A bit gruesome, to be honest. But I'm not sure it's any worse than what happens to a cow or goat that needs to be stunned senseless before its throat is slit and it can be turned into lunch."

Cora stared Drake down. Bainbridge put a hand on her shoulder as if to restrain her, and she shrugged him off. Burt wasn't sure that he'd ever seen anybody stand up to Drake like this before. It wasn't that he surrounded himself with sycophants, but he had a way of guiding people around to his way of thinking eventually. Or finding a way to break their resistance.

"People aren't going to pay money to watch these things... these almost-people get torn to shreds. It's like a snuff film. Nobody wants that. People certainly won't pay a subscription fee for that. It's awful," Cora continued.

"Maybe you should leave the business side of things to the experts, eh?" Bainbridge said.

"No, no," Drake intervened. "I want to hear all sides of this argument. Let her finish."

"There's just no way that anybody but freaks and sickos are going to want to see that. It's... it's a niche market. Only a handful of people will want to pay for something like that, and RexNetics isn't going to want to be associated with the types of people who do want to see it," Cora said.

Burt could see the wheels turning in her head, spinning her moral argument into a business argument so she could play to her audience. He guessed she was probably pretty talented in a courtroom. Of course, Burt knew that Drake already had a counterargument at the ready. Burt had heard it several times previously when he expressed his own doubts in the project.

"Oh, I think there might be an initial furor," Drake admitted. "But I think it will die down in a hurry. I think this will be quite popular, even if a few people cluck their tongues. As a matter of fact, I think this will be a modern Colosseum. The Romans came in droves to watch hunters and gladiators slaughter exotic animals. And they came in even greater droves to watch the lions rip apart prisoners. I've been told it was common for people to publicly disapprove of the spectacles, but as soon as the fights began, those very same people would flock to the stands and roar in delight each time someone's guts were clawed out onto the sand. Sort of the modern phenomenon of people complaining about reality television but watching anyway. Mark my words, pitting dinosaurs against our collection of cavemen will be the greatest entertainment event since the Roman Empire. And this will be far more humane. People will lose their minds to not only watch these events but to vote in online polls about which individual Piltdowns will square off against which dinosaurs. And of course it won't just be straightforward slaughter. There will be escape routes, so the Piltdowns can make it out alive to fight another day. They'll have access to rudimentary weapons. Viewers will have favorites. People will mourn when an old veteran finally runs out of luck and go wild when a plucky underdog escapes the jaws of death. The literal jaws of death, mind you. The stakes will be astronomical. And RexNetics will control the betting markets, of course. The entire event will be a combination of nature documentary, gladiatorial combat, unscripted reality television, and sporting event. First, people will tell us that they'd never watch such trash. But after word of mouth gets around, they won't want to miss a single event. This is the culmination of thousands of years of entertainment, and RexNetics will bring it to the masses, and they *will* pay for it."

Burt watched Cora's gaze switch from Drake to the investors, sweeping across them and recalculating. He could practically see a big cartoon lightbulb switch on over her head.

"There are animal cruelty laws. There will be investigations. Inspectors. Legal action. It'll slow down the opening of the park. It'll cost an ungodly amount of money. And it'll bring protestors, prosecutors, and lobbyists down on us with a whole ream of red tape."

She'd been parried when she played the business angle, so she switched tactics again and played the legal card. Yes, Burt suspected Cora knew how to draw blood in a courtroom.

Drake smiled. "Papua New Guinea does have animal cruelty laws, yes, though they aren't as stringent as they are in some other parts of the world. But if the authorities have the gumption to claim we're breaking those laws, they won't get anywhere. There are a dozen fatal flaws with any attempt to bring legal action over letting the Piltdowns and dinosaurs fight it out. Is it cruelty if they feel virtually no pain? Are the Piltdowns even animals? Or are they a product? Bainbridge will have them tied up in court for decades settling those issues. What's more, nobody in authority is going to want to enforce those laws. The tourism and tax dollars this park will bring in will see to that. Once we're open, closing us down wouldn't help anybody. We'll employ hundreds of local workers in relatively high-paying jobs. We'll have lobbyists wining and dining their legislature. Look at our competition. Global Fossil Fund is basically stealing the geological history of many underdeveloped countries. I'm investing in one. We're the good guys here. Primeval will be a huge boon to the local economy. Our projections show that I'll single-handedly be adding more than three percent to the nation's taxable income through jobs and tourism dollars."

Drake had led the group into the center of the main plaza, and he stopped now in front of the giant statue of himself holding a baby dinosaur. He put his hands on his hips, looking supremely self-satisfied.

"No," Suzanne said. "You won't be doing that."

Burt looked at her in surprise. Had the junior attorney actually managed to land a killing blow on Drake's arguments? If Cora had spooked the investors into pulling out, it would cripple Drake's short-term ability to get the funds he needed to reopen the park. And for Richard Drake, who was notorious for plowing money into projects to the point of massive debts and then rising back up on fat profits, losing his biggest investors now might be tantamount to pulling the plug on Primeval.

"You're not going to single-handedly do anything on this island. Because I'm going to help you. This is the greatest idea I've ever heard. I can't believe you waited until we got here to tell us about this part. You've really outdone yourself this time," Suzanne finished. Perry and Oleg looked at Suzanne, looked at each other, and then nodded at Drake.

And there it was. The Richard Drake signature pitch. He'd lured someone into objecting to one of his plans and then used that objection to rope in new loyalists.

Burt looked around at the park's pavilion, the central roundabout which would serve as the hub for all Primeval's operations. The hotel, towering over the surrounding jungle and offering views of most of the island. The closed gift shops and restaurants.

Burt had a lot of regrets about leaving Global Fossil Fund and signing up with Drake, but watching him build Primeval from nothing wasn't among them. It had been thrilling to watch Primeval rise up out of the jungle. At a glance, he could see the potential, and paired with Drake's easy-going charisma, it was easy to be blinded by that potential. Perry, Oleg, and Suzanne saw it, too.

This was all part of Drake's vast empire of bullshit. If things had gone as planned and the park was barreling toward Phase 2 and flush with profits, Drake would claim full credit. Now that things had gone wrong, Drake would find suckers to absorb the financial blows and distance himself until no one remembered he'd ever been involved with this boondoggle.

But Burt knew where the bodies were buried. Figuratively and literally. Florence's family held a funeral for her back in Texas, though that particular casket had been empty.

There were bigger problems with Primeval than just a moral quandary over feeding live prey to the dinosaurs, though. Burt knew there would be consequences for those other problems. He knew he'd eventually be Drake's sacrificial lamb when those consequences reared their heads.

And Burt also knew this was probably the last time he'd have anyone else opposed to the Piltdown idea inside the organization with him. He weighed his options. He could sit back like a good boy and let Drake work his voodoo, dealing with the fallout later. But Drake hadn't brought Burt on this expedition to help him pitch the park. He was here to help retrieve the genome data. He wasn't obligated to help in any other way.

Burt still didn't want to tell the whole truth about the problems at Primeval, since there would be hell to pay if he torpedoed the park all on his own. But if more than one person was undermining Drake's pitch...

Burt glanced at Cora. There was a chance she was a plant. Burt found it hard to believe that anyone on the legal team didn't know about the Piltdowns. It would be classic Drake to stage a little rebellion in his own ranks so he could squash it and look extra clever.

But the look of abject disgust on Cora's face upon hearing about the plan to feed the Piltdowns to the dinosaurs seemed hard to fake. And she looked genuinely upset to find herself alone in objecting.

Burt took the leap.

"Tell them about your plans for dealing with the second wave of fallout," Burt said. Drake's head whipped around to face Burt, and his eyes narrowed. "The Piltdowns are intelligent. Not human-level intelligence, of course. But they can use tools. We specifically kept them clever enough to allow them to escape or use simple weapons to defend themselves from the dinosaurs. Not as exciting for viewers if the programming is just wall-to-wall slaughter, after all. Right, Mr. Drake? Feeding creatures with basically dolphin-level intelligence to big lizards will upset people. We'll need to deal with that second wave of fallout, which will be a lot worse. I was hoping you could tell us all about how the park will weather that particular storm."

Burt had framed the issue like he was helping. He was not. Cora glanced at him. She seemed to guess the game he was playing at, even if she didn't understand why.

Drake hopped back in, drawing all the attention to himself again as surely as a practiced stage magician getting his audience to ignore his assistant as she swapped out the empty hat for one with a rabbit. But Burt could tell that he'd knocked Drake off his game.

"Look, yeah, these things are reasonably clever, sure. But so are pigs. Damn smart creatures, pigs. But no one is going to try to shut us down because we offer bacon as part of the hotel's continental breakfast. Or, here's an example. Think about this. If our technology wasn't genetics. Say, I had a time machine, and we simply grabbed dinosaurs straight from the Jurassic, right? If we used that same technology to go back and feed those dinosaurs exclusively on a diet of Hitlers, do you think anybody would object? No. Ticket sales would skyrocket. People would be fine with it. Leave intelligence out of this, Burt. It won't be an issue. The dinosaurs need to eat, and we can satisfy that need in a way that plays to our technological strengths and also provides convergent synergies to our entertainment division."

Burt knew he'd gotten under Drake's skin a little. Drake hated business-speak, even if he was fluent in it. Getting him to cough out a phrase like *convergent synergies* meant he was uncomfortable. It was like a sophisticated news presenter lapsing into her native Boston accent when surprised.

Suzanne didn't seem to care that Drake had been caught off guard. She was already sold and probably a lost cause. Oleg and Perry looked like they weren't done waving goodbye to their second thoughts, though.

Burt prevented himself from smiling. He'd landed a hit.

"How many of these creatures did you make?" Oleg asked, looking to Burt.

Drake butted in. "Given that they're essentially prey animals here, I expect that we just saw the very last Piltdown on the island."

"But how many were there when Primeval was evacuated?" Perry asked, also looking at Burt.

"About two hundred adults. We created a substantial population in anticipation of the park opening soon," Burt said. "It was essential we have a big population since we anticipated the dinosaurs would kill a lot of them quickly. Even with the extra muscle mass, it would be a massacre each time we streamed a feeding event. We'd need lots of warm bodies."

Suzanne probably liked what she was hearing. Perry and Oleg looked less and less sure.

Something big roared deeper in the jungle before Burt could continue. Everyone spun around, expecting the remaining Carcharodontosaurus to come charging out of the tree line. The BMP's autocannon swiveled from side-to-side, seeking a target.

Burt suddenly felt very exposed, standing in the middle of the big, abandoned pavilion. Some ancient instinct tickled the back of his brain, telling him to find a burrow and hide before the dinosaurs found him.

"We should get to the science center," Drake said, effectively ending further discussion. He grasped his enormously oversized anti-tank rifle. No one argued with him.

The entire group began moving again, walking faster than before. They reached the science center's broken front doors and peered inside. Behind them, the BMP rolled forward and parked itself outside the building's entrance. The huge vehicle couldn't go inside, but it could provide heavy fire support in case anything tried to follow the group through those doors.

Burt stared into the building's darkened entrance, its glass doors shattered. An inactive security badge reader was still attached to the gaping hole. This was the employee entrance. There was a learning center annex with a more prominent entry point further down.

Burt had worked in the heart of the science center for several years. It had virtually been his home. But he'd never seen it with the lights off and its hallways dark. He'd never seen the entrance without one of the security guards, Mark or Dwayne, checking IDs. He'd never seen the heavily polished floor scuffed and covered in shards of glass.

The way forward was bathed in shadow. Burt peered into the darkness within, gazing at familiar shapes and areas that now looked twisted and strange in the darkness. Ryder flicked on a flashlight, illuminating the hallway interior.

That's when Burt saw the bones.

SEVEN

MURDER, MANSLAUGHTER, AND CRIMINALLY NEGLIGENT HOMICIDE: A PRIMER FOR CRIMINAL ATTORNEYS

Cora stared at the science center's entranceway and the mess within. There was no sign that the Piltdown had passed through here. A reception counter sat immediately inside the science center's entryway. A phone, computer monitor, and desk printer that had once no doubt rested on the counter now lay shattered and trampled on the ground. A directory above the counter had listings for security, maintenance, administration, science, human resources, veterinary, and power supply departments, among others. There was also an entry for biological containment, but Cora wasn't entirely sure what that meant.

She knew all about the power supply situation, given her work on the patents. Seeing something, anything, she understood felt like a lifeline. This trip had been full of unpleasant surprises, and it was oddly comforting that she was familiar with at least one aspect of the island.

Several flashlight beams snapped on and played over the sign and the nearby security station. The security station looked like what Cora might see at the airport, with a metal detector, body scanner, and X-ray machine for bags. There was always the concern in these uncertain times that someone might try to sneak a weapon or a bomb into the science center. On-site security would always be an issue.

Still, Cora was a little surprised. This was the employee entrance after all, for vetted Primeval personnel. The people coming through here would be operations managers, scientists, and technicians, not random members of the public.

But then Cora remembered the real purpose of the security checkpoint wasn't to keep people from bringing harmful items into the science center. It was to keep people from leaving with valuable intellectual property.

If somebody left the facility with dinosaur genome data, it would let a business competitor catch up on years of research in a matter of months. The lab was a veritable gold mine for anyone with a mind for corporate espionage. Some of the most valuable trade secrets in the world were kept back there. That was the reason that Ryder's team was burning the bodies of the dinosaurs they shot. Otherwise, somebody with a pocketknife and a piece of Tupperware could carve off a sample and earn a duffle bag full of money as a corporate I.P. bounty hunter.

Surveying the disarray around the entrance, Cora didn't recognize the bones right away. In the gloom, they just looked like more debris to her. But then, several flashlight beams zeroed in on the skeletal remains. Cora took a step backward before realizing the bones weren't human. Or Piltdown, for that matter.

"A Massospondylus," Burt said, squatting down and picking up what appeared to be a broken hip bone. A few stringy pieces of sinew clung to the bone, but it had otherwise been entirely picked clean by scavengers and jungle insects. "At least two of them, actually. Some of the miniature ones. I was out with Florence with them when the park went down." The geneticist's voice got quiet, and his eyes went far away for a moment.

Cora had heard that name somewhere. Florence. Florence Bellfountain. She was one of the park's veterinarians. Cora recognized the name from the short casualty list compiled after Primeval collapsed. RexNetics had paid a substantial fee to her family without admitting any legal fault, just to make sure there was no lawsuit and subsequent bad press.

Cora wasn't sure why Burt would have been out with one of the paleo-veterinarians at the time the park's systems failed. She would have expected him to be here in the labs or grabbing a meal at the science center's employee mess hall.

But if he was out in the park when everything went to hell... He had been with somebody who didn't make it off the island. Cora realized she didn't know a lot about the geneticist. Cora had focused most of her attention on Drake and the investors when she wasn't avoiding Bainbridge, since they were the power players here. Burt was more of an enigma. But he might have his reasons for being kind of a jackass if he'd survived a dinosaur attack during the park's downfall.

Cora wasn't sure of her footing after her argument with Drake.

On the one hand, Burt had seemingly entered the fray on her side. It wasn't as if she needed rescuing. She had a law degree and could look out for herself when she didn't agree with somebody. But Burt had actually put Drake back on his heels a little.

On the other hand, Burt was the one who had done the dirty work in creating the Piltdowns. If anything, he had an interest in defending their existence. Even if he had some misgivings about the things, surely it was smarter to just keep his head down.

She thought about Burt telling her that he thought Drake wanted out of the dinosaur business, that this whole expedition was an excuse to grab the genome data and then offload the island onto the investors.

There was something going on here between Drake and Burt, and Cora didn't like it. As a RexNetics lawyer, she was likely to end up in the middle of it eventually, but right now, she wasn't sure who she trusted.

Burt had engineered the Piltdowns, but they were clearly Drake's pet project. Cora still didn't like the idea. Not one bit. She was fine with genetic manipulation. She wouldn't work for RexNetics if she was one of those weirdos that thought genetically modified blueberries would end human civilization somehow. But creating two organisms and then letting them fight it out in some sort of prehistoric Thunderdome was a step too far. People might pay to watch the Piltdowns get ripped apart by dinosaurs, but Cora didn't want her name attached to that in any way, shape, or form.

It had taken Cora a minute to figure out why Drake called the creatures Piltdowns, but then she realized they were named after the Piltdown Man, a famous paleontology hoax. A fraudster dug up some bones in Piltdown, England, and claimed that he'd discovered the so-called missing link between apes and humans in the evolutionary tree. The discovery was actually a collection of human skull fragments that had been hastily buried alongside an orangutan's mandible and teeth. Scientists spent most of the first half of the twentieth century debating the authenticity of the hoax.

These creatures weren't a mix of man and ape, though. They were monkeys that had been altered until they looked mostly human. Cora's first impression of the creature out by the main plaza's fountain was that it was a human being.

Perhaps that was why she was so troubled by the idea that Drake would feed the Piltdowns to his dinosaurs. Everyone else would be introduced to the Piltdowns prelabeled as an expendable product. Cora hadn't been introduced to them through that lens. She certainly didn't want to watch the human-like creatures torn to shreds by Drake's genetically altered murder-lizards, but she had no doubt he was right. Lots of people very likely would pay to watch such a spectacle. And any uproar from people opposed to the idea would only serve as publicity.

Perhaps she was upset because she originally went into law thinking it would be good to represent the little guy. That was why she was interested in becoming a prosecutor before her mother browbeat her out of the idea. Helping battered spouses, abused animals, victims of crimes, and single parents trying to collect child support had a certain appeal. Tossing the Piltdowns to dinosaurs like a Roman emperor deciding the fate of a fallen gladiator rubbed her natural instincts the wrong way. Even if the Piltdowns weren't exactly human, hell maybe because they were so close to being human without enjoying any of the benefits, it felt wrong to relegate them to contestants in Drake's Jurassic dog fighting arena.

And perhaps it was because she'd very nearly been Bitey McBiteface's lunch just a few minutes ago. She thought the last thing she would see in life was a set of gigantic teeth clamping down around her. Inflicting that fate on anyone else, *anything* else, suddenly felt enormously wrong. Sure, nature was red in tooth and claw, but Primeval wasn't nature. Even for all its advertised prehistoric ferocity, Primeval was more-or-less the opposite of nature. The creatures and the thrills were supposed to be entirely manufactured. Imposing nature's most vicious laws here for the sake of entertainment and profit made Cora feel spectacularly uneasy.

Should she resign? Was she still just shook up from her near-death experience? Would she realize that she was being hysterical after the last of the adrenaline drained out of her system?

Maybe. But she didn't think so.

"Stupid girl," her mother's voice echoed in her head. This job paid the bills. Cora was comfortable. Her work was reasonably fulfilling. She was upwardly mobile. Resigning would be insane.

"Eventually, we'll give tours through our operations center to our VIP guests," Drake said. "Good news. You get to be our very first VIP guests. The bad news is, I'm afraid we need to do a little housekeeping. Excuse me a moment."

Drake stepped behind the front desk and pulled open a slot in the faux-wood paneling. He reached a hand inside and yanked something. There was a noise like someone boiling a cat, but that faded into a low buzz and then a hum.

A single light blinked to life overhead.

"You still have power here?" Oleg asked.

"Indeed we do." Drake grinned. "State-of-the-art auxiliary power system. There are some giant batteries hooked up to a whole mess of solar panels and generators upstairs. Normally, they could handle all the emergency power needs of the whole park for up to a month. They were supposed to come on when the main system went down, but the hack scrambled that software. Staff tried to bring the backup systems online when they realized we'd been hit with a concerted malware attack, but the damage had been done at that point. We evacuated everyone when it became obvious that the dinosaurs were loose. Still easy enough to boot up manually, though."

Cora thought of the schematics for the backup power system that she'd helped patent. The electrical engineers would be happy that the battery backups could still provide a modicum of emergency power after months of neglect. The software engineers would be less pleased to know that the hackers had turned their code to Swiss cheese.

The overhead light snapped off.

"With the software busted, the emergency backup power will cycle on for a few minutes and then shut right back down. Hold on a second," Drake said. "We have power. Just not reliable power."

The overhead light flickered back to life and held steady before snapping off again.

"We'll need to wipe the system clean, but once we reinstall the necessary software, Primeval will be back and operational. With a new cyber-security suite, obviously," Drake said.

Just then, the satellite phone attached to Ryder's belt rang. He looked down at it in surprise. Drake looked annoyed as Ryder fumbled the phone up to his ear. He answered and listened for a moment before relaying a rapid string of instructions.

"That was our beachhead. They have the inner perimeter established. Sounds like maybe they saw your monkey friend, the Piltdown thing, hanging around the edge of the jungle. They want us back inside an hour, if we can manage. It's going to start getting dark soon, and the weather's shifted. We're going to get a storm overnight. I recommend we get in, grab the data, and bug out until the morning."

Drake nodded. "We should be able to do that. No problem. I'll give you all the short version of the tour now, and we can do a deeper dive tomorrow. For this trip, let's just focus on collecting that genome data."

"Good idea, Mr. Drake," Nella said, still making goo-goo eyes at her boss. But Cora noticed that Nella always kept one hand near the pistol on her hip.

"Perhaps you'll allow me to lead the way?" Ryder asked. He gestured at the bones scattered beyond the security station. He shouldered his compact submachine gun. "I have the equipment for any close quarters encounters with… whatever left those behind."

"Very well, Mr. Ryder," Drake said as if offering a great concession. "Might be a loose Spectrovenator or two running about. That way, please." Drake gestured past the security checkpoint and Ryder began to lead the procession.

Beyond the security center and reception desk lay a short hallway lined with framed modern art. But at the end of the hallway, the building opened up into a massive space. Ryder led them down a few steps, and Cora found herself in a giant atrium. Glass panels covered three sides of the gigantic room and the ceiling, allowing a magnificent view of the rugged jungle beyond. Open mezzanines on the upper floors featured office space, a company gym, and on the very top floor, the auxiliary power room.

The atrium was five stories tall, with the ground floor consisting of an employee mess hall and social hub. Tables lined the wall and there were counters for grab-and-go style dining. The glass panels allowed natural light to pour down and gave a view of the surrounding jungle, the lush greenery waving in the slight breeze. Outside, the sun had fallen lower in the sky, and the first orange and red hues of sunset had blossomed. It looked something like a utopic high school cafeteria. A grand staircase and elevator led to the upper floors.

The upper floors were recessed back, so the overhead space in the atrium went all the way to the ceiling high above. Each of the upper floors had a balcony overlooking the mess hall, sort of like a giant mall from the eighties, where everyone on the upper floors could look out over the food court and spot their friends below. The architecture reminded Cora of the tiered decks of a cruise ship.

It was a beautiful space, marred only slightly by the fact that some of the glass panels were broken. Bits of shattered glass lay here and there like twinkling diamonds. The broken windows had also allowed rainwater to pool inside, and Cora found herself sloshing through about a quarter-inch of brown water. It wasn't even enough to get her feet wet through her boots, but it was one more thing that would need to be cleaned up before the park could be reopened.

Drake pointed out various features and amenities top-level employees enjoyed at the operations center. It was all very important since employees had to live on the island, and he personally made sure that everyone's work-life balance was perfect, and on and on and on.

She didn't notice right away when Burt fell into line beside her.

"You don't like the Piltdown project?" Burt asked in a quiet voice, not much more than a whisper.

Cora looked at him. He looked like he was trying to decide something. He was clearly studying her. "No. I don't like it at all," she said.

"Did you know about them before you came here?"

"No," Cora said. "I've been wanting to get on the team working on the genome patents, but so far I've just been doing the intellectual property side of the auxiliary power system." The lights on the walls fizzled out and then came back on again. "Glad to see that works. Sort of. The hackers really did a number on the systems here, didn't they?"

Cora studied Burt right back. For being in a group, she was very much alone on the island right now. But did she trust Burt? No, absolutely not.

"Don't take this the wrong way, but you weren't originally supposed to be on this trip, were you?"

Cora bristled a little. She was relatively young and the higher echelons of the RexNetics legal department still leaned heavily toward older men. Nobody had ever told her to her face that she wasn't welcome, but she did often feel like she was on the outside looking in. Being invited on this trip was supposed to be a big break for her.

Only she'd found out that maybe Bainbridge wanted something in exchange for her big break. She'd found out that she didn't have any active assignments on this trip. She'd found out that she wasn't important enough to know about some of the big projects, like the Piltdowns.

"Maybe I phrased that badly," Burt said, apparently reading something in her eyes. "Let me ask what I'm getting at in a different way. How much do you know about how we developed the dinosaurs here?"

A hand landed on Cora's shoulder. She turned around and looked into the eyes of Arthur Bainbridge. "Mind if I borrow you a minute?" Bainbridge asked.

Cora shook her head and Burt nodded. The rest of the group continued on, and Bainbridge let them gain enough distance to enjoy a little extra privacy.

"I don't think it's wise to confide too much in the geneticist," Bainbridge said.

"Why not?" Cora asked. She didn't particularly like the idea that Bainbridge could tell her who on the expedition she was allowed to consort with. "I'd like to know as much about the types of intellectual property RexNetics has on this island as possible, since I might be working on it in the future."

"You'll be lucky if you have a job in the future," Bainbridge hissed. He still had his hand on Cora's shoulder, and his grip tightened. "That shit you pulled with Drake about the damn Piltdowns could have sunk this whole deal. All the intellectual property here is useless if RexNetics can't get the funds to reopen."

Cora closed her eyes. She didn't want to argue right now. She was exhausted after very nearly dying earlier. Frankly, she wanted to go back to the ship and sleep for the remainder of the trip. But she knew that if she didn't stand up for herself now, she *would* knuckle under once she got back to the office.

"Lucky if I have a job in the future? You mean as a lawyer for the company with the bloodsport subscription plan? Maybe I wouldn't be arguing with our boss in front of the investors if somebody told me what the hell was going on here. I have to come out here and almost get eaten to find out our business model is monster cage fights?"

"Cora, don't kid," Bainbridge said.

"I'm serious. This is not what I signed up for when I joined RexNetics."

"Alright, fine. Maybe we could have been more transparent with you and the rest of the team. You and I will have a discussion on the matter later, but I assure you the Piltdowns feel almost no pain. The whole thing is very humane. When that data is secure and we're all back safely to the office, I'll put together a little presentation and make sure the whole legal team is on the same page, alright? But I still think you should stay away from the geneticist."

"Why?"

Bainbridge sighed. "If he wasn't the person best equipped to verify the integrity of the genome data, we wouldn't have brought him on this expedition. When Primeval went down, he was here. And, well, I feel bad letting anyone know about this, but... he got his fiancée killed. He was out in the park with her, he made some bad calls, and a Suchomimus got her. Ultimately his fault at that point. I've gone over the incident and I assure you that RexNetics is legally blameless. But he's damaged goods at this point. I think he has an agenda all his own. Drake and I are keeping a short leash on him for that very reason. Personally, I wouldn't believe a word he says."

Bainbridge had a little tic when he was in full lawyer mode. His hand gestures became much more dramatic, and he gesticulated more frequently. It didn't mean he was lying, but it did mean he was putting some facts in their most favorable light. There had been a lot of hand gestures while he explained Burt's history.

"Thank you for telling me this," Cora said. She glanced at Burt as he continued along with the rest of the group.

"Stick with me in the future. Alright, kid?" Bainbridge winked. There was still the faint odor of booze around him, though it had faded considerably.

Cora nodded back at him, doing her best impression as if she trusted him implicitly.

"Let's catch up to everybody before something else jumps out at you, okay?" Bainbridge held up his big, shiny revolver in a *don't-worry-I'll-protect-you* gesture.

"Good idea." She scampered ahead, leaving Bainbridge a few steps behind. Her feet kicked up little sprays of water as she moved.

Drake and the rest of the group were approaching a hallway under a prominent sign announcing the way to the gene lab. A huge plexiglass window was meant to provide a view of Primeval's scientific nerve center, where computers should have been whirring and humming like protective mother hens over batches of embryos.

But the window only provided a view of a vast, dark room. Cora could see a handful of small LED lights blinking on and off around the room where equipment and computers were booting up. But there were no overhead lights coming on.

Cora could see just far enough to make out the nearest wall-mounted light. It had been smashed. Little pieces of glass flashed on the floor each time the nearest LED blinked to life.

Cora had seen a handful of publicity photos featuring the gene lab. After all, the place was as much an advertisement for the scientific know-how behind RexNetics as it was an actual work space. She knew that the room was quite large, but she couldn't see the far side in the darkness.

There was a single red light on what appeared to be a main control console, illuminating a tiny circle in the center of the room. Deep, black shadows extended away from the ominous red light. Cora knew that the light meant the computer system was in standby mode after being shut down improperly, but Cora couldn't help but be reminded of any number of evil robot movies.

"Are we going in there?" Perry asked.

"That's where the genome data drive is located. It's plugged into the main unit. All the genome data is on there. It was supposed to be removed when the island was evacuated, but it got left behind in the chaos," Drake said.

"How do you know the data isn't corrupted?" Oleg asked. "Seems like the hackers got into most of your other systems."

"It's not corrupted," Drake said with seemingly complete confidence.

"Why's it dark?" Suzanne asked. "They on a different circuit in there? Some sort of different backup system we need to turn on?"

"No, everything is run on the same system," Cora said. Everyone turned to look at her. "The backup system will run the whole island if it's activated anywhere. If the system got corrupted, maybe that would cause certain areas to remain without power, but we can't fix that just by flipping more switches somewhere. The problem here is that the lights are all smashed. Look."

"So who smashed the lights?" Perry asked.

"Nobody smashed the lights," Suzanne said in a tone that indicated that she thought the suggestion was stupid. "Some creatures got in there and fought it out at some point."

"Just stick close to me and use your flashlights. We'll move in real steady and then saunter right back out," Ryder said. The pair of grenades on his belt clinked together as he started to move in the direction of their goal.

Cora did not have a flashlight. She didn't have a gun. She didn't have a satellite phone. She didn't have any of the equipment that everyone else had been supplied with. She hadn't minded being unarmed on the beach. But that was before something almost ate her. Now, she wouldn't have minded a pointy stick. She just felt exposed in her sweat-soaked pantsuit.

"Yeah, stick close to me," Bainbridge said, holding his revolver with one hand and a small flashlight in the other in a way that he'd probably seen in a television show. Cora looked around and caught Burt's eye. He was also unarmed.

"Follow me," Ryder said, holding his stubby, mean-looking submachine gun. He started into the gene lab and the group set forth after him. Drake went immediately after Ryder, since he still wanted to maintain the illusion that he was in charge of every aspect of the expedition. Nella followed him. Then the three investors, then Burt, then Cora and Bainbridge with his revolver.

Flashlight beams danced across the walls as the group proceeded among the workstations in single file. Desks, embryo cabinets, and computer stations created a rough grid network. The gene lab was a real workspace, but it was also something of a Potemkin village meant to impress the VIP tourists. Cora knew that most of the work in this area could have been done just as efficiently in a small lab like those in hundreds of mid-level university basements all over the world. Drake had put great effort into presenting the science center as a cutting-edge facility that could not be matched anywhere else. But the actual architecture and layout of the room was designed first and foremost to impress rather than for functionality.

Suzanne must have been right. Animals had gotten into a fight in here at some point. Flashlights illuminated individual desks and pieces of equipment as the group moved toward the central processing tower's red glow. Some of the desks appeared frozen in time, as if someone would be back in a couple of minutes to finish what they'd been doing. Others were a mess, with equipment and computer screens swept onto the floor and smashed. Some office chairs had been smashed down to bent struts and ruptured stuffing. Blood and excrement stained the floor.

The room had a terrible animal reek to it as well. It smelled like sweat and urine and musty water damage. Cora did her best to breathe through her mouth, but the smell had an unpleasant thickness to it.

Cora saw a pair of tiny lights blink on and off in the nearby darkness as the group approached the central console. Other LED lights flicked on and off. Some were red. Some were green. Some were yellow. The effect in the darkness was oddly beautiful, almost like being surrounded by a field of fireflies.

The whole group circled around the central console, huddled in the red glow of its standby light. The console consisted of a wide, circular workstation with one large screen and a bevy of smaller monitors. A pillar rose up from the center of the workstation like an obelisk. The obelisk housed Primeval's central computing system and served as the island's brain. In theory, a crew of scientists could monitor the final stages of gene assembly from the workstation and other staff could simultaneously operate the park's core functions on the other monitors.

Only one monitor seemed to still be operational in any way. It had a large crack running down the face of the screen, and one corner showed a screen with blue background and white text. The other monitors had all been smashed. Red LED lights shone all over the central workstation, bathing the area around it in a little pool of crimson.

"Burt?" Drake said.

"Got it," Burt said. He reached into his shirt and pulled out a lanyard. The lanyard had a RexNetics employee ID card and a single silver key. He grabbed the key and inserted it into a compartment on the main console. There was a click, and Burt pulled the data drive out of the console's ports. "Here." Burt handed the data drive to Drake.

"That's it?" Suzanne asked.

"That's it," Drake said, hefting the flip phone-sized data drive.

"I was expecting something more... exotic," Oleg said.

Cora wasn't exactly sure what she'd been expecting. A shining ray of brilliant light. An angelic chorus, maybe. The data drive contained a trove of intellectual property. It was probably worth more than the actual island itself. Cora had somehow expected a bit more ceremony. The plastic casing should at least sparkle dramatically in the light like cartoon pirate treasure or something.

There was a muffled sound from somewhere nearby. Something wet sloshed in the darkness. Cora glanced around. Something wasn't right.

"Guys?" Cora tried to figure out what it was. The deep nasty funk pervading the room seemed to grow heavier and more oppressive.

"I know it doesn't look like much, but that data stick is the linchpin of the whole park," Drake said. He handed the data drive back to Burt. "The genomes are huge chunks of data obviously, but it's still just a file. It's just instructions for how to build the animals' genetic code. You can fit that information on a data drive the same way you could a... Do you smell that?"

Ryder's satellite phone rang. He checked the screen, which burned brightly in the darkness inside the science center. Cora jerked her head around as several of the blinking lights shifted in the direction of the phone. It was almost as if...

"It's the team on the beach," Ryder said. "They must need permission to take the cargo barge back to the ship for more supplies." He started to answer.

Cora realized what was wrong. Perry wasn't in the tight circle of red light anymore.

Ryder seemed to realize it at the same instant. He swung his flashlight around, pinning it on four figures next to one of the desks. The first figure was Perry. He had a long-handled knife lodged in his throat and chunks of meat had been bitten off his forearms. Perry twitched, and Cora realized he wasn't quite dead. Several sets of strong, hairy hands held him down, preventing him from thrashing and making more noise. The satellite phone tucked in Perry's shirt pocket came free and clattered to the floor, tumbling off into the darkness.

The other three figures were Piltdowns. One of them swallowed a gobbet of meat that had recently been attached to Perry's face. The Piltdowns' eyes reflected in the flashlight beam. Some of the lights Cora had been seeing in the dark room weren't lights at all. They were eyes, reflective and blinking as the Piltdowns stalked them from behind the cover of the workstations.

The Piltdown that had just swallowed Perry's cheek grinned with huge, bloodied teeth. It was a female, and she had a fireman's axe. Caught off guard by the creature's sudden appearance in Ryder's flashlight beam, it took Cora a moment to figure out that the hulking female figure wasn't smiling. Most of her face had been ripped away, revealing scabby flecks of meat clinging to yellowed bone. What was left of her face was black and crusty, where it wasn't weeping pus and red-tinged sputum. But the thing's eyes were intact and alive and full of both hunger and crazed hatred.

How was the creature still standing? How was she not a mewling ball of agony? But then Cora remembered something Drake said earlier. The Piltdowns had been designed to feel virtually no pain. Their nerves were intentionally damaged, so they could be "humanely" fed to the dinosaurs. Whatever fight or accident that claimed the female's face, it had been little more than an inconvenience for her.

The female held up a hand to shield her eyes from the light, and she smacked the nearest male Piltdown with the shaft of her fire axe. The male grunted and wrenched the knife out of Perry's throat with a wet ripping noise. There was a little wheeze of air, and Perry stopped twitching.

Showing his teeth, the huge, muscular Piltdown drew the knife across his own chest, leaving a smear of Perry's blood. Cora recognized it perfectly well as a threat display. The female Piltdown, apparently the little band's matriarch, had just ordered her henchman to take care of these interlopers, and he was happy to oblige.

A burst of gunfire stitched across the male Piltdown's chest in parallel with where he'd wiped Perry's blood. The monstrous figure took a half-step backward, staggered by the impact. He looked downward at his own viscera, his guts trying to unspool from his torn belly, foaming blood bubbling out of his chest. He looked back up and sneered, unbothered by whatever deadened pain managed to reach his senses. Still holding the knife, he took two purposeful strides forward and then toppled over onto his face as his body simply gave out from the damage it had received. Ryder shifted his submachine gun to cover the next nearest Piltdown.

Hoots and shrieks filled the science center, and Cora realized there were more than three of the genetically upgraded macaques in here with them. A lot more.

A piece of sharpened rebar whizzed past her head, thrown like a makeshift javelin, and lodged in the wall on the far side of the room.

"Run!" Drake yelled, and the group of survivors dashed for the nearest exit.

EIGHT

IMPEACHING EXPERT WITNESSES: WHEN SCIENTISTS AND PROFESSIONALS GET IT WRONG

"Run!" Drake yelled, and he began leading the group toward the wrong exit, a corridor that led deeper into the science facility. Amid the darkness and the confusion, it was difficult to tell the best way out of the building. But now, Drake was taking everyone the wrong direction.

"Not that way!" Burt yelled. He waved his arms and tried to get everyone's attention. Cora seemed to notice him, her steps briefly faltering, but then a gigantic brute of a creature loomed out of the darkness, a screwdriver in one clenched fist and a hammer in the other.

Cora squealed and pivoted, avoiding the murderous creature's swing. She took off after the rest of the group, leaving Burt in the rear.

Burt knew he could turn around and run the correct direction, but then what? He didn't have a weapon. If he got cornered or tripped over a stray electrical cord in the darkness, he was done. The Piltdowns would be upon him, and he would die screaming. It was as simple as that.

So Burt ran after the others. He saw reflective eyes in the darkness. *The Suchomimus.* He heard bare feet pounding behind him. *Oh God, it's got Florence.* He could smell the ape house stink around him now, and the scent of death. *That wet crunch. The bulge of something large sliding down the beast's neck, forced into its gullet, like a snake that had swallowed a baby chick.*

He ran like he did that night. He ran expecting giant teeth to snatch him up into the air. He ran expecting the blade of a knife to sink between his shoulder blades. He ran expecting to never see the sun again.

Drake and the others burst through a doorway and into a corridor. Unlike the gene lab, this was a purely practical maintenance area. The concrete floor was damp, and the walls dripped with condensation. Somewhere nearby, a long-broken pipe dripped a steady trickle of water.

Some of the lights were broken in the corridor too, but not all of them. Burt could see handprints on the walls. Bloody handprints. Many of the handprints could have been incidental, the result of many bloody palms pressing against the walls. Others appeared more purposeful. A scattering of handprints were in mediums other than blood. He spotted a few yellow ones created with what might have been mustard. Others were a shade of off-putting pink that Burt recognized as the primer paint used all over the hotel when it was being constructed.

The Piltdowns were making... art? Or was it all just a mess, the natural result of chaotic, filthy creatures running amok in their den? Burt didn't know the answer to that. But he did know that this building was where the Piltdowns had established themselves. This was their space now. And the longer he and the others ran around like chickens with their heads cut off, the more likely they'd be cornered and killed.

The corridor split at a right angle. "There's an emergency shelter this way," Drake shouted, running directly past the corridor that led to the emergency shelter.

Burt chased after the rest of the group, still yelling for everyone to follow him instead. His feet crunched on a number of bones. Birds. Lizards. Fish. Small dinosaurs. The corridor was piled high with refuse and stinking filth.

"Not that way!" Burt yelled.

Behind him, the door exploded open and a group of Piltdowns thundered into the hallway, each one carrying some sort of weapon. Hoots and screams echoed behind him like voices from the depths of the underworld.

The survivors charged down the corridor and then up a short half-staircase. There were fewer signs of the Piltdowns at the far end of the corridor. Fewer handprints on the walls. Fewer gnawed skeletons of small animals.

All the lights blinked off for a second as the power hiccupped again, casting the corridor into utter darkness. Burt resisted the urge to screech to a complete halt, but he slowed in surprise, every instinct in his body warning him that he was about to trip or slam into some obstacle. The lights flickered back on again. Burt glanced behind him. The Piltdowns filling the corridor behind him hadn't slowed down in the least.

Why should they? Their bodies didn't particularly care if they slammed face-first into a concrete wall at full speed. They felt no pain. Just hunger and bloodlust. Because that was exactly the way he'd engineered them. They'd taken the opportunity to gain on Burt and the rest of the group. Their shrieks of excitement grew more frenzied as they saw they were catching up, winning the race.

Burt's heart jackhammered in his chest. The creature's odor, some combination of bodily funk, rotten food, and festering meat, clung to the inside of his mouth and made him want to gag. He breathed hard as he ran, sucking down more of the awful smell with each breath until it felt like it was coating the inside of his lungs.

The group turned a corner and faced a gigantic steel door, like something that might seal off a military nuclear bunker. A keypad hugged the wall next to the door. The door was sealed shut.

"Is this the emergency shelter? What's the code to the door?" Ryder asked, breathing hard.

"Uh..." Drake said, evidently realizing his mistake. This was not the shelter.

Burt knew what this place was. Biological Containment. Once upon a time, it had been the most secure location on the island. One of Primeval's many dirty little secrets. There was no turning around now, though. But there was an exit to the building's exterior on the other side of the containment unit. The only way out was through. *Keep digging 'til you reach daylight.*

It was probably safe enough inside. Probably. But Burt knew he'd assumed that the Piltdowns would have all been eaten by the dinosaurs by now, and that particular hypothesis had been proven catastrophically incorrect by the data. Burt could hear the data charging down the hallway after them, weapons clattering. The data was going to eat the flesh off their bones if he didn't do something.

Burt skidded to a stop in front of the keypad and slapped in his personal code. There was a clank. And then a hiss. And then a sound like someone rolling a boulder up a hill. The giant blast door began to swing open.

The door opened enough to admit one person at a time. Drake squeezed through the widening gap first. He yanked Bainbridge in after him.

With a roar, the first Piltdowns rounded the corner. They stopped dead when they saw the door opening. The nearest one's eyes widened.

Ryder sprayed the group of creatures with submachine gun rounds. The roar of the weapon was deafening in the concrete tunnel. Burt leapt through the door, but not before he saw torn flesh and bits of bone spray away from the crowd of Piltdowns like a red wind. In the cramped confines of the corridor, Ryder couldn't miss. The Piltdowns didn't even seem to notice. They lumbered forward on shattered limbs, blood seeping from mortal wounds. Only those Piltdowns that had been killed instantly ceased their pursuit. And they were soon replaced by more Piltdowns pouring out of the gene lab.

Ryder came through the huge door last, firing a few more controlled bursts of fire. Burt caught a final glimpse of the female Piltdown with the missing face waving her fire axe like a general rallying the troops. What little remained of her face was a mass of lesions, boils, gangrenous meat, and bloody scabs. But her eyes shone clearly from her ruined face, spearing Burt with a look of abject hatred and hunger.

Burt tapped out his code again on a keypad inside the room, and the door began to close. A few seconds later, the massive door sealed itself shut like a bank vault protecting some vast treasure. Even through the thick metal, Burt heard several heavy bodies collide against the door and begin pounding and scraping with tools and weapons.

Burt leaned against the wall, directly beneath a dozen different bright yellow warning signs, and tried to catch his breath. His heart felt like it was doing a gymnastics routine, and his legs were suddenly shaky. The scratching, banging noises on the other side of the door began to taper off.

The world was quiet again, except for the ringing in his ears from Ryder's gunfire. But there was still a smell in the air. It was a different smell than the Piltdowns. Almost like they'd just unsealed an ancient tomb. And in a way, they had.

Cages of varying sizes lined the walls. Some were small enough to house a guinea pig at the pet store. Others could have held a small circus's menagerie. Some were clear plexiglass. Others were cold steel. Most were empty. A few held old carcasses of twisted, gnarled things that could not be described as dinosaurs. The desiccated remains looked like things from another world.

The cages were stacked in rows, almost like a shipping warehouse. In some places the stacks had been toppled over, limiting visibility and creating a sort of rudimentary maze. Some of the cages were intact. Others were broken open.

"What the hell happened out there?" Nella asked. She had her pistol out and was scanning the room for threats, no longer pretending to be simply Drake's personal assistant. Any trace of her California accent was gone. A new accent had replaced it. Israeli, maybe? With her pistol out and the no-nonsense scowl on her face, Burt would have believed she was ex-Mossad or Special Forces. Her demeanor had switched to a posture that reminded Burt of a coiled rattlesnake.

"You said those fucking things were all dead," Drake hissed at Burt, gesturing in the direction of the closed door.

"I said I assumed they were dead. They were created to be eaten. You don't leave a flock of sheep in the wolf's lair and expect to come back and find they've kicked the wolves out of their den. They've found a way to survive, and I suggest we do, too. We shouldn't be in here. There's a door at the far end of this containment unit that will lead us outside. We should go before the Piltdowns try to circle around and cut us off," Burt said.

"You said those things were modified macaques? They were eating Perry. *Eating* him. Macaques mostly go for fruit," Ryder said.

"Mostly," Burt said. "They're omnivores, like us. They'll eat a few good-sized rats every year to supplement their diet. But the Piltdowns are bigger and have increased muscle mass. They require a much greater protein intake. And this is not a natural ecosystem. The ratio of predators to prey is completely unsustainable. They probably ran out of easy meat months ago, and now they'll take anything they can get. Now can we *please* get out of here? I don't like it here."

"What is this place?" Cora asked.

"Biological Containment. It's where the genetic failures were shuffled off to for additional study before they were euthanized," Burt said. He turned to Drake. "Did you tell her why there were so many difficulties with the gene modifications? Did you explain that particular problem to your legal department?"

"Actually, I really don't--" Cora started to say.

Drake cut her off. "Is everything in here dead?"

"It ought to be," Burt answered.

"Yeah. Some clown told me something similar about a bunch of gene-edited macaques living on this island, too." Drake crossed his arms.

Burt felt a bubble of anger rise inside him. He didn't want to be here. He didn't want to speculate on questions about what was alive on the island when he had zero data. He didn't want to be eaten by prehistoric *or* man-made horrors while sitting around arguing about it. He wanted to get off this damn island. Right now, if possible. He reached into his pocket and felt the reassuring weight of the data drive.

"We could make a stand here," Suzanne said, hefting her rifle. "Remember the Alamo and all that."

"I seem to remember the folks in the Alamo were slaughtered to the last man," Bainbridge said.

Suzanne's grin faded, though she still looked as though she liked the idea of a glorious battle to the death against a horde of simian freaks.

Drake pulled out his satellite phone. "We are not going to make some sort of last stand. And we are not going to just open a door to the outside and make a run for it. I hired a small army of very big dudes with very big guns to keep all of us safe, and I'm going to make sure they earn their keep."

He dialed and stuck the phone to his ear. He waited. And waited. And waited. He pulled the phone away from his ear and frowned at it.

Burt felt a sense of dread stir deep in his guts.

"Your team on the beach isn't answering," Drake growled to Ryder.

"Might be busy. Big Suzanne is still out there, somewhere. Let me get Nikolai to bring the BMP around." Ryder pulled out his own satellite phone. He dialed. And waited. And waited. And waited.

"We're behind a giant steel door. Might be blocking the signal," Oleg offered.

"Yeah. Maybe," Drake said.

Burt kept looking around. Many of the cages in here were broken. Metal bars were bent. Plexiglass was starred and shattered, scratch marks etched on the inside. This place was the morgue of ambition. So many of the initial organisms created for Primeval had not worked out. Plans had been changed to accommodate for the difficulties encountered with the dinosaur genomes. Corners had been cut. Many of the animals were stillborn. Others were simply wrong. This place was built to study and dissect the creatures that could never be shown to the public in any capacity.

The fact that any of the cages were broken was a bad sign. The fact that many of them appeared to be broken into from the *outside* was worse. Because that meant something big had been responsible, something that came through and smashed through metal bars to eat the smaller creatures inside.

"We should leave," Burt said. The words came out calmer than he felt. Inside his head, images of Perry being eaten by Piltdowns too hungry to bother waiting until he was dead played over and over again.

The lights guttered out again. Burt made an extremely undignified yelping noise. Something moved in the darkness. Burt heard the clatter of metal as a heavy object was tipped over further in the containment unit.

The lights flashed back on. Burt and everyone else glanced in every direction. Those with weapons held them at the ready, but there was nothing to shoot at.

"I agree," Ryder said. "Time to leave. What's the fastest way out of here?"

"There's an exit on the north side of the building," Burt said. "Follow me." No one else volunteered to take the lead, even though Burt was really, really hoping somebody else would step forward.

Ryder nodded, accepting Burt's knowledge of the terrain. Oleg and Suzanne held their rifles, looking around nervously. Of the two, Suzanne looked a lot more sure with her gun. Oleg's hands were shaking slightly. Bainbridge made a small production of cozying up to Cora, his oversized revolver in his hands. Drake made a slightly less dramatic show of getting closer to Nella, but he was still pretending that he was protecting her and not the other way around.

Burt patted his pocket, making sure the data stick was still there. Such a little thing, and yet it was indirectly responsible for so much trouble.

Burt looked up the first aisle of cages and containers like a shopper in Hell's supermarket. The way to the far end of the room was blocked by an avalanche of debris. Equipment, cages, and a forklift lay in a jumbled mass. He moved to the next aisle and saw a similar scene.

Something big had crashed through here at one point. Burt had a pretty good idea of what it was, but he hoped he was wrong. A peek into the third aisle proved he was right.

Well, shit.

"What in God's name is that?" Ryder asked.

"It's the Tyrannotitan," Burt said.

"The *what*?" Ryder asked.

"Is it... dead?" Cora asked.

It was a good question. Burt looked at the enormous mound of flesh and meat. It didn't move. No, wait. Actually, he could see movement through its mostly translucent skin. Something slowly but rhythmically pulsed and squelched inside the creature.

The monster looked something like a bus-sized transparent trash bag that had been filled to overflowing with slaughterhouse offal and teeth. Its blobby, amorphous shape made Burt's eyes want to throw up. Its enormous size made his knees want to buckle. Its translucent, vaguely slimy skin made his brain dredge up old middle school textbook diagrams of single-celled organisms engulfing each other in a microscopic battle for supremacy and survival. Except the Tyrannotitan was anything but microscopic.

The thing had been locked in Biological Containment when Primeval collapsed. With both the main doors sealed, it had never escaped. Burt was shocked the creature had survived several months in here, but then he remembered the broken cages. It had been eating the other specimens, giving it some basic nutrients as it harvested their corpses.

Shifting its weight slightly, the Tyrannotitan knocked into the side of the aisle and sent a small metal cage toppling to the floor. Burt cringed at the noise it made, but the monster made no move to attack them.

Even knowing exactly what it was, even having helped create the thing, Burt couldn't think of it as anything other than a monster. Because what else was a monster but some living thing that had no business being alive?

The group condensed into a tight huddle against the far wall away from the monster, their voices dropping to harsh whispers. Something heavy banged against the door, and the Tyrannotitan twitched at the noise. But it didn't lunge toward them. It seemed weak and tired, like a snail that had been caught in the hot sun. It had been locked in here for a long time now. Burt eyed the creature from across the room, trying to gauge if it was even aware of them.

"It's not dead. I'm not sure it knows we're here either, though. Its senses are pretty rudimentary," Burt said. "Limited vision. Maybe some smell and hearing."

The lights blinked out, and there was a thrashing noise, like the sound of wet bean bag chairs being mashed together. More cages fell to the ground or screeched across the floor. The lights came on again. The Tyrannotitan was no closer to the group but it had repositioned itself, apparently reacting to the change in light.

"Why did you make this?" Oleg asked, gesturing at the godless sack of meat.

Drake gave Burt a dirty look, as if this was all his fault somehow. It sort of was, but not entirely.

"The Tyrannotitan was a big South American carnivore, very closely related to the Carcharodontosaurus. Since they're such close cousins, we figured we could tweak our Carcharodontosaurus genome and produce another major star attraction with minimal investment. Nobody else has a Tyrannotitan on display. We'd differentiate Primeval from everything else on the market with something like that," Drake explained.

"I thought Phase Two of the park was to brew up some classic dinosaurs like a T. rex?" Cora said.

"We had more than two phases," Drake said acidly, as if Cora was the dumbest worm on the planet. "The paleo-zoo business is 4-D chess. Sometimes you need to get Phase Five off the ground before you start working on Phase Two. Someday we're going to have Primeval: Zanzibar, Primeval: Cyprus, Primeval: Galapagos, Primeval: Catalina. And then we'll eventually have fantasy parks built off tweaked versions of the dinosaur genomes. Primeval: Camelot with dragons. Primeval: El Dorado with that Aztec thing. Quetzal-quantum or whatever. A Japanese park with goddamn copyright-free Godzilla knockoffs. They'll all need different attractions. But instead of building each genome from scratch, we'll cheat and build off the work that's already been done. We just need a single tyrannosaurid genome. A single spinosaurid genome. A single carcharodontosaurid genome. Everything else will flow from that starter template. This is simply a Carcharodontosaurus where we got too far off from that base template."

"That does not look like a Carcharodontosaurus," Suzanne said. "That doesn't even look like a dinosaur. It looks like a disturbed child wished a booger to life, and then it ate all that child's enemies until it was the size of a whale."

"Our gene editing team was altering the very fabric of life," Drake said. "You don't just spin a dial to make a brand-new dinosaur, even when you're just adjusting an existing genome. Something went wrong with the Tyrannotitan project, and we ended up with that. I believe the Biological Containment team was keeping it alive in here to better understand which genes needed to be altered on the next attempt. This thing is a sort of rough draft dinosaur."

"A very rough draft," Oleg observed, looking at the vaguely maggot-shaped creature.

"Can we discuss business plans later?" Ryder asked. "I don't trust those Piltdown things not to find a way in here eventually, and I only have so much ammunition with me. You said there were originally about two hundred of them?"

"Yeah," Burt said.

"Christ on a trampoline. That's a small town."

Burt eyed the Tyrannotitan. There was one more aisle leading to the far side of the building. He walked over and checked it. A few fallen cages and some equipment lay scattered around, but the way was essentially clear. He breathed a sigh of relief. He could see the massive vault door from here. From the outside, they could hopefully call the main security force. If the worst-case scenario happened and the Piltdowns had figured out to cut off that route, firing off a few shots would draw the BMP. It didn't matter how many Piltdowns were still on the island, then. Some knives and tools were no match against an autocannon.

Ryder saw what Burt saw and gestured. "Let's go." He took over and led the way. Burt gladly handed over the role of forward scout.

Picking his way down the aisle, he avoided as best he could the fat snail trail of dried slime that covered the floor in many areas. In places there were splashes of blood or partially dissolved bones where the Tyrannotitan had consumed some of the other failed experiments locked in Biological Containment. Burt had the image of prisoners left in an abandoned jail turning to cannibalism until only the biggest, strongest, most vicious sonofabitch remained.

If Burt had known what he was getting himself into by signing on with Drake, he would have run screaming in the opposite direction when RexNetics first approached him. If he had known the sort of mistakes that came from being the lead geneticist at a startup paleo-zoo, he would have given up his career and taught middle school science in a quiet corner of the Midwest somewhere. And if he'd known his creations would one day devour his fiancée, threaten his life, and bind his fate to Richard Drake's forever, he probably would have switched his expertise from biology to physics so he could try to build a time machine with the express purpose of going back and beating the living shit out of his younger, greedier, stupider self for signing up with Drake.

Burt's view of the Tyrannotitan kept shifting. He could see it through a plexiglass cage. And then he couldn't because a cargo container

81

blocked the view. Then he could see it again through a set of metal bars. Then, he couldn't due to an upended, slime-covered water tank. It just kept getting closer and closer each new time he saw it.

The creature was long and tapered, more like a giant slug than the bipedal dinosaur it was supposed to be. Stunted limbs of various shapes and sizes sprouted from its body at odd angles, all of them limp and boneless. He had seen the creature plenty of times, but it still turned his stomach to see its insides churning and gurgling under its skin. Behind him, Burt could hear muffled sounds of revulsion as the rest of the group got a better look at the monster as well.

They said that the two things you never wanted to see being made were laws and sausages. But perhaps dinosaurs needed to be added to that list. Because things like the Tyrannotitan, the missteps and miscalculations and mistakes, were vile to look at. Burt and the genetics team had played God here. And you weren't supposed to ever see what happened when God accidentally fucked up an animal design.

The lights went out again. That should have been a relief, but the Tyrannotitan thrashed blindly again. Something heavy crashed. Someone grunted in pain. There was a wet noise.

The lights came back on again, and the Tyrannotitan had repositioned itself so it was now directly facing Burt. It only had rudimentary eyes, little more than photosensitive blobs of glop embedded near its mouth. But those eye spots were now looking directly at Burt.

He froze. Could it see him? Did it know he was here? Or was he just one more shimmer of color among many others?

The Tyrannotitan opened its leech-like mouth, revealing ring after ring of needle teeth. It lurched forward like a tidal wave, pressing against the freight car-sized plexiglass enclosure separating it from Burt. The enclosure shifted a foot across the concrete floor with a screeching noise.

"Go!" Drake yelled. He swung his oversized German anti-tank rifle around, and Burt realized what he was about to do a second too late. Drake fired the massive gun, staggered, and fell on his butt from the massive recoil. Nella dragged him back to his feet before he could even start to pick himself back up.

The armor-piercing bullet blew through the plexiglass, turning most of the view white with a star-kiss of fractures, shot through the length of the Tyrannotitan, and blew a fist-sized hole in the far wall. The sound of the gunshot seemed to fill the whole world.

Foul liquid sprayed out of the Tyrannotitan's wound, but it didn't seem to mind. It reared back and made a noise like two big rig trucks mating, and then it started forward again, bashing through the first panel of compromised plexiglass. Drake reloaded his gun. Bainbridge opened fire. As did Suzanne and Oleg.

The Tyrannotitan made more furious noises as high-caliber rounds sailed through it, but it was like poking an amoeba with a stick. The creature's body rippled with the bullet impacts, but its organs were already a hodgepodge of barely coherent systems with redundant backups growing like tumors all through its body. The Tyrannotitan was less of a dinosaur and more of a cancer, a collection of uncontrolled cell growth and seething organic chaos.

Burt started running toward the end of the aisle. He reached the giant steel door and keypad on the far wall and entered his code as the Tyrannotitan smashed through the second pane of broken plexiglass. Everyone else with a gun kept firing at the monster.

The monstrosity surged forward, shoving the last edges of broken plexiglass aside and bulling its way in among the survivors. The group broke and ran, fleeing the horrible creature as it writhed toward them.

Oleg tripped over a piece of debris on the floor and went sprawling.

The Tyrannotitan shimmied forward, and its mouth closed over Oleg, engulfing him. Burt could hear a faint, muffled scream. Rearing back, the Tyrannotitan choked Oleg down. A dark, kicking silhouette squirmed inside its body, clearly visible through the creature's transparent flesh.

The Tyrannotitan lurched forward, not yet satiated. It didn't move as fast as a Carcharodontosaurus, since it didn't have proper legs. It could slither forward at about the pace of a brisk run. Fast enough that it would catch up to them.

Everyone scrambled for the door. The huge vault door swung open on its mechanized hinges, letting a crack of daylight into the containment unit for the first time in months. The sun had grown low in the sky, almost dipping below the edge of the horizon. It would be dark soon, but for now, there was still a brilliant orange hue in the sky.

Burt ran outside into the daylight after everyone else and stopped dead in his tracks. A group of Piltdowns stood directly in front of the door, having clearly anticipated where the group of survivors would emerge.

And *she* stood in the lead, her face twisted into a permanent, leering grin due to her missing lips. The Piltdown's matriarch held her fire axe with an aplomb that a mob enforcer would admire, clearly ready for business.

And then the matriarch's eyes grew wider as she saw what was behind Burt. She gave a warning shriek at the same time that the other survivors came bounding through the widening gap. Maybe the Piltdowns couldn't really feel pain, but that didn't mean they couldn't feel fear.

The matriarch took a step forward as if to hold her ground, or at the very least planning to plant the blade of the axe between Burt's eyes, but the rest of her troupe turned and scattered as the Tyrannotitan reached the doorway and began to muscle its way through the gap. The matriarch looked at Burt, looked at the seething, wretched abomination escaping its way through the door, looked at Burt again, and then very obviously decided he wasn't worth it. She gave him a look that communicated something to the effect of "meet me behind the gym after school so I can give you what's coming" only significantly more terrifying since the face that was giving that look was a pitted, half-rotten ruin of flesh and exposed bone and simian fury.

Burt turned and dashed over to the keypad on the exterior side of the door. He started to enter his code, and then the screen went dead. The power had gone out again. The door stopped opening wider, but it was already too late.

The Tyrannotitan wriggled bonelessly through the gap like an octopus escaping through an impossibly small gap in an aquarium. Burt froze, watching as the hulking creature paused for a second, assessing its surroundings.

Burt felt like Dr. Frankenstein truly seeing his creation for the first time and realizing just how badly he'd miscalculated. Nothing on this island was supposed to exist. The dinosaurs should have been extinct. The Piltdowns were a crude imitation of the past. But this thing was a cruel mockery of the natural order. And Burt was responsible for making it. Inside its belly, Burt could see a vaguely human-shaped silhouette kicking and thrashing as it began to dissolve in the beast's stomach juices. A sort of red haze seeped out from around the shape like dark ink dribbled into a cup of water.

The Tyrannotitan zeroed in on the movement of a Piltdown fleeing into the jungle, and it seethed into action, digging a slimy furrow in the dirt and uprooting small shrubs and trees as it went. It left behind a trail of ectoplasm-like slime as it vanished from sight. A Piltdown shrieked somewhere in the nearby jungle and was then silenced.

"Let's get the hell out of here," Ryder said.

Burt nodded. He looked up just in time to watch the sun slip fully beneath the horizon, and the last light of day began to bleed away.

NINE

COPYRIGHT AND COPYWRONG: DO'S AND DON'TS FOR NEW INTELLECTUAL PROPERTY LAWYERS

Cora looked at their diminished group. Perry was dead, his throat torn out by the Piltdowns. Now, Oleg had been swallowed whole by that... that thing.

She felt sick to her stomach. Primeval was unlikely to reopen at this point. Two of its top backers were dead.

And it wasn't just the deaths that bothered her. It wasn't even the fact that it could have just as easily been her that died horrifically, though that might have been why her knees felt like rubber.

The thing that bothered her most right now was that she had pushed so hard to be on the RexNetics intellectual property team. She'd specifically wanted to be on the crew working to protect the genome data, so that Richard Drake and his company could profit from it. But she knew the only person she could blame for being here was herself.

Once upon a time she'd justified to herself that it would be a bad idea to be a prosecutor. Could she really see herself recommending to a judge that somebody should go to jail? That somebody should have their freedoms taken away? Cora, who had always been too timid to raise her hand in class even when she knew the answers, loudly objecting to improper evidence in the middle of a trial and throwing down with experienced defense teams while a jury was waiting for closing arguments? Conducting cross-examination on rapists and murderers?

Not on her life. She'd make a terrible prosecutor, she'd told herself. Her mother was right. Better to slide into a less confrontational, lower stake field. And if it paid oodles more? Well, so much the better.

But now she saw the world of intellectual property wasn't just a quiet academic backwater of the legal field. Everyone at Primeval had been playing with fire, and she had been scrambling to bring them more matches.

Before, Cora had liked telling her friends that she worked on intellectual property for a theme park. It sounded so benign. People told her they pictured her in court with the park mascot as a witness. They were always surprised that she did something as dull as power system patents.

Cora had always thought of Primeval as essentially a zoo. But zoos didn't need to compete in the same way RexNetics did. They cooperated on breeding programs and veterinary expertise.

But Primeval wasn't about preservation. It wasn't even about innovation. It was about exploitation. Richard Drake had brought in a bunch of specialists and then asked them to flog their scientific expertise until they made something that could generate sufficiently gigantic profits. Drake's approach to scientific innovation was to jump out of a dark alley at it and then rifle through its pockets after it was subdued. Only this time, it had not been subdued.

Primeval was an assembly line, selling bigger and better products to a public with a short attention span. They built their products to order, but their products were living organisms. And in the race to acquire the best, most crowd-pleasing organisms, everyone had lost sight of the fact that the intellectual property here was alive and it was dangerous.

Cora felt like a scientist who had just discovered a new type of bomb and watched it used in anger for the first time. Patenting a string of DNA seemed perfectly reasonable in theory. Somebody assembled it the way they would a new widget or gizmo, so it deserved the same protections. But that process created strange, strange market incentives. Once somebody owned a living attraction down to its very genes and could profit from it, the race was on to find the best exchange rate between custom-designed flesh and cold, hard cash.

Drake took off his hat and wiped the sweat off his forehead. "Burt, still got that data drive?"

Burt patted his pocket. "Right here."

"Maybe you should let me hang onto that?" Drake said.

"You know what? I think I will let your legal team handle it," Burt said, pulling the data stick out of his pocket.

To Cora's surprise, Burt handed it to her. She paused for a second. Then, she saw the sour look on Drake's face, as if he was about to snatch the data drive out of Burt's hands. She took it like she might an ancient and holy artifact.

"Since nobody bothered to give her a weapon for this snipe hunt, that'll give everybody an extra incentive to keep her safe," Burt said. "After all, retrieving that data was the whole purpose of coming out here, right?"

"Burt, you know damn well that--" Bainbridge started to say.

"Arthur, shut up," Drake interjected. He eyed Bainbridge as if the man had committed some great faux pas. Then Drake gave Cora a stern look that was probably supposed to convince her to give the data stick over to him.

Cora decided she trusted Burt. She wasn't sure she *liked* him in the least. But she trusted him. Right now, she did not trust Drake. She took the data drive and placed it in her own pocket.

"I'll keep it safe," Cora said. She felt the weight of the thing, no heavier than a stick of butter. It held such power. Wealth almost beyond imagining. Destructive potential *fully* beyond imagining.

Suddenly, she felt like she'd been tasked with ferrying The One Ring to Mount Doom. Except, instead of casting it into the flames, she was to hang onto it for safekeeping until it could be put to profitable use once again. She almost wilted at the combination of responsibility and frustration and vague revulsion that settled over her.

She considered taking the data drive out of her pocket and just smashing it with a rock. Such a little thing, and yet so full of troubles. Pandora's box with terabyte upon terabyte of storage. But breaking the thing wouldn't solve anybody's problems, least of all hers.

Much as she didn't like the forces that had been unleashed on this island, part of her still quailed at the idea of such expensive intellectual property. The data drive was undoubtedly the single most valuable thing she would ever touch. The thought of destroying it felt like snapping the arm off a statute in a museum or tossing paint on a Renaissance mural.

But breaking it might also feel like defusing a bomb.

Ultimately, she kept the device stowed in her pocket. She consoled herself by remembering that she didn't have any legal right to break the data drive, regardless of her personal feelings. She needled herself because she knew she didn't have the courage.

"Daylight's burning. Let's get the hell out of here before the sun sets," Suzanne said. "I don't fancy being out here at night."

"Right," Ryder said. "Follow me. We'll get back to the BMP and the beachhead. I don't feel as though I was properly briefed to keep everyone safe on this expedition. I'll reconvene with my men and figure out if we can continue here or if we need to withdraw everyone." The hint of distaste in his voice was unmistakable.

Cora felt bad for Ryder. He'd had nothing to do with the creation of this place, but he was probably going to have two deaths on his conscience going forward.

The whole group moved around the side of the building, tramping through landscaping that had been chomped and crushed by prehistoric herbivores in some places and become overgrown in other areas. Cora wondered how many herbivores were even left on the island.

She thought back to that tree stake she'd seen buried in the dead Atacamatitan. She was pretty sure that was a sign the Piltdowns had hunted the massive beast, like Neanderthals driving spears into a mammoth's flank. In another few months, the island's population might be reduced to a few starving predators all stalking each other through the jungle.

The group rounded a corner and Cora could see the science center's atrium again. The moon reflected off the glass plating, except where some of the panels had been broken, leaving gaps like missing teeth in a smile.

Cora could see clouds gathering on the horizon, blotting out some of the stars as they began to dazzle to life in the darkness. A storm was brewing.

She wanted to be off this island before the storm hit. She wanted to be on the cargo tug, pulling away from the docks. She wanted to be in her cramped little cabin, with the lights on, where she could work on trying to forget the sight of Carcharodontosaurus teeth rushing at her. And the sound of Perry's final, wet gasps as a knife was yanked from his throat. And the image of that godawful thing Burt had called the Tyrannotitan devouring Oleg. Soon, this whole island would just seem like a distant nightmare. She could get back to her real life. Maybe salvage her career doing trademarks for an advertising firm or something. Anywhere but another bioengineering company.

"There's the BMP," Ryder said, pointing.

Cora could see the big, boxy armored personnel carrier parked in front of the operations center. The machine rumbled softly but didn't move.

Ryder pulled out his satellite phone again and dialed. In the distance, Cora could faintly hear an answering ring from the direction of the BMP. The ringing continued. And continued. No one picked up.

"C'mon, Nikolai. Pick up the phone, dammit," Ryder said.

"Let's just run up and pile in," Bainbridge said. "I don't want to be out in the open any more than we have to be."

"It's dark. We'd surprise them by running up. They have a machine gun. That's a good way to get shot," Nella answered. She wasn't bothering with the California accent anymore. There was no point in pretending she was just Drake's personal assistant now. Nella was his bodyguard, and she didn't have any patience for plans that would get her boss killed.

"Ah," Bainbridge said.

A head appeared in the gunner turret. For a moment, Cora thought it was Nikolai. But then she realized that the head belonged to a Piltdown. The heavily muscled figure lifted itself up until it was sitting on top of the BMP.

It held a ringing satellite phone in its hand. The figure poked at the ringing phone and then bit it, testing to see if it was edible. When the phone proved less than tasty, the Piltdown smashed it on the vehicle's armored chassis.

Ryder sighed and put his own phone back down.

Then, the Piltdown reached in and grabbed something from inside the BMP. Cora squinted, trying to make out what the object was. It looked hairy. A big rat maybe? The Piltdown peeled a portion of the object away and chewed contentedly.

Cora got a better look at the object and realized it was Nikolai's bearded jaw. The Piltdown had plucked out and eaten the man's tongue like a particularly succulent grub. Despite everything she'd seen today, Cora felt a surge of disgust. She suddenly felt far too warm and realized that she needed to take some deep breaths, or she was going to puke.

The creatures must have attacked the BMP while everyone else was inside the operations center. Nikolai and Maryna had stayed with the vehicle, but they would have been on the lookout for dinosaurs. If they saw a human-like form, they wouldn't necessarily shoot right away. And even once they realized that the figures were like the one that had been by the plaza fountain earlier, they wouldn't immediately realize just how dangerous and blood-thirsty the creatures were.

"Son of a bitch," she heard Suzanne mutter, apparently also realizing what the Piltdown was munching on. Cora heard the sound of metal sliding against cloth.

"No!" Ryder and Nella said at the same time.

The Piltdown atop the BMP looked over at the sound of the voices. It picked up a bloodied wrench, evidently used as a crude club. And then the upper third of the Piltdown's body flew away in an explosion of liquified viscera as an incredibly loud gunshot rang out. Cora felt the world seem to suddenly expand and then contract around her as Suzanne's elephant gun roared.

"How do you like that?" Suzanne whooped.

From the nearby jungle, a bellow answered.

The remaining Carcharodontosaurus. She'd heard the sound, and she knew exactly what it meant.

"Get to the BMP," Ryder shouted. Drake pushed past Cora, and then the whole group was running. Cora ran as much to avoid being trampled as because she could now hear the sound of thunderous footsteps fast approaching.

Two more Piltdowns popped out from inside the BMP, these two appearing from the open rear hatch. Their arms and faces were caked with gore, and they looked surprised by the sudden commotion. Nella dropped both of them with her pistol, two rounds to the center of mass and a third to the head for each. As far as Cora could tell, the other woman didn't even break her stride. The two Piltdowns collapsed, but they both thrashed and kicked for a moment, refusing to die right away.

At the front of the group, Ryder peered into the vehicle's interior. His face screwed up in disgust, but the way was evidently clear. He waved everyone else forward.

Cora heard a crashing noise and the jungle parted. The remaining Carcharodontosaurus, Big Suzanne, slammed through the trees like a bulldozer.

Regular Suzanne stepped forward and raised her rifle. She pulled the trigger. Nothing happened. She hadn't reloaded after blowing away the Piltdown on top of the BMP.

Big Suzanne's jaws clamped down over her namesake, snapping closed like a bowling alley claw machine latching onto a stuffed animal. There was a sound like hedge trimmers snapping through green wood as the dinosaur bit through bone and cartilage. For a second, Cora could see the investor's legs kicking and thrashing where they dangled from the dinosaur's mouth. Then, Big Suzanne chomped down again, and the pair of legs fell separately to the ground with a pair of heavy thuds.

Ryder grabbed Cora's arm and heaved her into the BMP. Cora tripped and landed flat on her stomach next to the remains of Maryna, who had been pulled apart like string cheese by the Piltdowns. Nikolai and Maryna would have to be cleaned out of the crew compartment with a hose.

A second later, the vehicle's rear door slammed shut and Ryder shimmied through the crowded space toward the BMP's controls. Cora pulled herself to her knees just as the vehicle lurched to the side and rang from a heavy impact.

Big Suzanne was shoving at the armored personnel carrier, trying to bust it open to get at the people inside. Everyone screamed. Cora landed right back on her stomach as the vehicle shook again.

Something rolled across the floor and toward Cora's face. She tried to swat the blood-streaked thing away before realizing it was a satellite phone, probably Maryna's. Instead of tossing it away, Cora grabbed it as she picked herself up again. For just a second, she thought she would call the police, but then the sheer absurdity of that idea struck her. They were on an island in the middle of nowhere. There were no police.

She pulled herself together and hauled herself onto one of the seats lining the sides of the vehicle. Her blouse and pants, so carefully selected to maintain the right air of professionalism and propriety, were now smeared with pieces of the BMP crew.

The vehicle lurched again, not to the side but forward this time as Ryder worked the controls. Big Suzanne roared as the armored war machine clanked away from her.

"Shoot that thing!" Bainbridge yelled.

"With what?" Ryder yelled back.

"The big gun thing. The autocannon!"

"I'm not stopping this thing to stick my head up to fire the gun," Ryder said.

"Nella, you do it, then," Bainbridge said.

"Like hell," Nella said back.

As if to underscore Nella's point, Cora looked up through the open gunner's hatch and caught a glimpse of teeth. Big Suzanne chomped down on a section of the BMP's armor and tried to slow it down like a hyena with its teeth sunk into the haunch of a fleeing gazelle. The vehicle's engine briefly made a strained noise, but then the dinosaur's grip on the armored personnel carrier broke, and they accelerated away.

In short order, the thundering footfalls faded until they could no longer be heard. Big Suzanne roared once and then even that sound was drowned out by the roar of the armored personnel carrier's engine. The giant machine had moved slowly on the way into the park so Drake could work on his sales pitch. Now, they were tearing ass out of the park, sans sales pitch and several members of their expedition.

The BMP picked up speed, its treads tearing up the pavilion's carefully laid paving stones. Cora sat on her seat as the vehicle shook and rattled, trying not to get bounced around too much and mostly failing. She tried to brace herself with her feet, but her boots slid in the blood smeared across the floor.

Cora looked down at herself. Her pantsuit was a mass of red ruin. Her palms were streaked with gore where she'd picked herself up off the floor and grabbed the satellite phone. She looked like she'd just been dunked in a slaughterhouse slurry pit. She made a choked sound somewhere in the back of her throat that was partly a scream and partly a sob. She knew she wouldn't be able to stop if she started now.

Everyone spent a moment in silence, not out of respect for Suzanne Fischer, but because no one knew what to say after all that. Finally, Bainbridge broke the quiet. He turned to Cora.

"You have the genome data?" He looked at her expectantly.

Cora patted her pocket and felt the angular shape within. She pulled out the memory stick just to make sure it hadn't been damaged in her tumble. Her pocket was gummy with drying blood, and she squeezed her eyes shut as she forced her hand inside. Her fingers found the data stick and pulled it out. She held it up like she'd just performed a magic trick. Is *this* your intellectual property?

"I'd really be more comfortable if I held onto that," Bainbridge said. "I am the senior attorney on that project after all."

Cora bristled just a little. She'd have to hand the memory stick over anyway, if Bainbridge hadn't come right out and asked for it. But the "senior attorney" comment rubbed her the wrong way. It only seemed to emphasize that he'd never brought her along for her expertise or to help train her up. *You had your fun, but it's time for the real lawyer to take over.*

She also caught Burt's eye. He was looking at her and very clearly trying to telepathically tell her to hang onto it. She wasn't sure why exactly Burt didn't want Drake and Bainbridge to have the data stick, but right now, she trusted him more than them. And also, she was feeling petty after being taken to the ass-end of the world, almost eaten by several different monstrosities whose existence probably offended God, and then being told she couldn't hold the golden ticket anymore.

"I think I'll hang onto it for now. I'll feel safer if I know you're completely focused on protecting me with that." Cora pointed to Bainbridge's revolver.

Burt smiled to no one in particular.

Bainbridge made a face. He looked like he wanted to argue the point further, but the BMP began to slow. They had made it back to the beach in record time.

Cora briefly debated if she should run into the water before boarding the cargo tug back to the boat. She felt sticky and unclean. Probably because she *was* sticky and unclean. She kept her arms stiff and out to her sides so she wouldn't accidentally touch any of the blood on her blouse and pants. She'd realized she even had some matted into her hair. Running into the water and washing some of the gore off herself would feel wonderful, but she decided against it. She didn't want to delay leaving this place by even a second. The boat had showers, and she could toss these clothes overboard later. *Goodbye, pantsuit. Bon voyage, cute blouse she really liked.* She couldn't imagine wearing either of them again now.

Ryder parked the BMP and the rear doors opened. Cora stepped out of the vehicle and onto the edge of the pier and immediately realized that something was wrong. She'd expected a team of heavily armed men to greet her and the rest of the group.

There were several barricades set up, including a small wall of sandbags topped with the biggest gun she had ever seen in her life mounted on a swivel. Crates of supplies sat open all along the pier and across the beach.

Had the rest of Ryder's team left and abandoned them? No, the cargo tug was still tied up at the end of the dock. That was the only way back to the boat.

A figure suddenly stood up on the cargo tug, just a silhouette in the deepening gloom. Another figure joined it a moment later.

Oh no, Cora thought. Maybe it was all okay. There had been some big, burly dudes on the security team. But these silhouettes were slightly off. The proportions were subtly wrong. The limbs a bit too long. The heads a bit too small for the bulky bodies. Cora squinted, hoping to make out a few more details, hoping she was wrong.

The first figure picked up what appeared to be a severed human leg and took a huge bite out of the thigh meat before dropping it to the deck. The shadowy figure hopped off the cargo tug and onto the dock and began to stride purposefully toward Cora and the others. It was holding a broken table leg like a medieval mace. The second figure followed the first, and Cora caught a brief image of their reflective eyes coming toward her like a pair of feral cats.

Cora's mind raced. How had the Piltdowns taken down the whole security team? There were only two of them against a whole encampment of men armed to the teeth. Two Piltdowns couldn't wreak that much havoc all on their own.

Ryder saw the two Piltdowns as well. He checked his submachine gun before raising it to a firing position. He touched the cylindrical grenades dangling from his belt as if debating using one and then thinking better of it.

"Everybody back in the vehicle," Ryder said a moment before the length of sharpened rebar exploded out of his chest. The simple spear had been flung from the jungle. Cora whipped her head around and saw reflective eyes in the shadows now. Big, muscular shapes began to push the foliage aside and lumber onto the beach. They picked up speed as they cleared the jungle, charging forward.

Ryder looked down at the crude spear that had popped out of his chest like a Jack-in-the-box. He touched the end of the spear, which had been ground against some surface until it formed a pencil-sharp point. Blood now dripped off the slightly blunted end.

"Oh," Ryder said in a voice like he'd just had a particularly bad joke explained to him in great detail. Then, he fell flat on his face and more Piltdowns poured out of the jungle in a shrieking mass.

Oh, Cora thought dumbly. That was how they did it. It did take more than two Piltdowns to overrun the encampment. It took a bunch of them.

And now that Cora was looking in that direction, she could see where a bunch of heavy, bloody objects had been dragged through the sand and into the dense foliage. There were about as many drag marks as there had been members of Ryder's team.

It probably hadn't even been hard for the Piltdowns to overtake the men, who hadn't been briefed about the creatures. They thought they were here to fight dinosaurs. So when a few cavemen emerged from the nearby jungle, they didn't immediately fire, confused. Cora thought back to that call Ryder received in the science center, right before their own group was attacked. That had been the security team seeking clarification about what they should do. Then a few more Piltdowns appeared. And then a few more. And then there were Piltdowns on every side. What happened next was probably fast but nonetheless very unpleasant.

And now it was about to happen again.

Piltdowns poured out of the jungle near the BMP, running pell-mell toward the group. Most of them had fresh blood around their mouths from feeding on the security team. Some had grievous injuries, whole limbs flopping where they were attached by only a length of sinew. Machine gun fire had ruptured organs and pulped muscles, but the injured Piltdowns showed no sign of pain beyond running a bit slower than their compatriots. Blood loss or infection would spirit many of them away later, but for now, they weren't about to let a little thing like a shattered arm prevent them from ripping out Cora's spine.

Nella opened fire with her pistol and dropped three Piltdowns in quick succession. But the creatures shrugged off mortal wounds like they were fly bites. Anything that didn't immediately kill them was only an inconvenience. One big male Piltdown absorbed a shot to his gut, paused for just a second as if he needed to stifle a fart, and then he kept on coming even as his intestines began to leak out the hole in his ruptured abdomen. Bainbridge also opened fire with his cowboy revolver, missing every shot.

Cora didn't see the Piltdown matriarch anywhere. Perhaps she was still fleeing the Tyrannotitan somewhere deeper in the jungle.

The BMP wasn't an option. The Piltdowns were too close, and it took too long for everyone to file in and seal the doors shut. That took precious seconds they didn't have. Even if they could make it into the BMP, everyone who knew how to operate the machine was dead.

Cora looked down at Ryder's still form, a red puddle forming on the sand around him. The grenades were still on his belt.

Cora didn't have anything else. She decided that if she was going to go down, she was going to go down fighting. She ripped the grenade off

Ryder's body as another spear sailed past her, landing harmlessly in the sand.

She pulled the pin on the grenade and tossed it in the direction of the densest knot of Piltdowns. It landed in front of them and promptly burst.

Cora had been expecting a bigger bang. Or some type of fiery explosion like in the movies. Instead, the grenade sort of popped, seemingly without inflicting the least bit of harm on the Piltdowns, and then it began to hiss smoke like Cora's first car when it finally gave up the ghost and died on the side of the highway while she was in law school.

The thick fumes were a strange reddish color, and Cora realized that what she'd thrown was a smoke grenade. The rapidly expanding cloud of colored smoke engulfed the nearest Piltdowns, turning them into little more than shapes in the red mist. But it did slow them down. The lead Piltdowns skidded to a stop, surprised by the noise and the sudden cloud.

Suddenly a hand grabbed her shoulder, and she thought it was all over. The next thing she would feel would be another hand on her scalp, getting its grip so the Piltdown could wrench her head off her shoulders. But instead of the sensation of tearing muscles and popping vertebrae, a voice shouted in her ear.

"This way!" It was Burt.

He pointed and then took off, almost bowling over Drake and Bainbridge. Nella didn't need to be told to run. She fired a couple more shots at the nearest Piltdowns and then began running, too.

Burt tore through the smoke and into the jungle. Cora ran past the nearest Piltdown. It grabbed at her in surprise, but then it too was lost in the red smog. Shrieks and cries filled the air around her.

Cora ran. She felt the sand under her feet give way to more solid soil, but she couldn't see anything more than vague shapes to tell her she was any closer to the edge of the jungle. Suddenly, vines and brush leapt out of the smoke and tried to smack her in the face. She stumbled over a root but managed to keep her balance and continued running. Other figures ran beside her, and as the smoke began to thin, she saw that they were humans and not Piltdowns. Behind her, confused and angry snarls sounded as the Piltdowns tried to figure out where their prey had gone. She ran harder, putting more distance between herself and the sound of the Piltdown hunting band.

She wished she could pretend she was running toward safety, but she was fully aware that she was simply running deeper into the dinosaur-infested jungle. There was no safety on this island.

TEN

LABOR LAW FOR DUMMIES: NAVIGATING EMPLOYEE SAFETY STANDARDS IN LITIGIOUS TIMES

Burt ran, just hoping he hadn't somehow gotten turned around in the smoke and the jungle. His mind kept conjuring images of those blood-streaked, not-quite-human faces coming toward him. He ran until his legs burned. He ran until his breath came in strangled, choking gasps. He ran until he saw little spots in his vision. But he kept running. He continued toward his goal, only throwing a glance over his shoulder to make sure everyone else was following, hoping he wouldn't see those awful, loping figures in pursuit.

He saw Cora and Nella. He craned his neck a little further, and then he saw Drake and Bainbridge. That was everyone. Their once sizable group had been reduced to just five people. He shifted his head around to what was in front of him again, just in time to slam into the chain link fence at full speed.

He grunted as the chain link bowed inward and then catapulted him backward onto his butt. The jungle had begun to grow up around the fence without the grounds crews to machete it back every few weeks. Vines and creepers had reached out and now clung to the fence. In another few months, they might engulf it, creating an impenetrable wall of metal and foliage.

Burt picked himself up and looked at the buildings that lay beyond the barrier. Unlike the sleek architecture that dominated most of the park, these structures were boxy and utilitarian. The largest one resembled a runt-sized Soviet apartment block. The BMP would have looked right at home in front of it.

The building took up about the same area as a compact city block. It was composed of three wings arrayed at right angles, like a square missing one side, and had a little courtyard for recreation in the center. The design principles said "large college dormitory." The architectural style said "maximum security insane asylum." An industrial-sized trash chute hung from one wall like a giant stick insect.

Some of the lights were on inside the structure. They blinked out a moment later as the auxiliary power's corrupted software ground to a halt and restarted over and over again. The fact that not all the lights had been turned off before the system was shutdown was a testament to just how quickly chaos had overtaken Primeval and necessitated an evacuation.

"What is this place?" Cora asked.

Burt looked through the fence, memories flooding through him. He'd never loved this place, and he'd barely thought about it since leaving the island. But now that he was here again, a hundred phantoms tugged at his thoughts.

An evening spent with Florence, stargazing into the tropical night sky. His first official "date" with Florence in the commissary after they'd both signed the lengthy paperwork with Human Resources to start a workplace romance. Their date had consisted of eating the same cafeteria food they ate every day because none of the fancy tourist restaurants were operational yet. But they'd talked and talked and talked.

Florence had a future elsewhere. She'd originally planned to do just one tour with Primeval, but she'd signed a contract for another year here to stay with him. He knew that she sometimes regretted ever coming to the miserable little island. He knew she enjoyed looking forward to the day when RexNetics no longer needed him and she could take her turn to spread her wings. Several universities wanted her to spearhead new paleo-veterinary medicine programs. He knew full well that he was the one holding them up, but he just needed to stay a little longer to get things up and running so he could wriggle out from under Drake's thumb.

And then the park failed. And Florence died. And Burt lived.

Burt felt something cold coil around his heart and squeeze. The smell of her apartment after she burned those scented candles she liked. The table she always claimed for them in the back corner because it had a view of the whole cafeteria, and she liked to people-watch. The dog they'd talked about getting together someday. She wanted a Lab or Golden Retriever she could go on hikes with. He wanted something smaller that could sit by his desk, like maybe a Pug. Each memory hit him like a tidal wave until he felt like he was being swept out to sea.

"Staff quarters and amenities," Drake said, answering Cora's question and interrupting Burt's spiraling thoughts. "Primeval operated more like a cruise ship than a traditional theme park. We weren't in the middle of Orlando or Anaheim. Our people couldn't just drive to work every morning. By design, we're miles from the nearest inhabited island. Staff needed to live on-site. There's a gym, a couple of cafeterias, and some other basics. I try to make it as comfortable as possible for my employees here."

"That's just peachy, but does anybody have an extraction plan? We're still stuck on this island, and in case anybody forgot, our backup is dead," Nella said. She did not seem winded at all by the long sprint through the jungle.

To Burt's enormous surprise, Bainbridge spoke up. "I might have a little something up my sleeve. Let's get somewhere safe first, though."

Burt eyed the nearest apartment block. "I know a place we can hole up and gather our thoughts. Maybe get a plan together. We'll be safer inside."

He looked around and saw a spot where the chain link fence had been flattened. The barrier was meant to keep curious tourists out of the staff locations, not to keep hungry dinosaurs at bay. Something big had wandered through at some point and flattened the fence, leaving behind only some bent and twisted metal.

"We don't know what's in that compound," Drake said. "Maybe we should try to circle back to the BMP."

"I would *not* advise that," Nella said. "You're welcome to try, but at least inside the structures we'll have some protection from the dinosaurs. The big ones, at least."

"But there could be more Piltdowns in there," Drake protested.

"There could be more Piltdowns anywhere," Cora said, speaking up. "I would prefer that we only have to worry about them and not the Carcharodontosaurus as well."

Drake hefted his giant German anti-tank rifle. "I can deal with Big Suzanne. But if we run into twenty Piltdowns in there, well, I'd much rather have a couple of inches of armor between me and them than some drywall and a deadbolt."

Nella scowled and gestured with her pistol. "Fine, go back to the vehicle. But we know for a fact there are more of those creatures back there, and you'll have to sneak around them to get to the BMP. You don't pay me enough to go back with you, though."

Drake looked surprised to find himself in an argument. He was not a man used to receiving pushback. "Fine. But Nella, you and Burt are taking the lead on this. If there's something in there, you two get to bump into it first."

"Oh, good idea, Mr. Drake. I'll get right on it." Nella used her fawning airhead voice again for the first time since she'd given up pretending she was merely a personal assistant. She checked her pistol and nodded with grim satisfaction.

Drake looked like he wanted to argue the point further, but Burt simply started walking toward the section of downed fence. He stepped over, being careful not to get his feet tangled up in the metal, and found himself on the employee campus again. He fought back more memories and started toward the nearest building.

The structure was drab, water-stained concrete. A few jungle plants were trying to find purchase and climb up the wall, making the place look a bit like it was trying to disguise itself as a medieval ruin.

"This way," he said. "We'll cut through." He pushed open the door, and peeked inside. He heard rather than saw Nella following a few steps behind. The big, industrial laundry area featured a wall of washing machines and dryers. A couple of colossal spiders peered back at Burt from the room's corners, but the place was otherwise abandoned. A pile of half-sorted laundry lay on one of the tables.

Burt crossed the laundry room, his footsteps sounding far too loud in his own ears, and opened the far door. There was a narrow gap between the laundry room and the nearest apartment block. He looked to the left, in the direction of the checkpoint where employees were supposed to sign in and out. He could see the entrance to the security tunnel there. He remembered a half-dozen safety drills in which the employees practiced evacuating to the tunnels.

Every major location at Primeval had an entrance to the tunnels so tourists and staff could quickly run to a secure area in the event of a dinosaur escape, terrorist attack, or other major disaster. The tunnels all led to the central bunker beneath the science headquarters at the center of the park. The tunnels and cross tunnels were also used for utilities, storage, and the quick transport of supplies across the island.

Were the tunnels still secure? Maybe it would be better to take shelter down there? But then Burt remembered the ambush in the darkness inside the gene lab. If there were Piltdowns in the tunnels, they could corner everyone and butcher them with ease. No, it was better to stick to the buildings.

He hoped.

Burt scrambled across the open area between the laundry room and the apartment block just as the first drops of rain began to fall from the clouds gathering overhead. In the distance, he heard a rumble that was probably thunder. But on this island, it could have been something alive.

He pushed a door open and stepped into the cafeteria, the others following on his heels. A couple of windows were busted out, allowing water and debris to gather on the floor. And something had ransacked the kitchen, leaving behind only torn wrappers and packaging.

But the cafeteria only smelled of damp and disuse. Normally, that odor might have tickled his gag reflex, but this time he welcomed it. The building didn't have the thick animal stink of the Piltdowns. That seemed like a good sign. He trudged through the cafeteria and into the central hub of the building.

The lights were on in the main lobby. Burt stepped onto the soggy carpet and listened, but he didn't hear anything except for the increasingly loud rain outside. Some abandoned luggage sat nearby. A light fixture had crashed to the ground at some point. But the place seemed well and truly unoccupied.

He looked at the abandoned luggage briefly. Burt had been out in the park with Florence when everything happened. He never had a chance to make it back to the employee zone. He never saw this place evacuated and abandoned. Some part of him still half-expected to see a work colleague stroll out of the cafeteria. Or Florence.

The elevator light was actually lit up. Burt briefly wondered if the elevator itself was functional. Probably, if the backup power was able to supply light. But he wasn't about to take the elevator anywhere. The last thing in the world everyone needed was to get stuck in the elevator in case it failed in-between floors.

"Let's head up," Burt said, angling toward the stairs. He turned toward the door and paused briefly. There were claw marks on the wall, scratching up the wallpaper. They didn't look recent, but like the ransacked kitchen, it meant something *had* been here. Maybe the employee area wasn't the Piltdowns' turf, but something else had paid the building a visit. He looked at the size and spacing of the claw marks. Most likely a Spectrovenator.

One Spectrovenator wasn't so bad. One would probably run away from them. A group of them was another thing, though. A group would be trouble.

As quietly as he could, Burt pushed open the door to the stairwell. More luggage sat just inside the door. One duffel bag had been torn open and the contents spread helter-skelter over the first stairway. Burt wondered why, and then he saw the shredded foil of some candy wrappers. Something had sniffed out the morsels of food. Probably the building's Spectrovenator visitor.

Burt turned and looked at the faces behind him. Nella kept glancing around, keeping her situational awareness dialed up.

Burt probably should have been doing that more. He should probably have a gun. He should probably have run screaming into the night when Drake first told him that he was being recruited to go back to Primeval. Burt probably should have done a lot of things differently.

Drake just looked grim and petulant. Bainbridge had his oversized revolver out again. He'd gotten some of his swagger back since announcing that he had some sort of secret plan to get them off the island. Cora had the expression of someone who'd recently realized they left the oven on at home. A mixture of concern, reevaluating one's choices, and *oh-shit-oh-fuck*.

The rainfall had washed some of the BMP crew's blood off her, but she still looked a bit like she'd just spent all day chainsawing cows down into dog food-sized bits. She was red from head-to-toe.

He moved up five flights of stairs, his knees starting to protest as they reached the top floor, and then opened the door to the hallway where all the genetics staff had their rooms. Nothing was waiting for them in the hallway. A few doors stood open, but the hallway looked otherwise almost normal. The lights blinked off, and Burt jumped, but they snapped back on a moment later. Just the power continuing to hiccup. He was breathing hard, both from the hike up the stairs, and from the tension he felt building inside him.

Burt debated just popping into one of the open rooms as a place of temporary shelter, but that felt somehow wrong. At this point, probably no one on the genetics team would mind, but Burt still wanted *his* room. The one he had shared with Florence. It was probably the closest he would ever get to being able to say goodbye. He walked down the hallway and pulled out the key he still had all these months later.

He slid the key home, and the door swung open. Burt immediately felt the taut rope that had been holding his emotions together since that night begin to fray. A picture from happier days hung on the wall next to the door. He and Florence at the workplace New Year's party. It had been taken a few weeks before he proposed. He'd only recently convinced her to stay at Primeval with him for another year. Scattered all over the room were more reminders of her. More photos. A shelf of her books, neatly arranged by author. A closet full of her clothes, Burt's own wardrobe relegated to a small dresser. Florence always had a lot more clothes than he did, but it was because she was a lot more likely to get covered in dinosaur diarrhea in the course of her work as a paleo-vet than he was as a geneticist. She brought a few changes of clothes with her every time she reported to the veterinary office.

Everyone filed inside, and the apartment suddenly became cramped. By the standards of Primeval, where real estate was at a premium and almost all of the space needed to be reserved for attractions and guest services, the apartment was relatively spacious. Lower-ranking staff residing on the lower floors lived in much more restricted quarters.

He saw Cora looking at the picture of him and Florence. Had he told her about Florence? He didn't think so. Then she looked at Burt with a pitying look, and he knew she knew. Somebody told her. Maybe Bainbridge. He looked at Cora, bedraggled and covered in blood.

"Cora, would you like to borrow some clothes?" Burt asked.

"Oh my God, yes, please," Cora said. "I mean, if that's alright with you."

"Yeah. You might need a belt. Florence was a little taller than you, so the sizes will probably be off. Bathroom's through there. Feel free to get cleaned up. Take what you need."

"I...," Cora started to say something and then looked back at the photo on the wall briefly. "Thank you," she said. She fished a couple of things out of her pockets. The first was a satellite phone that she must have gotten off one of the dead BMP crewmembers. The second was the data drive with its dinosaur genome sequences.

Burt took them both and stuck them in his own pockets. He noticed the look that Drake and Bainbridge gave him as he put the data stick away. Like hungry dogs watching a rabbit.

"So what's this plan to get us off this island?" Nella asked as Cora began to pick out some clothes that might fit.

Burt also wanted to know about this grand rescue plan, but he watched Cora select clothes from his dead fiancée's closet. Florence's favorite t-shirt came off the rack. Cora held it up to herself, being careful not to get blood on it. Burt almost asked her to pick something else, but he forced himself to hold his tongue and pay attention to Bainbridge instead.

Bainbridge pulled out his satellite phone and scrolled to a number he'd saved in his contacts. "Well, when I was working with the authorities of Papua New Guinea on the legal side of getting Primeval up and running, I made quite a few contacts, including in the military. Papua New Guinea isn't exactly a world-class military powerhouse, but they have a teeny-tiny air force, including a single Huey helicopter that could be used to evacuate us. One call to their Defense Department, and the cavalry comes running."

"There's a helipad on top of the hotel for VIPs," Drake said.

"Right. We're not even that far away. We could take the security tunnels. The animals won't even know we're moving out to be evacuated right below their feet," Bainbridge said, clearly pleased with himself.

Burt could see that Nella was trying to find the flaw in the plan. Could it work? Maybe. Burt had never served in the military. He didn't know a good tactical escape plan from a hole in the ground. But being ferried off the island in a helicopter sounded better than Burt's next best idea, which was to hide until the crew of Drake's yacht contacted somebody a lot less important than whoever Bainbridge was calling and begged for help.

He moved over and opened a drawer in the cramped kitchenette, half-listening to Bainbridge as he pushed the call button and started a series of transfers to someone important in Papua New Guinea's military. Burt fished around in the drawer until he found what he was looking for. He pulled a meat tenderizer out of the drawer. Then he took the data drive out of his pocket and laid it on the counter.

Bainbridge finished a brief explanation of the situation, leaving out a great many details that might make RexNetics and Richard Drake personally liable for the deaths of quite a few people today.

Cora had picked out a few clothes that looked like they might fit. The shirt, some pants, and a light jacket. She caught Burt's eye and nodded her thanks. Burt nodded back as she ducked into the bathroom and shut the door.

Burt waited until Bainbridge ended the call, a big grin on his face, before he took the meat tenderizer and began to smash the hell out of the data drive.

ELEVEN

HOT TOPICS IN INTELLECTUAL PROPERTY: DIGITAL RIGHTS MANAGEMENT, BIO-PIRACY, & THE FUTURE OF I.P. THEFT

Cora had only just finished marveling at how good it felt to be wearing clean clothes, and at just how odd it felt to be wearing clothes that belonged to Burt's dead fiancée, when an unholy racket arose from the other room. She threw the door open, expecting to see Piltdowns bursting into the room like some sort of prehistoric SWAT team.

But there was only Burt, standing in the apartment's micro-kitchen, holding some sort of hammer and pulverizing something. She saw a small amount of shattered plastic, some bent metal, and the gleam of electronic innards. Then, she realized it was the data drive.

The piece of intellectual property that she and the others had come all the way out here to retrieve, the one that she had planned to eventually form the centerpiece of her career. The one worth about the same amount of money as several winning lottery tickets all glued together and wrapped in gold leaf. The one several people had inadvertently died for today. *That* intellectual property.

Part of her was absolutely horrified, as if she'd just watched someone vandalize a museum's most prestigious masterpiece. And a little part of her was savagely glad to see it obliterated.

Burt looked up and must have noticed the look on her face. "Holy shit. They really didn't tell you, did they?"

She looked around. Drake and Bainbridge looked shockingly nonchalant for having just witnessed the destruction of the intellectual property that undergirded Primeval. Drake had even said they were eventually going to use that DNA data as the basis of new dinosaurs in the future, like their failed attempt to make a Tyrannotitan. The data contained on that drive was supposed to be the mojo that would drive decades of innovation and expansion at RexNetics, and Drake looked like someone who'd just noticed the milk in his fridge was expiring slightly sooner than he expected.

"Want me to read her in on the secret?" Bainbridge asked.

"Holy shit," Burt said again. "They brought you all the way out here to this little slice of paradise and they really didn't tell you? Oh my God. It's like a surprise party planned by imbeciles."

"Tell me what?" Cora asked, hating the strident urgency in her voice but needing to know nonetheless.

Drake looked at her. "I guess the cat's out of the bag. The data's worthless," he said.

"But... you... we..." Cora sputtered, trying to figure out where to even begin.

"It's pirated," Bainbridge said, as if that explained everything.

"You can't pirate dinosaurs," Cora said, flabbergasted.

"I used to work for Global Fossil Fund," Burt said. "And their star attractions are the Carcharodontosaurus, the Suchomimus, and the Spectrovenator. Exactly the same ones that Primeval was going to showcase."

Cora looked to Drake. "But you told the investors before that you were using the same dinosaurs as Global Fossil Fund as a mark of quality. If you could make the same dinosaurs, it would prove that the RexNetics technology was up to the task."

"Oh, yeah. That. I lied," Drake said. He shrugged. "We copied the Global Fossil Fund roster because those were the only dinosaurs we could actually make from the data Burt stole."

Cora looked at Burt. The part of her that had studied so hard to get into law school and worked her butt off to master her law classes and slaved away ahead of the bar exam and sought out a carefully curated career path, sat down and committed ritualistic suicide. She was working for fucking I.P. pirates? RexNetics was just bootleg music downloads for dinosaurs? And she'd nearly died working for these people?

She must have misunderstood. That couldn't possibly be right. This was some sort of joke.

"I was a junior geneticist at Global Fossil Fund. I had access to all the data, but I was a small fish. RexNetics made me the proverbial offer I couldn't refuse. More than enough pay to kill my student debt. A huge jump up in my career. A bullet-proof retirement package. The resources to run interference on any sort of investigation into the copied data. I figured I'd be indispensable. It also meant that RexNetics would pretty much own my soul for the foreseeable future, but I didn't think that through at the time," Burt said. He gave a sort of embarrassed shrug.

"Yeah, I drafted your new contract," Bainbridge said. "You really should have consulted with a lawyer before you signed that."

"Probably," Burt said. "But then I'd have to explain that I copied several terabytes of genome data onto a memory drive without permission and handed it over to a rival company."

Drake nodded. "It was probably the most successful corporate espionage scheme of all time. And it was surprisingly easy. In retrospect, it was too easy," he said. "Global Fossil Fund had become a major operator in the entertainment industry, but it was still mostly operated by scientists, not business people. They had a lot of blind spots. They didn't have all that many safeguards set up against a snatch-and-grab operation from the inside. We probably should have asked why. But by the time we figured it out, it was too late to fix the problem."

Burt flicked a few pieces of mangled plastic off the countertop and into a wastebasket. "Global Fossil Fund didn't have a lot of physical safeguards. There wasn't much to prevent me from downloading all the data and dropping it off with my RexNetics contact. It was like a Cold War spy leaving classified documents wrapped up in a newspaper on the park bench. But even if there weren't many physical security measures, there were some digital safeguards. They didn't tell the genetics team about the digital ones. That was something the IT department worked on. You ever hear of digital rights management software?"

Cora nodded. The topic came up in her law school intellectual property classes, but she had never been directly involved with digital rights management. "It lets copyright holders control how their material is used once it's out in the wild. Sort of a leash for users. Maybe you pay for a song and download it to your computer, but the software won't let you download it again to another computer until you deactivate the download on the first computer. Means there's only one copy per user."

"More or less, yeah," Drake said. "Shows up a lot with video games, too. Somebody buys a game, and the software does a handshake with the game company to verify that it's a legitimate sale. If somebody pirates the game, the handshake fails, and then usually the game won't play. Maybe a little message pops up telling the player to either go buy a legitimate copy or piss up a rope. Doesn't have to deactivate the entire game, though. Sometimes, the game company gets clever. Instead of refusing to play, the game just kills your character every time you use the jump button or something. You can still technically use the software, but it's fundamentally broken in some obnoxious way that wastes your time. Global Fossil Fund had a similar idea."

"The genome data was loaded with malware, something that nobody outside their IT security division knew about," Burt said.

"You can't put malware in DNA," Cora said.

"You'd be surprised. DNA is just four repeating nucleotides. Adenine, Cytosine, Guanine, and Thymine. You can build a whole dinosaur out of that. Or a person. Or a cabbage. Compare that to computer binary. It's all ones and zeroes, and you can make the whole internet out of that. With a digital copy of a DNA sequence, you can dress a few ones and zeroes up in a trench coat and pretend they're nucleotides and just hide them in the dinosaurs' junk DNA. A pretty substantial chunk of the dinosaur genetic code doesn't really do much of anything. Same with human beings. A lot of it is evolutionary dead ends that never got snipped out, or ancient retroviruses that injected themselves into our gene pool back when mammals were still fresh off the drawing board. At a glance, you can't tell which part of the genetic code is essential to organ development and which part gives you a greater tolerance for spicy foods and which part does absolutely nothing. And since there's so much of it and you can't tell what anything does right away, it's the perfect place to hide malware," Burt said.

Cora thought through everything she remembered about Primeval and why it shut down. As if on cue, the lights flickered out before coming back on again. "There was no international hacking group, was there? You accidentally uploaded a malware virus from the Global Fossil Fund data, and it crippled the park."

"That's the short version of events, yes," Drake said. "The genome data had a hidden digital rights management program tucked away, carefully packaged as just another bit of genetic code. All the Global Fossil Fund systems have a corresponding bit of software in them somewhere. If the genome data goes through a system that doesn't have that bit of code, if it reaches out and doesn't get the secret handshake in return, it'll start wheedling its way into every computer and subsystem it's connected to. But slowly. Insidiously. Ever hear the phrase 'computer cancer?' By the time we realized it was there, it was already shutting systems down at random. It had metastasized, and it was in absolutely everything. Everything. We'd led the big wooden horse right through the city gates and didn't even think about it until it was too late. The malware wormed its way into the central system and corrupted the whole park," Drake said.

"And then there was the bio-malware," Burt said.

"Bio-malware?" Cora didn't like the sound of that.

Drake brushed an invisible bit of grime off his designer jacket. "Yeah. The Tyrannotitan? Like I said, we wanted a different lineup than what Global Fossil Fund had. We decided to tweak the Carcharodontosaurus into a related genus, the Tyrannotitan. The Suchomimus was going to become a Baryonyx. The Spectrovenator was going to be some bigger abelisaurid. Carnotaurus, maybe. Or a Majungasaurus. Something with some charisma. Some oomph to it. Not a pissant like Spectrovenator.

"But there were some other insertions into Global Fossil Fund's DNA. If you try to change the genome and you don't pass that secret handshake test, you get something like our Tyrannotitan. Most of those animals were stillborn. But some survived. They were just... wrong. We thought it was something we were doing incorrectly. Dinosaur DNA doesn't come with an instruction manual. We'd try to tweak the creature's color patterns, easy stuff like making an albino Carcharodontosaurus, and we'd just get monsters. Global Fossil Fund's bio-malware wasn't as sophisticated as their computer malware. We eventually figured out how to circumvent some of it, but we still thought that our difficulties were due to rushed experiments or botched samples. If you tinkered with the DNA on a system that didn't pass the digital handshake test, it would randomize swathes of genetic code you didn't touch. You could play whack-a-mole with the errors, but each time you altered something, another piece of genetic code would change somewhere else. And if you *didn't* start tinkering with it, you could only make carbon copies of the Global Fossil Fund roster. I finally managed to make a herd of miniaturized Massospondylus, and we probably would have fully worked our way around the problem if the park didn't go down when it did. We made a good number of Global Fossil Fund clones to study and show off to investors, but they would have all been euthanized as soon as we could get our own templates working properly. They couldn't be allowed to live. If we exhibited exact copies, Global Fossil Fund's lawyers would instantly suspect we'd stolen their genomes, and they'd only need a single vial of dinosaur blood to prove it."

Bainbridge spoke up. "If everything had gone according to plan, we would have taken the data drive back to the yacht, plugged it into a laptop to show the investors everything was in order and then chucked the laptop into the ocean. It would be so infected with malware by that point that we couldn't connect it to anything else. Show the investors we have the goods, convince them to buy their way in, and then milk them for everything they have once they've tied their wagon to Primeval. Depending on market conditions, we could either offload the problem onto them and wash our hands or leverage their assets to fully start over."

"Jesus," Cora said, taking in the scale of the fraud Drake had tried to pull. "That's why you wanted to host a hunt here. Each day the dinosaurs were loose was another day somebody might figure out what RexNetics had done. This whole expedition was a cover-up."

Bainbridge gave a smile that wasn't a smile at all. "We paid off a few fishermen who landed on the island at one point. We think Global Fossil Fund encouraged them to try to collect a sample. They could shoot one of the little dinosaurs, toss it in the same ice they were using to preserve their fish, and ship it off to Global Fossil Fund. Of course, they almost got eaten, so they were happy to take our money and disappear. But the fact remains that we're fairly certain Global Fossil Fund suspects the truth. That was the impetus for doing this now instead of waiting until more of the animals starved. People were starting to poke their noses around the island. We needed to destroy the evidence. Both the dinosaurs themselves and the genome data. Clean slate. The genome data was still worth an enormous amount of money, but mostly because it would be the key piece of evidence in the largest lawsuit you've ever seen. The hunt was a way to raise funds and eighty-six any evidence of wrongdoing at the same time."

"But why steal the DNA in the first place?" Cora felt like screaming. *This* was what she'd dedicated her career to? She'd dragged herself through law school to become basically the fancy equivalent of a Watergate goon, helping clean up messes the big man left behind when he wanted to steal some files from his enemies? "You have the money to start a dinosaur entertainment park from scratch. You're goddamn Richard Drake. You're, what, the tenth richest person on the planet?"

"Eighth," Drake corrected.

"That's not better in this context," Cora said, trying to keep her voice steady. She was quivering with barely suppressed anger. "Maybe it was cheaper to find somebody like Burt to whore out some intellectual property to you, but the risks. The liability!"

"For the record, I was a very expensive whore," Burt said.

"He was," Drake confirmed.

"Again, that's not better!" Cora said.

"The reason we bought ourselves a pet geneticist is actually quite simple. Speed," Drake said. "There are already two major players in the dinosaur entertainment market, and there's a half-dozen other firms champing at the bit to fight their way in. But most of them will fail. There's only room for a handful of players in this particular game. We're not running a budget motel at the edge of a big city. We're not opening a chicken farm in the middle of a rural area. This market is more like a giant defense firm. You don't just have mom and pop tank factories springing up overnight. There are huge barriers to entry due to the investment required, and there are only so many customers to go around. This is a race to gain market share. Being an established, trusted brand will be enormously helpful in the long run when new players try to enter the market. Getting Burt to simply give us a decade's worth of Global Fossil Fund's research was a huge head start. It allowed us to go directly to a stage where we could build a park because we could roll out proof-of-concept dinosaurs almost immediately. Unfortunately, things didn't work out quite as planned."

"But you did manage to make original creatures in that time," Cora said. "The Piltdowns weren't stolen from Global Fossil Fund, right?"

"That's right," Burt said. "We developed those in-house. But it's a lot easier to make macaques beefier than it is to turn a chicken embryo into a Tyrannotitan. If we'd been starting our dinosaurs from scratch, we'd be on about the same page as SaurCorp or Epoch Studios, dicking around with enzymes in test tubes and preparing for yet another round of CRISPR edits."

"With Primeval off the ground and bringing in funds, we could have carved out a space for ourselves and defended it from the latecomers," Drake said. "Hell, the other parks probably wouldn't have been financially viable once a third major power entered the field. Primeval would have been able to scoop up their staff and intellectual property when they failed. Not only would we have cut them off at the knees, but we'd be able to fuel our own expansion by gobbling them up. But that would only work if we got to market before they did. By a significant amount."

"Of course, there was always Plan B," Bainbridge said. "If the park was unsalvageable, we'd offload it and leave someone else holding the bag. Just quit-claim all the intellectual property. It's like selling someone the Brooklyn Bridge. If life gives you lemons, make lemonade. If life gives you rat turds, tell people they're chocolate chips and get out of town before anybody tries the trail mix you sold them. We'd clear out, but Suzanne Fischer and company would almost certainly go bankrupt before they figured out what had gone wrong."

"But since Primeval's chief investors are no longer available to purchase the park..." Drake gestured at the smashed memory stick. "We can dispense with the illusion."

Cora stared, still absorbing the situation. She was exhausted. Her brain didn't want to fully process any new information after running from genetic abominations and seeing people killed by man-made horrors earlier.

But all those incidents had been in the moment. They had been fast and terrible and largely out of her control. But there was an awful deliberateness to the information she'd just learned. This wasn't nature, however corrupted by genetic manipulation and profit motives, being red in tooth and claw. This was intentional, dangerous fraud. And people had died because of those choices.

And then Cora realized with dawning horror that she'd gotten exactly what she wanted when she set out for this island what felt like a lifetime ago. She'd been elevated to the inner circle. She'd seen behind the curtain and made complicit in what was going on back there. She was in the big leagues now.

Bainbridge hadn't let her on the dinosaur patent project earlier to keep the conspiracy as contained as possible.

Drake launched this whole expedition to retrieve his intellectual property so he could hide the evidence of the fraud.

Even Nella had probably been in on the secret before Cora. If any of this information was news to her, she didn't show it. She'd stationed herself near the window and was keeping watch over the outside.

And Burt? Burt really was just some asshole on Drake's payroll. Goddammit. Somehow that one stung the most. But now Cora understood what Burt meant when he said that Drake owned him. RexNetics had elevated him and compromised him at the same time. Telling anyone meant destroying himself along with Drake.

And now Cora was part of that chain. She was part of the cover-up. She knew the secret, and it made her want to scream.

Rain pattered against the apartment window as Cora tried to think of something to say. She felt flattened. She thought she'd been working for, well, maybe not the good guys. But she thought she was generally on the side of law and order. Clear legal rules about who owned what intellectual property and how it could be used kept the gears of business turning, and when there were conflicts, they were orderly, adjudicable conflicts. But no, she was working for intellectual property scofflaws. Honest-to-goodness, USDA-certified asshats. And now she'd found out she was among their ranks.

If anyone found out about this, she'd be disgraced and radioactive in the legal community. Hell, she'd be lucky to keep her law license. Actually, she might be lucky to stay out of prison, now that she knew about all this.

"Well, shit," she finally said.

Burt chuckled. He gave her the knowing gaze of the damned. He'd already made his bargain with the devil.

Cora briefly considered if this knowledge at least gave her any leverage. Probably not, if Drake managed to clean up the island. The genome data was already toast thanks to Burt. If she tried to extricate herself from this mess and blow the lid off RexNetics, she wouldn't necessarily have any proof. Bainbridge would bring down one almighty lawsuit upon her head. And Drake obviously wasn't above playing dirty. He could probably have documents forged showing that she had engineered most of the wrongdoing and then throw her to the wolves. She was caught in Drake's web as surely as Burt.

She considered if she even *wanted* to extricate herself. If necessity had made her a part of the inner circle, there would be certain bonuses. There'd no doubt be an official promotion and a large pile of money waiting for her. Even if Primeval shut down entirely and Drake simply had to write it off and eat the expenses out of pocket, he probably wouldn't tumble out of the list of the twenty-five richest people in the world. There'd still be a lot of other opportunities for a young lawyer who knew too much. She could be shuffled off to some cushy position in another part of Drake's business empire. He'd have to buy her off. She wouldn't exactly be put out to pasture and left to chase ambulances for 1-800-LAWMART. All she had to do was keep quiet.

A noise slowly drew her attention. At first, Cora thought it was thunder, but then she realized that it was the steady beat of a helicopter's rotors. The others noticed too, and everyone raced to the window.

The noise intensified and a light flew overhead, passing them by, growing more distant again. The helicopter was heading toward the center of the island.

"They only sent one?" Burt asked.

"It's a Huey. They can fit up to fourteen kitted out soldiers," Nella said. "There's a lot fewer of us than that now."

"Do they know we're here? Are they going to land?" Cora asked. She felt a stab of panic at the idea that the helicopter might buzz by, not see them, and fly away again.

"They're going to the helipad on top of the hotel," Bainbridge said. "Safest place to set down."

That sounded well and good and perfectly reasonable to Cora except for the teensy-weensy detail that she wasn't at the hotel. Acres of monster-infested jungle stood between her and the hotel.

"What's the safest way for us to get to the hotel?" Cora asked. For the moment, she shelved further thoughts about where her career all went wrong and what she wanted to do about it. She couldn't spend any of that sweet, sweet hush money if she was dead.

Drake spoke up. "The shelter tunnels. They go to every major point on the island. Designers told me they're like the London subway system during the German blitz. Easy to access. Can withstand an impact from anything short of a nuclear detonation. We pop down, follow the signs, pop back up in the hotel basement and then make our way up to the helipad. We'll bypass everything up at the surface."

"That… might just work," Burt said, rubbing his chin.

"Let's get moving then." Bainbridge held himself a little higher. The stolen genome data was destroyed, taking a big chunk of potential incriminating evidence with it. And now he'd called in the cavalry and probably saved their collective bacon. No matter what financial fate befell Primeval, Bainbridge was getting a raise out of this fiasco.

For the first time since fleeing the gene lab, Cora allowed herself to feel a little excitement. All she had to do was get back to the hotel and then she could get the hell off this island. Maybe it wasn't exactly a hop, skip, and jump away, but there was a plan and a route that sounded relatively safe. Although a warzone would probably still be safer.

"Wait," Nella said, and her tone made Cora freeze. "Did you hear that?"

"No. What was it?" Bainbridge asked.

"*Shhh*." Nella held a finger to her lips and drew her pistol.

Cora strained her ears, but she couldn't hear anything over the sound of the rain outside. Not for the first time today, she wished she had a weapon. She saw the satellite phone she'd grabbed from the BMP sitting on top of the table next to the closet, right where she'd left it before she changed clothes. She grabbed it just to have something to hang on to. It felt better to have something than to sit and wring her hands. Then she saw a block of knives near the sink. She clipped the phone to her shirt and pulled out the largest knife. It looked like something a serial killer might use to chop up horny teenagers in a slasher movie.

Would the gleaming metal blade help her against a Piltdown? Against the Piltdown's matriarch, with her ruined face and fire axe? Against a whole horde of the flesh-hungry brutes as they screamed for her blood? Probably not. But it was something. And Cora would take anything she could get right now.

Nella moved across the apartment with the quiet ease of a cat. She walked on the balls of her heels, each footstep lost in the constant drum of rain against the window.

She stepped up to the apartment door. The barrel of the pistol touched the faux-wood veneer with a faint noise, the first sound inside the apartment for several seconds. Nella stuck her eye to the peephole.

The door exploded inward off its hinges, falling inward on top of Nella. She held up her arms in surprise, but it knocked her flat on her back, the broken door landing on top of her like a flyswatter. A Spectrovenator shoved its way through the now open doorway and hissed at the people inside. It took a tentative step forward.

Gunfire exploded upward through the door. A couple of shots punched harmlessly through the ceiling. The rest buried themselves in the dinosaur's neck and gut. The creature toppled over with a shriek, its clawed feet kicking wildly before it went still.

Nella pushed the door off her. Cora had the brief mental image of a vampire shoving the lid to her coffin open to greet the night.

Somewhere downstairs, more Spectrovenators shrieked. The noise they made was somewhere between a yap and a cluck, surprisingly high-pitched and grating.

"Time to go," Nella said, reloading her pistol. She stepped out into the hallway and waved everyone out.

Cora stepped past the dead Spectrovenator. The dinosaur's mottled black and tan hide was now splashed red with blood. Its mouth hung open, revealing an array of sharp, curved teeth. The Spectrovenator wasn't huge. Nowhere near as large as the giant Carcharodontosaurus, but it was bigger than most large dogs.

What had Burt told her earlier that afternoon on the beach, back when her biggest concerns were keeping sand out of her shoes and avoiding Bainbridge? A single Spectrovenator wasn't too dangerous on its own, but in numbers...

More furious yelps and chuffs from downstairs. They were in numbers now. And like every other animal that had been abandoned here, they were hungry.

Cora stepped out into the hallway along with Drake and Bainbridge. She looked back and saw Burt pause in the entryway of his former apartment. For a second, she thought he was stopped because of the dead dinosaur partially blocking the exit. But no, he stopped, took one last look at the framed picture of himself and Florence, and then shuffled past the dead dinosaur.

"Come *on*," Drake said.

"The elevator's this way," Bainbridge said, pointing.

"No," Nella said. "We don't want the doors to open and find ourselves looking at a bunch of hungry dinosaurs and nowhere to go. Stairs. Move." Cora was more than happy to follow Nella as she dashed toward the stairwell.

Below them, the Spectrovenators yowled and bellowed. The hunt was on. Again.

TWELVE

THE RIGHT TO BEAR ARMS & YOUR CLIENT: PERSPECTIVES FROM EXPERIENCED ATTORNEYS

Burt and the others dashed down several flights of stairs. It felt insane to be rushing headlong toward the source of the horrible noises coming from the first floor, but what other choice did they have? Maybe Bainbridge could call in more favors and get most of the rest of Papua New Guinea's military out to the island, but it would take hours to mobilize and transport a large-scale force.

Burt wasn't holding out much hope that he and the others would still be alive by the time rescue arrived now that the dinosaurs knew where to find them. And that was assuming that the military brought the resources required to actually reach the apartment. Troops on foot were as likely as not to meet the same fate as Drake's security team, ripped apart by things in the jungle before they even realized the magnitude of the threat they faced.

Staying put and hunkering down wasn't an option, not when the Spectrovenators knew they were here. Drake and Bainbridge both had guns, but so far as Burt could tell, Nella was the only person here who knew how to actually shoot. And any shooting would only draw the attention of more of the island's inhabitants. Burt remembered how Big Suzanne had tracked them down after they shot at some of the Piltdowns outside the science center. If this turned into a siege, every dinosaur left on the island would gather around the building to wait for their chance to corner and eat the remaining survivors.

No, that Huey helicopter was their only shot. And that meant making a run for it *right now*.

Burt cursed to himself. Everything he touched on this island seemed to turn to hot, bubbling shit. Florence was long dead. His own creations were trying to eat him. And he'd completely alienated the one person on the island who might actually understand his position.

Cora had obviously been taken by complete surprise to learn about the stolen dinosaur genomes. She'd been played just as readily as he had, and he hadn't even realized it until he carried out Drake's bidding by smashing the data drive.

Seeing Cora in Florence's clothes made Burt's heart lurch sickeningly. He could tell that he had probably lost whatever grudging trust she might have had in him by smashing the data drive when she still seriously thought that her career depended on protecting it. And now, she'd been inducted into the little group of conspirators against her will.

Burt finally had company in his little circle of Hell. Someone had been duped even worse than he had into coming back to this wretched island. But now that he had the company, he wished he could undo it all.

Maybe there was something he could do. He'd just have to survive first.

He was panting as the group raced down the stairs to the second floor. He could smell mildew and something else now. Something musky and pungent. It smelled a little like the turkey farm at the edge of town where Burt grew up.

The stairwell door burst open at the ground floor and three Spectrovenators barreled inside. The smell instantly intensified. The dinosaurs looked up, and their eyes collectively locked onto the group. Their nostrils flared, taking in the scent of human prey, and their lips curled back to reveal wickedly curved fangs. The creatures loosely resembled small tyrannosaurs, each the size of a large dog.

Nella fired her pistol down at the bottom landing. The rounds were deafening in the confined space, and a high-pitched ring immediately began to whine in Burt's ears. One of the Spectrovenators went down, a gout of blood spurting out of its head. A second screamed and snarled, lurching out of the stairwell. The third screamed as an ugly wound sprang into existence on its flank, but it didn't retreat. And another Spectrovenator was already muscling its way into the stairwell to occupy the space its companion had just fled.

Nella's pistol clicked dry. She reached into her pocket and froze. Her hand patted her thigh, trying to find something that wasn't there. Burt groaned inside. He knew what that meant. He knew exactly what that meant. Nella was out of rounds.

Bainbridge yanked out his big revolver and fired off a round in the direction of the dinosaurs below. Burt saw something spark off one of the concrete steps near the bottom of the stairwell, and then something blew past him. It took him a moment to realize that it was a round ricocheting back in his direction. Nella swatted Bainbridge's wrist upward before he could fire again.

The wounded Spectrovenator took a step up the stairs, favoring its right leg but clearly undeterred. It made a deep rumbling noise down in its throat. Its talons clicked on the cement steps.

Burt looked around. There had to be something they could do other than simply run back up the stairs. That might buy them a few minutes, but it sure as hell wouldn't help them any in the long run.

The helicopter that would take them out of here wasn't even that far away. All they had to do was get back to the hotel at the main pavilion. That was it. Safety was less than fifteen minutes away at the pace of a brisk stroll. But that helicopter might as well have been on Mars.

He knew this island better than anybody else here. There had to be a way. There had to be something he could do. If he could just think of something other than the threat of being eaten alive.

And then he had something.

"Back upstairs," Nella said. "Maybe we can get to the roof and barricade it for a final stand."

"No, this way," Burt shouted. He threw open the door that led to the second floor's main hallway. This level housed lower ranking staff, including a lot of the maintenance and groundskeeping people. Most of the workers were unskilled labor from Papua New Guinea instead of imported specialists like himself. The rooms were smaller and had bunk beds three-high.

Burt always felt a little guilty when he came down to this level. The quarters were still basically decent, but they were more like overcrammed college dorms than the comparatively luxurious room he shared with Florence. They weren't exactly slums, but RexNetics had a literal underclass of employees living at the lower levels.

Normally, Burt didn't come to the second floor unless he had to. But sometimes he did have to. Because the second floor had the best access to the trash chute. Technically, the chute ran to all five levels, but there was a snag at the third floor, and trash bags that were supposed to be destined for the dumpsters tended to get caught and back up there. After the fifth time it happened, the third-floor residents threw a minor revolt and hung signs on all the other floors asking people to use the second-floor chute or just walk their damn trash down to the dumpsters. The smell of the backed-up trash chute convinced even the lazier residents to use the second-floor chute.

There at the far end of the hall was a little door built into the wall, almost as if it was the drawer to a large filing cabinet. Burt knew it was big enough for a human being. An IT guy had been fired for getting drunk and riding down the chute one time. Of course, he got stuck at the third floor in a giant knot of trash, which might have saved his life since it was mostly a straight plunge down to the dumpsters. It had taken most of a day to extricate him, though.

Burt suspected there were probably supposed to be safety regulations that prevented people from tumbling their way down the trash chute like they were on an Olympic luge team, but everyone who worked at Primeval had signed ironclad liability waivers. Burt had mostly been picturing dinosaur attacks when he signed on the dotted line promising to arbitrate rather than sue if he was injured on the island. But substandard building safety standards probably fell under that category as well. Burt was pretty sure he could thank Bainbridge in some way for that little clause. But now he *actually* needed to thank Bainbridge for allowing Primeval to install shitty employee amenities. Bless the little weasel's heart.

"This way," Burt shouted, waving everyone toward the end of the hall.

"It's a dead end," Nella shouted, slamming the stairwell door behind her after everyone else ran through.

"Not quite," Burt said. "The trash chute."

Nella visibly debated overriding his admittedly crappy plan. Burt saw the exact instant she rifled through alternative options and came up with nothing. She nodded and took two strides forward only for the stairwell door to explode open behind her.

The wounded Spectrovenator darted forward as Nella tried to spin around. The dinosaur's head darted forward, and its jaws clamped onto Nella's arm just above the elbow. She gritted her teeth in a suppressed scream and tried to jab her elbow into the creature's throat, but the angle was all wrong.

The Spectrovenator shook its head, shredding skin and muscle alike, its teeth sinking deeper at the same time. Nella tried to wrench her arm out of the dinosaur's grasp when the second Spectrovenator nosed through the door and bit her calf, latching on with the tenacity of a wolf trying to drag a caribou down by the throat.

Burt took a step toward Nella, unsure what he intended to do, exactly. Punch the dinosaurs? Kick them right in their scaly shins? Use harsh language?

He just knew he had to do something. Too many people had died in front of him. Too many people had died partly because of him and his work here. He launched himself forward, intending to jab the nearest dinosaur in the eye. He vaguely remembered reading that that was supposed to dissuade sharks if they accidentally attacked a person.

Nella exploded.

Blood, shredded tissue, and shattered bone sprayed backward down the hallway. Nella's entire midsection had simply disappeared in a burst of red. Her upper torso dropped, only held up by the jaws of the first Spectrovenator. Bits of viscera spooled out of her upper half. Her legs, only attached to the upper half of her body by a bit of skin, fell to the floor.

Drake held his anti-tank gun, his eyes, very, very wide behind the sights. "I... Oh my God... I was aiming for... She got in the way. You all saw. She got in the way of the dinosaur." His voice cracked.

Nella's eyes bled. Her ears bled. Her nose bled. She stared dumbly down at where her guts used to be, already dead from the impact. The impact of the anti-tank round had ruptured her veins and arteries. Even though the bullet had hit her in the abdomen, the brute force of the anti-tank round had likely whisked her brain like an egg.

The Spectrovenators dragged Nella's two halves into the stairwell, disappearing from view. The only sign they or Nella had been there was the growls and snarls and ripping noises coming from the stairwell and the fan of crimson across the floor.

"I didn't mean to..." Drake was still saying. He had a lost look in his eyes.

"Come on," Burt said, taking Drake by the arm. He led the man down to the end of the hallway. Even if the Spectrovenators were temporarily busy, Burt was sure they would eventually come looking for seconds.

Burt wanted to be sick. He wanted to punch Drake in the nose. He wanted to find a brick wall and bang his head against it until he forgot all about the things he'd seen today. But there was no time for any of that.

Cora caught Burt's eye. She was pale and grim-faced.

"It's going to be okay. Trust me," Burt said, even though he didn't believe it himself right now. Cora nodded.

Burt stopped in front of the trash chute and opened the hatch. He peered inside, not quite sure what he was expecting. He couldn't see much at all through the dark, nearly vertiginous chute, but it didn't look like there was a mouthful of teeth waiting for them at the bottom. That would just have to be good enough.

"Let's get out of here," Burt said, gesturing to the chute.

"Is the coast clear?" Bainbridge asked.

"As far as I can tell," Burt said.

"You should go down first and let us know if it's safe," Bainbridge said.

"Maybe the guy with the guns should go down first and let the rest of us know it's safe," Cora said.

"Don't get cute with me," Bainbridge said.

A Spectrovenator stuck its gore-streaked head out of the stairwell door at the sound of the voices. A second head appeared a moment later, licking blood from its chops.

"Right. See you at the bottom," Bainbridge said. He lifted one foot up and then the other, balancing himself on the edge of the hatch almost like a kid about to go down the waterpark's biggest slide. He pushed off and disappeared into the darkness. There was a muffled thud at the bottom, and then a distorted shout. The words were hard to make out, but something about being fine and heading for the security tunnel.

Burt offered Cora his hand to help her up onto the ledge. Drake grabbed his hand instead and hoisted himself up before sliding down. There was another thud at the bottom.

"Bainbridge? Arthur? Wait for me," Drake shouted from below.

Throwing a glance toward the stairwell door, Burt gestured for Cora. Cora hoisted herself up and got into position. She gave him a nod, and then she vanished down the chute after the others. Burt clambered up onto the chute's ledge, dangling his legs into the angled shaft.

The Spectrovenators had moved into the hallway now, realizing that their prey wasn't cornered after all. Burt heard a thump at the bottom of the shaft and released his grip on the edge of the chute at the same moment the Spectrovenators broke out into a charge.

Darkness consumed him. His clothes tried to catch and snag on any imperfections in the metal seams or globs of old trash from long-burst garbage bags. But he picked up speed, banging roughly against the side of the chute once before tumbling out into a freight car-sized dumpster.

Burst garbage bags cushioned his fall as he landed. His feet hit the ground first, but he landed on an uneven mound of trash and fell on his butt among the refuse. An avalanche of rain-slicked plastic and debris tried to bury him, but a hand reached down, and he grabbed it. Cora pulled on his arm, trying to help him to his feet.

Burt thrashed and fought, trying to right himself. His right hand landed in something cold and squishy. He sliced his left hand on something sharp and yelped. Finally, he found his footing and managed to pull himself upright with Cora's assistance.

Burt breathed a sigh of relief. He looked around and saw Drake clambering out of the giant dumpster. He was struggling to both climb upward and keep his giant gun in his hands, and he fell backward into the trash heap below him. "Arthur, wait," Drake wailed.

"Let's go before those things figure out where we went," Cora said. In that moment, wet trash clinging to her already soaked clothes, she looked like the most formidable lawyer he had ever seen. She looked determined as hell, and Burt pitied whatever poor fool underestimated her in the courtroom.

Rain spattered onto Burt's head as he nodded.

Just then, there was a gunshot. Burt jumped and almost fell into the trash heap again. The first shot was followed by two more in quick succession. That was Bainbridge's revolver. The Spectrovenators. There were more out here.

And then a head-splitting roar sounded through the storm. Drake jumped off the side of the dumpster and disappeared from view, apparently running toward the sound of the roar.

Christ. It was the remaining Carcharodontosaurus, Big Suzanne. She must have heard the gunshots and come running. She'd associate the sound of gunfire with people, delicious, protein-packed people. Of course, she probably also associated them with the death of her mate and offspring. And all of that meant that every time they had fired a gun on this island since killing her family, they had been broadcasting their location directly to Big Suzanne, who was highly motivated to come and, if Burt properly understood the technical term the paleozoologists working for RexNetics used, "wreck their shit."

"We have to get Drake and Bainbridge," Cora said.

"I mean, do we? The Carcharodontosaurus is out there," Burt said. The way he saw it, hunkering down in their smelly bunker here had its appeal.

"If they get to that helicopter before us and don't see us right behind them, how long do you think they'll wait before telling the crew to take off?"

Burt guessed about five seconds. No, Cora was right. If they didn't stick together as a group, bad things would happen. Worse things than were currently happening.

Damn lawyers and their damn rhetoric. Much as he'd like to just be a coward and hide in this trash bunker, eventually the Spectrovenators would catch their scent and surround them. At least Bainbridge and Drake had weapons. Cora had a satellite phone and a knife she'd taken from his apartment. Burt had jack and squat in abundance, but otherwise, he wouldn't be much help.

"Point taken," he said. He and Cora climbed up the side of the dumpster in time to see Drake turn around a corner of the building in the direction of the security tunnel entrance. And the direction the gunshots and roar had come from.

Burt dismounted and landed on his feet next to Cora, and they took off after Drake. They rounded the corner and nearly slammed into his back.

Drake stood stock still in the rain, his giant rifle aimed at a huge shape in the process of disappearing into the trees. A shredded, limp form dressed in the remains of a Hawaiian shirt hung from the creature's jaws. Drake pulled the trigger, only for the anti-tank gun to click dry. He hadn't reloaded since shooting Nella.

Drake cursed and pulled the bolt back on the enormous gun. Rainwater beaded on his faux-adventurer jacket as he slammed an oversized bullet home. He brought the big rifle up again and aimed it at the tree line. Burt swatted the rifle upward before Drake decided to take a potshot at some shadow.

"Gunfire is what drew her in the first place. If you fire, she's going to come right back," Burt said.

"Good. I can reload before she gets to us," Drake said, jerking the rifle back.

"Maybe. But if you miss, we're all dead. And if you hit her but don't drop her immediately, we're probably all dead. And if you land a perfect kill shot and drop her where she stands, we might still all die because the Spectrovenators already heard those gunshots earlier and are almost certainly going to start looking for us. Let's just get out of here," Cora said.

Drake paused for a second, as if he was going to fire blindly after the Carcharodontosaurus anyway, and then he let the rifle drop. He looked tired and far older than his years now. He looked like he'd finally realized just how far out of control the situation really was. For a man who had built his entire financial career on bold risks and a devil-may-care attitude, it was not easy to look at the situation and realize how bad it really was. For a man who had been insulated from any real consequences for years thanks to lawyers and money, the dire straits he found himself in now were apparently quite the shock. He looked like a frat boy who found himself in a police cell after doing something dumb on spring break, finally sobering up enough to realize that the charges leveled against him would have real consequences. It was a look of fear, desperation, and anger, like a wolf resolving to chew its own paw off to escape from a trap.

Burt didn't like that look one bit. It wasn't a completely sane look.

"Let's get to the security tunnels," Burt said, taking Drake by the arm. Drake jerked a little, as if being touched had startled him, even though he was looking right at Burt.

Burt and Cora started moving, and Drake shook some of the strange, dazed look off his face. As they moved, they passed a dark puddle on the cement. In the deep gloom of the storm, the puddle looked almost black, but it was dispersing as the rain continued to pound down. Burt could almost have pretended he didn't know the dark puddle was really red and not black, but the shreds of fabric, the giant, saurian footprints nearby, and the shoe with a human foot still inside told him the whole story.

Their group was down to three survivors. Drake pointedly did not look at the meager remains of his old friend and business confidant.

Burt ran up to the security checkpoint that separated the employee zone from the rest of the park and opened the door to a reinforced concrete shelter. Red emergency lighting illuminated a ramp downward and a dark, cement tunnel filled knee-deep with dark water.

And there on the walls were strange markings. Handprints made with paint and crusted blood. Somewhere out in the tunnel network, other security entrances were open. The Piltdowns had made the tunnels their own.

Burt looked over his shoulder and saw the first Spectrovenator emerge from the apartment now that Big Suzanne had left, searching for the origin of the gunshots and no doubt hoping there would be scraps leftover.

He briefly looked at the path that led to the center of the park and the hotel, where the helicopter awaited them. The jungle grew thick and untamed on either side of the path. An attack could come from any direction at any time. In the tunnels, an attack could only come from the back or the front.

Burt descended the ramp into the flooded tunnel, into a world of dark water and red emergency lights. The lights fizzled out as the park's power supply rebooted again.

Burt stepped into the darkness.

THIRTEEN

DUTY OF CARE IN AN EMERGENCY SITUATION: A REFRESHER FOR ATTORNEYS

Cora waded through the black water. The freezing water came up to her knees, and it was slowly, slowly rising. A constant, steady roar filled the tunnel as more rainwater dripped, poured, and sloshed into the tunnel from hundreds of grates and vents. Pieces of trash and debris floated on the surface. Cora's foot bumped something, and a bloated, partially eaten rat carcass bobbed to the surface.

Cora resisted the urge to gag. She resisted the urge to panic and climb up a nearby set of rungs bolted into the wall and flee to the surface. But she couldn't resist her imagination's urge to picture the tunnels filling with black freezing water until there was no air left. Or the constant, paranoid fear that something would reach out from the water and grab her ankle with cold, dead fingers.

Perry's bloody corpse, black water gushing out of his severed throat.

Ryder, the rebar spear sticking from his chest clanging against pipes and damp concrete as he wandered the tunnels' black corridors.

Nella's ruined torso dragging itself along under the water, her guts trailing behind her like a ruptured jellyfish.

Cora shook her head, trying to dispel the awful images. But the dark, mostly featureless tunnels felt like some awful, unreal underworld. A place where the dead might gather for one final stop on the highway to Hell.

The buzzing emergency lights cast red reflections off the water's surface, which danced and swirled as the group moved down the tunnel. The reflections gave the impression that the ground was alive and squirming, and it made Cora vaguely nauseous. The emergency lights cast everything in a ghastly shade of red, adding to the funhouse effect. Burt had taken the lead, since he'd lived here and done some workplace emergency drills. He had the best familiarity with the tunnels.

Not that it was easy to get lost down here. The tunnel was mostly a single, straight shot. They'd passed a cross tunnel that led to the south and north ends of the island, back toward the docks and to the planned Phase 2 expansion area, respectively. But they were heading west toward the island's center and to where the whole tunnel network ultimately converged.

Sometimes, Cora's boots touched something in the dark water, and she would jerk her foot away. She was pretty sure some of the objects were abandoned luggage or equipment. They would shift a little when she kicked them or she'd simply stub her toe. Other times, she stepped on something that crunched. Cora hoped those were just sticks and not the bones of creatures the Piltdowns had dragged down here. It was impossible to tell in the dark, dark water.

Her legs were cold, and her feet were starting to go slightly numb. Wading through the water was slow and exhausting. She wished she was under a cozy blanket, warming her toes in front of a crackling bonfire. She wished she was back at the office, responding to mundane emails and drinking too much iced coffee. She wished she was back in law school so she could talk herself out of ever becoming an intellectual property lawyer.

But she was here in a flooded security tunnel, hoping genetically altered macaques didn't storm out of the red-tinged shadows and rip her face off.

There were signs of the Piltdowns everywhere. The walls were covered in crude handprint art like the hallways behind the gene lab. In places, large dinosaur bones breached the surface of the water. They had come from animals too large to find their way into the tunnels on their own, so they must have been dragged inside in pieces. Machinery had been smashed. Pipes had been wrenched off the walls and ceiling. The place looked like a subway station after a hurricane.

Cora, Burt, and Drake had passed a number of rooms attached to the main tunnel. Most of them had been for storage or small staff areas. But one of them had been a pump room. The tunnels should have remained mostly dry, even in a storm. But the pumps were either shut down or broken, like most everything else on this island. The auxiliary power system she'd helped patent could barely handle running the light system off its enormous battery array, and those kept failing and restarting as the malware mixed in with the dinosaur genomes continued to wreak havoc on every single automated system in the park.

They'd also passed a handful of emergency access points. These weren't the large, sloped, disability-approved entrances meant for easy guest access. They were little more than alcoves with rungs leading up to a manhole cover.

Cora wanted out of these tunnels. She wasn't normally claustrophobic, but the perfectly straight walls disappearing into red-tinged darkness made her itch for the open air.

She stared ahead, hoping to see their exit magically materialize in the distance. But all she could see was the seemingly endless sets of flickering emergency lights converging in the far distance.

She forced herself forward. She wanted to find that helicopter and ride it all the way back to her old life. Maybe it could ferry her off the island, but she knew her old life was toast. She knew she couldn't work for Drake in any capacity after this. Drake could set her up for life, but Cora didn't want to ever see him again.

Maybe she shouldn't think about what she'd do later. Maybe it was better to focus on the here and now, keeping all her attention on getting off this island. But she was exhausted. And focusing on *right now* meant she had to implicitly acknowledge all the awful things she'd seen today.

But for the first time in a long time, she wasn't really sure what she was going to do about her future. She'd always studied hard to go to a good university and then studied harder to go to a good law school and then studied even harder to find a good career. And now she wanted to drop kick all of that out the nearest window. Looking to the future and not knowing where she was going was liberating. And terrifying.

Still, she was handling the situation better than Drake, who currently seemed to be stuck in the past. Or maybe dreaming of a lost future that had slipped beyond his grasp.

"Those goddamn bastards at Global Fossil Fund. They can't do this. They can't build a death trap into their data and just set it loose. People could die. People *did* die. I'll sue their balls off. They're responsible for what happened here. We'll take them for everything that they're worth," Drake muttered to himself. He was a bit hunched as he walked, rubbing at his shoulder every so often where he'd absorbed the recoil from his giant anti-tank gun.

Cora fully believed that Drake would sue Global Fossil Fund for rigging their data. Like a lot of people in the field of biotech, Drake's favorite hobby was aggressive litigation.

He might even have a semblance of a claim. Cora remembered a case from her first year of law school's tort class where somebody knew he had frequent trespassers on his property, so he set up some shotgun traps. Surprise, surprise, some trespasser got injured and surprise, surprise, sued the living shit out of the property owner. The property owner lost, since the law did not look kindly upon people who deliberately created a risk of harm. And nothing stopped someone from suing a company that made a defective or dangerous product, even if they'd been injured after shoplifting the item.

But would a judge or jury look favorably upon a multi-zillionaire stealing corporate secrets, abusing the technology in hopes of turning a quick buck, and then trying to cover up the resulting mess by sending in a team that wasn't adequately warned of the danger, resulting in a large number of preventable deaths?

That wasn't Cora's field of law, but she wouldn't want to touch that case with a pole. It didn't really matter what sort of liability waivers RexNetics had everyone sign, Drake was coming out of this the worse for wear.

Good. Cora's job was technically to zealously advocate for her client, no matter how far in the wrong they were. But in this case, the attorney code of duties and ethics could pound sand.

She had decided. It didn't matter what he offered or what kind of contract she'd be breaking. She wouldn't work for Drake or any of his ventures in the future. Her sense of justice wouldn't allow her to. Of course, she still had to live long enough to stand on her principles later.

Burt stopped in his tracks at a cross tunnel. To Cora's eyes, the cross-tunnel just looked like all the others, a big, concrete tube like a subway route without the tracks.

"Are we lost?" Cora asked.

"No, the hotel is still that way. It's just..." Burt took a few steps down the cross-tunnel, and then Cora saw it too. There was some, for lack of a better word, goop on the wall. In the red emergency lighting, it almost looked like someone had flung jam onto the wall.

"I think the Tyrannotitan was down here," Burt said.

Cora looked at the slime and remembered the slug-like body and texture of the thing from Biological Containment. She looked at the ooze on the wall. Her guts tightened.

"Do you think it's still down here?" Cora asked.

"No way to know. I'd think as the water rose, it would decide to go elsewhere. But I'm not sure how smart it is. It might not easily find its way out. Or if it found some food down here earlier, it might stick around for a long time looking for more."

"Why the hell did you grow that thing?" Drake asked.

"Some dipshit ordered me to make a Tyrannotitan using the Carcharodontosaurus genome," Burt said.

"And does that thing look like a Tyrannotitan? It's an abomination is what it is. Morons. I'm surrounded by morons." Drake continued to talk, muttering more to himself than anyone in particular.

Rather than argue further, Burt gestured forward. The red emergency lights stretched away into the distance, perspective causing them to converge into a little red pinprick.

"It's not much further now," Burt said. He paused and stretched. Something in his shoulder made a popping noise.

Cora stood next to him. Despite the effort of trudging through the water, she was cold. The black water seemed to leech all the warmth out of her body. She stamped her feet, trying to get some feeling back into her toes.

"You have any big plans after we get off this rock?" Cora asked. Cora wasn't good at small talk and never had been, but she wanted to hear a human voice right now and not just the gurgle and roar of icy water flooding into the tunnel.

Burt looked at her with apparent surprise in his eyes.

"What?" Cora asked.

"I'm just a little surprised you're speaking to me. I'm partially responsible for everything that's happened here today. I wouldn't want to speak to me," Burt said.

Cora glanced at Drake and then back to Burt. "Listen, you are so far down on my list of problems right now. Let me pencil you in for the silent treatment a couple of months from now."

"It's a date, then." Burt smiled.

It was a grim smile, but it was probably the first genuine smile Cora had seen since she set foot on the island. She smiled, too.

"Jesus. Will you two come on?" Drake started forward, and Cora followed in his wake next to Burt.

They'd taken another ten paces when the lights sparked out again. Something far behind them made a startled squawking noise.

Cora stopped, breathing in the dank air for a moment. She strained her ears, but all she could hear was dripping, swirling water. The lights snapped back on, and she spun around. She couldn't see a thing in the darkness.

Maybe the noise had simply been a burst pipe or a piece of electrical equipment frying out. And maybe Santa would let them all ride his sleigh the rest of the way to the hotel.

"Did you guys hear that?" Cora asked. Her voice was little more than a whisper, but it still seemed to carry and echo in the long tunnel. Maybe the dripping water would swallow her voice before it went too far. Or maybe not.

"Yeah," Burt said, also looking behind them.

Drake raised his rifle and winced as he cradled the stock to his shoulder.

"Spectrovenator?" Cora asked.

"Yeah," Burt said again.

Damn. The creatures must have picked up their scent, even in the rain, and tracked them down here. Their scent was probably washed away wading through the water, which would slow the Spectrovenators down, but there were only so many directions to run. For an instant, Cora pictured the scene in old movies where an escaping criminal splashed through a creek to throw off the police bloodhounds. Of course, the bloodhounds didn't usually eat the prisoners if they caught up to them.

Cora shuffled forward, doing her best to move quietly but quickly through the water, now up to her mid-thighs. Her cold feet felt like cinder blocks tied to the end of her legs. She almost immediately stumbled over something and nearly went face-down into the black water. Her jerking movement to save herself sent a little wave through the water like a ship's wake passing through a harbor.

There was another angry squawk from behind them. Was it closer now, or was that merely Cora's imagination? It was impossible to tell in the echoing confines of the tunnel. She threw a glance over her shoulder, but she couldn't see anything except the emergency lights and their crazy, reflected ripples in the water. It was probably good she couldn't see anything, since anything close enough to see could also see her.

"Just a little further," Burt said. "All we need to do is…" Burt's words trailed off.

Cora looked forward again, expecting to see a Spectrovenator or maybe a group of Piltdowns directly ahead of her. But there was nothing except the glow of maybe five sets of emergency lights.

Wait a minute? Hadn't she been able to see the emergency lights stretching off into the far distance just a minute ago? Had just a part of the island's power grid failed? Was the auxiliary power system only supplying electricity to individual subsystems and parts of the park now?

As she looked, the most distant pair of emergency lights went out. It didn't flicker or give any warning it was about to fail. It just went out.

And then Cora realized what had happened. The set of lights had been eclipsed. Something was blocking them. Something had emerged from the next cross-tunnel. Something big enough to fill the entire tunnel and block the view of the lights. Something that was now coming in their direction.

The water surrounding Cora began to flow past her like the stream of a lazy river. Before it had swirled and churned as they moved through it, but it hadn't flowed. Now, that same something that filled the tunnel ahead of them was pushing the water out of the way.

The Tyrannotitan.

"Turn around," Burt said, his voice oddly flat.

"But the Spectrovenators," Drake protested.

"The nearest exit is behind us. We can make it. Go," Burt said.

Drake held his rifle. He started to raise it in the direction of the encroaching darkness but then apparently thought better of the idea.

129

Cora reached down and grabbed the hilt of the knife she'd taken from Burt's apartment. It was tucked awkwardly through her belt. It wasn't much, but it was all she had to defend herself. She told herself it wouldn't come to that.

They'd just boogie down to the nearest exit, pop up to the surface, and walk the rest of the way to the main pavilion's hotel and the military helicopter. Bingo bango bongo. Easy as pie. A literal walk in the park.

Another set of lights was blotted out as the Tyrannotitan, still hidden in the blackness, moved closer.

Cora started wading forward with the others, trying to work on building some momentum without splashing around like an injured seal. Her legs felt heavy and awkward in the water. Her whole body ached from a day of running, falls, and harsh treatment. She felt like an orange rind that had been squeezed dry and thrown away. For now, she focused on putting one foot in front of the other.

The group reached the cross-tunnel where Burt found the slime.

"We should split up," Drake said suddenly. "They can't get all of us that way."

"What? No. The nearest exit is this way," Burt said. He pointed back the way they had come. Toward the sound of the Spectrovenators. Cora also didn't want to go that way, but she sure as hell didn't want to split up.

Cora glanced behind her, in the direction of the hotel. Another set of emergency lights vanished from view. And now Cora thought she could see the barest outline of something inside that darkness. Something that pulsed and writhed. Something slick and drenched in mucus. Something groping blindly toward them as it filled the entire tunnel.

Nope. That decided it. She was following Burt to the nearest exit. No splitting up. Nothing clever. She wanted out of here *right now*.

Burt had also caught a glimpse of the Tyrannotitan. He gestured frantically. Cora splashed toward him. She almost didn't see the access ladder to the surface. It was tucked into a shallow alcove, rainwater dripping down from above in a steady trickle.

She completely missed the Spectrovenator. The dinosaur leapt out of the nearby shadows, snapping at her. Cora yelped and yanked the knife free from her belt. She held the weapon like a slasher villain, with the handle and blade pointed straight down. Cora knew that almost certainly wasn't how you were supposed to use a knife. She was even more certain that you weren't supposed to get into knife fights with dinosaurs.

"Drake, shoot it," she yelled. The gunshot might attract more animals here, but Cora wouldn't much care if she was already dead. No gunshot rang out.

The Spectrovenator took a step closer, a string of drool dangling from its mouth. Then, its eyes focused on something behind Cora. Its entire body language changed, recoiling backward. It turned around and ran for its life.

That should have been a relief.

It wasn't.

Cora risked glancing behind her and saw a huge shape looming in the darkness. The shapeless form looked more like a magnified piece of plankton than anything that was supposed to be a dinosaur. In the dim, red light, Cora could see bones suspended inside its body like veggies in some old gelatin salad recipe. Some of the bones were smaller dinosaurs. Others appeared to be small island creatures. Others were vaguely humanoid, and Cora assumed those had been from Piltdowns. And Oleg. The defleshed bones bobbed and sizzled inside the monster's body as it trundled toward her, its mouth a gaping, hungry pit.

Cora had enough time to realize that she didn't see Drake anywhere. Had the Tyrannotitan gotten him? No, there would have been a gunshot or a scream. She'd be able to see the silhouette of his writhing body where he had been sucked into its unctuous, gummy depths.

Drake had split off at the cross-tunnel, taking the only gun between the three of them with him. He was striking out on his own.

That bastard.

"Cora, this way," Burt said. He waved her over to the ladder. She looked at the Tyrannotitan one more time as it slithered closer. Then, she grabbed the cold metal rungs bolted into the side of the tunnel and started climbing. Muddy water piddled down on her head as she scrambled the ten or so feet up toward the manhole cover capping the exit.

She heaved upward, and the lid lifted a little before settling down again. Burt patted her calf rapidly from below, telling her to hurry the hell up.

Shifting her tired, half-numb legs, Cora planted her feet and angled her whole body into her next effort. She grunted, heaved, and shifted the manhole cover more, creating an opening. Sliding her fingers through, she pushed the manhole cover out of the way, the metal grinding across the ground. Pulling herself upward, she crawled out of the tunnel and lay panting on her stomach for a moment. Flopping over, she shot a hand back down the shaft. Burt grabbed her wrist, and she helped drag him to the surface.

Looking down, she saw something vast and slimy pass below a few seconds later. It was like watching an amoeba under a microscope that had been zoomed in too close. Cora briefly wondered if the monster was even a proper multicellular animal, or if it was just a single, flawed

Tyrannotitan cell that never divided but simply kept growing and growing and growing until it was big enough to park a semi-truck inside it. Surely, it couldn't really just be one giant, carnivorous cell, could it?

Cora slid the manhole cover back into place with what felt like the last bit of her strength.

She lay on the muddy ground, the rain pounding down onto her. Maybe she was dead. Maybe Bitey McBiteface had chomped her in half hours ago, and this was Hell. Maybe this whole thing was just the last, illusory misfiring of her neurons as her body succumbed to massive trauma and blood loss. But, no. Hell was supposed to be warm, and if her brain was hallucinating some sort of fever dream before shutting down for good, she would have at least picked a good dream. Something with ice cream sandwiches and a sunny weekend, maybe.

Cora groaned and sat up, getting her bearings. She and Burt sat on a concrete slab. A couple of overturned four-by-fours lay nearby. More sat in a line near the main path, next to a small hut. This was a vehicle depot for motorized park tours. Tourists could rent one of the glorified golf carts, driven by a member of staff, who would ferry them around from one end of the park to the other, snapping off dinosaur trivia and hocking overpriced bottles of water the whole time.

Beyond that, Cora could see the lights of the main plaza's hotel. They'd nearly made it. They were no more than a couple of football fields away. So close. So tantalizingly close. Not for the first time, Cora thought that maybe, just maybe, they were almost to safety.

She was wrong.

FOURTEEN
HOSTILE WORKPLACE ENVIRONMENTS: HOW TO TAKE AWFUL BOSSES TO COURT AND WIN

Burt moved through the jungle as quietly as possible. The rain pounded through the jungle canopy and streamed downward, covering the sound of his and Cora's footsteps as they trudged through the mud. He dared not walk on the actual path leading to the hotel, since that would leave him out in the open. Every instinct in his body told him to crouch and skulk and creep his way through the brush instead, presenting as hard a target to spot as possible.

It was only a short distance to the park's gargantuan ten-story hotel. The hotel was supposed to be a jewel of luxury and relaxation, with a health spa, several swimming pools, a massage center, fine dining, a Vegas-style casino, and the rooftop VIP bar and heliport. And it was indeed luxurious. But it was also designed as a sort of huge sieve to separate tourists from their money. Since Primeval was located on a remote island, it wasn't as if people could buy the day-pass and then drive across town to a cheaper hotel. So every room service delivery and pay-per-view movie had been priced with a captive audience in mind.

Burt had seen the business models. As the head of the genetics division, he had to attend meetings that could have been emails and was included in email chains that could have been a series of expressive grunts. The brilliance of Primeval wasn't in the science. Burt sure as hell knew that. The science was all either stolen or derivative. The brilliance of Primeval was how it was designed to use a few scientific gimmicks to wring money out of people.

There were the Piltdowns, designed as live bait entertainment, and that was probably Primeval's single greatest entertainment innovation. Everything else, including the dinosaurs, had been poached from elsewhere. A tiered subscription model to Primeval content, gatekeeping all the coolest stuff behind paywalls? Dinosaur NFTs that allowed investors to buy digital micro-shares in the dinosaurs, assets which had zero tangible value but which could be traded as commodities anyway? Plans for some sort of future Primeval social media site? A large language AI model so people could "talk" to their favorite dinosaurs? All hackneyed old gems from the most brazen robber barons of the digital age.

Of course, those plans mostly went out the window when the park went down and Drake realized that every single linked computer system in the park was corrupted with Global Fossil Fund's genome malware. Once that happened, the plan had shifted to offloading the tainted assets as quickly as possible to people like Perry, Oleg, and Suzanne. And now that those plans had been effectively scuppered as well?

Burt didn't know what would happen next. He didn't even know if Drake was still alive. He'd split off at the cross-tunnel, and Burt hadn't seen the man since.

Even after everything he'd been through, Burt didn't wish Drake dead. Maybe in jail and financially neutered or something, but not dead.

If Drake was still alive, he could protect Burt from the worst of the fallout from this. Maybe not forever, but Drake would have the resources to put up a long and grueling legal battle before he could be found liable in any way.

But that wasn't why Burt hoped the man was alive, since he figured Drake would throw him under the bus if it bought him ten minutes less in prison.

Burt wanted something else. He thought maybe he would get it when he smashed the data drive. Some sense of satisfaction. Some closure after what happened. Destroying the data he'd sold his soul for.

It hadn't. There had been no catharsis.

He was as restless and unsettled as before. The burdens of his past mistakes had not lifted simply because he destroyed the data drive. If anything, he had even more ghosts tugging at his sleeves after today.

Destroying the data had provided a revelation of sorts, though. He'd originally stolen the data for Richard Drake. And then he smashed it for Richard Drake. Both times, Drake convinced him that it was in his best interest, either securing his future or covering up his liability. But maybe it was time to stop doing what Drake told him today, even if it wasn't exactly in his own best interest.

Burt found that what he really wanted, what he really, really wanted, was to burn the whole thing down. Preferably metaphorically, but he wouldn't turn up his nose at doing it literally, either. He wanted to go public with all the dirty, grimy secrets that undergirded RexNetics and Primeval. He wanted to smash the idol's clay feet. Maybe there was some modicum of redemption if he unburdened himself of his legal sins in the form of a sworn affidavit.

Oh, sure. He'd almost certainly be sued down to his subatomic components. Drake would sue him for breaching one hell of a nondisclosure agreement. Global Fossil Fund would sue him for stealing their intellectual property. The families and estates of the people who died here today would probably sue him, just in case there was still the remote possibility there was any meat left on his bones. He'd be bankrupt about ten seconds after he went public with his story.

But at this point, he just didn't care.

He owed at least that much to Florence. He couldn't bring her back, but maybe he could wipe the slate clean and move forward. Either way, Burt knew he'd need a good lawyer after all this was said and done. He glanced at Cora, moving through the jungle next to him. She looked at him, briefly made eye contact, and then she went back to scanning the jungle all around them.

After this was over, they'd either be friends or mortal enemies. He wasn't sure where the chips would fall. He was hoping for friends, though. Because Christ Almighty, he was going to be in a heap of legal trouble no matter what.

Burt spoke in a whisper, barely audible above the sound of the pounding rain. "Are you, uh, going to stay with RexNetics after all this?"

Cora glanced at him, his voice apparently breaking into her own thoughts. "I… I don't think so. I don't see how I possibly could."

"Drake will probably offer you a wheelbarrow full of money and a pony if you stay. Assuming he's still out there, somewhere."

"A pony? No deal. A fairy princess unicorn or nothing. I've really got him by the balls on this one."

Despite himself, Burt laughed a little. Cora smiled. Burt ran a hand through his sodden hair and tried to fix it a little, but the rain just plastered it right back to his forehead.

"Drake could probably ask me to make a fairy princess unicorn. A horse genome. Some rhinoceros DNA. Shake well and serve with a wedge of lemon," Burt said.

"Would you do it?" Cora asked.

"Make a fairy princess unicorn?" Burt hadn't meant the statement seriously and was a little surprised.

"Well, not that, specifically. I mean more broadly, really. Would you do *anything* for Drake at this point?"

"I might spit on him if he was on fire, but generally, no. I'm done. I'd like to think I learned my lesson," Burt said with a shake of his head.

Cora put a hand on his shoulder. "Good. Me too."

Burt smiled to himself. Up ahead, he caught his first little glimpse of the hotel through the thick foliage, and he refocused his attention on sneaking his way forward.

Maybe it was all moot. He might very well be dead in the next ten minutes. But they were so close to the hotel and that military helicopter now.

135

The jungle began to thin slightly as Burt moved forward, and he knew that meant they were approaching the edge of the main pavilion, which seemed to be the heart of the Piltdowns' territory. Another few feet forward, and Burt saw the hotel clearly.

He held up a hand to stop Cora. He squatted down behind a fern and looked around, getting his first properly unimpeded view of the area. He didn't immediately see any dinosaurs or Piltdowns, which was great. But he still wanted to get a good, hard look before he stepped out fully into the open. The rain pounded down on him, running off leaves overhead in rivulets and soaking him as if he'd been walking through a cold shower.

He glanced at Cora. She had her arms crossed over her chest, clearly freezing. "For what it's worth, I'm sorry you had to be involved in all this," he said.

She gave a sort of grim chuckle through chattering teeth. "Could be worse. I could be stuck on the miserable, dinosaur-infested island that *didn't* offer a full Scandinavian sauna experience." She pointed to a torn banner hanging crookedly from the hotel wall.

"Yeah. Or you could be stuck on a miserable, dinosaur-infested island with only a lawyer for company."

Cora hit him on the arm.

He looked around. They were partially hidden behind a pair of benches near the edge of the path. They were facing the hotel's front entrance, which was lit up as if for a gala. Huge glass doors showed the lobby like a giant diorama. It was in relatively good shape. The hotel must have gone into lockdown mode when the park went down. Burt could see the bay of elevators, the front desk, and the large chandelier dangling from the ceiling. The main doors were locked, but the hotel had plenty of other ways in. A service door somewhere must have been jammed open, because animals had clearly been through the lobby at some point. Some of the tasteful furniture was smashed, and there was a huge hole in the drywall near the front desk where something big had crashed its way through. But the damage was mostly superficial, not the sort of destruction that resulted from prehistoric monsters living in there for months at a time.

"Do you see anything we should be worried about?" Burt asked, squinting into the darkness. The rain slashed through the night, limiting his vision more than he liked. But it also meant that anything out there would have a harder time seeing him, too.

"No, and that worries me," Cora said.

"Yeah. I'd almost feel better seeing something we should steer clear of. But I think this is probably our chance. I have an employee code that'll get us through the front doors even if they're locked. I say we run across the plaza, get inside, and make our way to the roof."

"Works for me. Stairs or elevator?" Cora asked.

Burt thought for a second. After the Spectrovenators tried to corner them in the stairwell at the employee quarters, he didn't much fancy that route. But if the elevator broke down and they became trapped, they would be well and truly stuck.

But on the third hand, if they got stuck in the elevator somehow, they were relatively safe. If they managed to drag themselves up ten flights of stairs, and Burt didn't remember the last time he'd gone up ten flights of stairs all at once, and they suddenly needed to run for their lives...

"Elevator," Burt said.

He started to creep out of the jungle when he heard the screech of a furious animal. He and Cora both ducked down low to the mud and looked around, trying to figure out where the sound had come from.

Then, they saw a figure charge across the pavilion. It was Drake. And behind him, at least one hundred Piltdowns came chasing after him. A fencepost that had been whittled into a spear sailed past Drake and embedded itself in the earth. The Piltdowns kept coming, nearly all of them wielding weapons of some kind.

They reminded Burt of the angry mob that stormed the castle in the old Frankenstein movies. Except instead of a horde of superstitious villagers coming together to destroy the creature, it was a throng of creatures determined to destroy their creator. Of course, these things didn't want to corner Drake and have a discussion salon about his duties as their surrogate father and the dangers of scientific hubris. They wanted to rip his flesh off and stuff it down their gullets until he was nothing but a screaming, bloody skeleton. And if they didn't catch Drake, then they'd settle for anyone else in the general area.

Drake ran up to the front doors of the hotel and pulled out a keycard, swiping it across a reader next to the door. Burt saw a little light blink green, and Drake threw the door open, launched himself inside, and slammed the door shut a couple of seconds before the first Piltdown hurled itself against the shatterproof glass. The glass doors vibrated, rattling in their frames, but they didn't break.

Drake unslung his rifle, and for a second, Burt thought that Drake was going to do the dumbest thing possible and shoot through the glass. The anti-tank gun had the penetration to shoot through the reinforced glass, and the bullet would probably pass through about twenty Piltdowns as well. But it would also destroy the structural integrity of the glass, and the remaining Piltdowns would come pouring in. But Drake didn't fire the gun. He slid the long barrel through the door handles, further reinforcing the doors. Then, he turned and ran to the bay of elevators. He smacked the call button, and an elevator door opened just as the first big crater appeared in the glass at the hotel's entrance.

The glass didn't crack. It was multiple layers of glass, plasticized resin, and sheets of woven polymers. It was designed to take multiple direct hits from small arms fire and even absorb small explosions. So when it started to break, an outer layer would buckle before the next layers absorbed the rest of the impact. Drake's giant rifle could no doubt punch through, but even then, the glass wouldn't fracture all at once.

But the glass wasn't impervious to damage either. The Piltdowns hammered on it with fists, with tools, with knives, with clubs, with the full weight of their bodies, heedless to the effects of the impacts. Burt heard fingerbones, ribs, and even big, thick arm bones snap as the Piltdowns attacked the glass with savage disregard for their own well-being.

Impact craters started to pock the glass in big, white indents where the outermost layer of glass had been broken but the inner layers absorbed the rest of the force. Soon, the entire bay of windows was white with impact points. It looked as if dense spider webs had sprung up and engulfed the entire hotel entryway.

Finally, one of the Piltdowns broke a hole all the way through a section of glass. The glass still didn't shatter completely. It was like poking a hole through a sheet of tinfoil with a pencil. Hairy, bleeding hands grabbed at the edges of the hole and pulled and wrenched, slicing fingers down to the bone in the process. But after a moment, the hole was bigger, and Piltdowns streamed into the lobby like rioters looting an electronics store. Some of them went to the elevators and banged on the metallic doors, but then they apparently heard the elevator moving somewhere up above them, and they streamed for the stairs.

A few Piltdowns lingered downstairs. Some had grotesque injuries which slowed them down. Some had been trampled in the scrum to get inside the lobby. A few others, their bellies perhaps full of Drake's security team, seemed content to inspect the hotel's interior, looking for any secret stash of food.

Burt recognized the Piltdown he'd pegged as the group's matriarch, a big female missing most of her face. She wandered around the lobby, holding a fire axe like an old time-y gangster wielding a baseball bat while offering a business "insurance." Her face, little more than a scabbed skull, leered at the hotel lobby's interior. She pulled a decorative pillow off a chaise lounge and took a bite out of it, testing if the colorful pillow was maybe some kind of strange fruit. She spat the stuffing out, looked at the pillow with obvious displeasure, and then ripped it apart with her bare hands, spreading more stuffing across the floor.

She seemed in no hurry to get to the roof. Her position in the group likely meant that she was guaranteed a share of meat, even if she wasn't there for the kill. For now, she seemed content to explore this new area, which meant that she was also blocking any chance Burt and Cora had of reaching the bay of elevators.

"We have to get up to the roof before they do," Cora said in a quiet voice.

"I know." Burt knew the helicopter crew would take off if their landing zone was compromised, with or without them. He fished around in his brain for a plan. They needed to get to the roof before the Piltdowns, but they were as good as dead if they strolled into the lobby with the matriarch.

Burt racked his brain, but it mostly seemed to be full of angry static and curse words. They were so damn close. If Drake hadn't split off, he'd be here with them right now, and he wouldn't have brought every Piltdown on the island down on the hotel like a plague of locusts.

He tried to visualize the hotel plans in his head, but the entertainment and management side of Primeval had never been his concern. The plans were little more than squiggles in his overworked brain. There had to be a shortcut. There had to be a quick way up to the roof.

A trash chute? No, he'd played that card once and it was a lot easier going down a trash chute than up. A fire escape ladder? No, all access to the hotel was internal for security reasons. A damn dumbwaiter, maybe? No, the hotel didn't even have dumbwaiters, but it did have...

"I've got it. Come with me," Burt said, scurrying through the muck parallel to the hotel. "There's a service elevator around back for the housekeeping and maintenance crews." Burt spoke in a whisper, his mind flashing back to a meeting he'd been forced to attend but had mostly zoned out of.

They moved as quickly as they dared, hunched over to make themselves less visible. They circled around to the side of the hotel, and they passed through a smashed employees-only gate. A handful of electric carts were parked under an awning, awaiting staff who would never return.

Burt ran past the carts and to a side door with a prominent sign warning the entrance was for authorized personnel only. He tapped in a code on the keypad next to the door, and there was a loud click. He shoved the door open and stepped into a dark corridor lined with shelves of cleaning supplies, towels, and travel-size soaps, shampoos, and conditioners.

He went to the end of the corridor and spotted the freight elevator. The industrial-sized elevator lacked the polished stainless steel and carpeted floor of the guest elevators. It looked more like something a morgue would use to transport gurneys.

Burt jumped in, Cora a step behind him, and he punched the button for roof access. The elevator dinged, and Burt heard something in the hotel grunt in response to the noise. A simian hoot echoed from down another hallway. Then, the doors closed, and Burt felt the gentle tug of acceleration as the elevator thrummed upward.

"Do you think we'll beat them to the roof?" Cora asked.

"God, I hope so," Burt muttered. He knew perfectly well that if they didn't, they were dead meat. This was their final chance to get off the island.

Burt hoped they made it. He hoped to hell they made it. Not only because he didn't want to be torn apart by a hundred angry, blood-streaked monkey paws, but because he had unfinished business.

He had mistakes he needed to fix. He needed to repent for the things he had done. He'd been greedy and stupid and people died because of his choices. And he was going to take Richard Drake down with him for their shared responsibility over this catastrophe. Burt felt his lips peel back into a nasty little grin, but there was no humor in it.

He watched the numbers on the elevator's display, and then he heard it. The steady *thwock-thwock-thwock* of the helicopter's rotors starting up. Drake had made it, and they were evacuating him.

And then he heard gunfire.

The elevator came to a stop, and the doors parted, revealing the scene on the roof. Drake sat in the third-hand Huey helicopter, gesturing wildly for the pilots to take off. Rain pelted down, creating puddles on the roof that reflected the chopper's lights. The puddles nearest the aircraft began to ripple as the rotors spun faster. Two dead Piltdowns lay sprawled in front of the helicopter, their bodies riddled with bullets.

Two soldiers crouched in the passenger area, rifles to their shoulders. One of the soldiers spotted Burt and Cora and yelled something at the pilots. That made Drake's head whip around, and he locked eyes with Burt. The look of surprise on Drake's face was almost comical. He had probably told the chopper crew that he was the only survivor, and he had maybe believed it, too.

More gunfire erupted as Piltdowns streamed out of the stairwell and sprinted toward the helicopter as its rotors spun to life. More Piltdowns collapsed mid-sprint. Others simply absorbed the hail of gunfire, staggering but not immediately going down. Their deadened nervous systems wouldn't keep them alive for long with their organs pulped and their lifeblood gushing onto the ground, but the Piltdowns would keep right on coming until their bodies physically could not function anymore.

The altered macaques came at the helipad in a tidal wave of primate fury. The soldiers with Drake gave Burt a pitying look and then yelled something at the pilot. The helicopter lurched, and its landing gear heaved off the ground. But not quickly enough. Moving with the fury of the damned, the Piltdowns surged forward.

The soldiers screamed, firing wildly into the crowd as the first Piltdown hurled itself into the helicopter's passenger compartment. Despite taking several point-blank rifle shots that sent huge globs of meat and bone spewing out of its back in baseball-sized exit wounds, the Piltdown still had the strength to jab a machete into the first soldier's guts all the way to the hilt. More Piltdowns launched themselves at the helicopter as it rose. Four or five managed to leap directly into the passenger compartment or catch the floor and haul themselves up. Two more grabbed onto the landing gear.

Hooting, grunting, screaming figures ran up to the helipad, throwing things at the Huey as it continued its ascent. The last Burt saw of Richard Drake was a horrified, wide-eyed face peering down at Burt before a press-gang of hairy bodies fell upon him and the remaining soldier.

A second later, the helicopter lurched violently in the air. Burt caught the briefest glimpse of the pilot's face through the windscreen as his head was wrenched free from his shoulders. The seat restraints kept his body in the seat, manning the controls, even as his head was passed to the Piltdowns in the crew compartment like a bowl of bean dip making the rounds at a party.

The helicopter began to spin and Burt realized that it wasn't going to stay in the air much longer. It dipped and bobbled in the air, weaving back and forth and losing altitude. It swung out over the edge of the hotel and disappeared downward, out of sight so Burt could only hear the increasingly uneven sound of its rotors.

There was a sound like the end of the world but louder, and the whole building shook under Burt's feet. A gout of flame belched up from the side of the hotel like hellfire grasping at sinners' feet, and thick, greasy black smoke immediately began to bellow into the night sky. Some of the Piltdowns screamed, either in surprise or bloody triumph, Burt wasn't sure.

Somewhere in the distance, Big Suzanne roared, hearing the sounds of the gunfire and explosion. She would no doubt come to investigate soon.

And then the Piltdowns still on the roof noticed the two people standing across from the helipad. A couple of them grunted, and all eyes turned toward the freight elevator.

Burt took a step backward into the elevator with Cora and thumbed the "Close Door" button. The elevator dinged, and the doors slid shut.

Burt didn't say anything.

Cora didn't say anything.

The elevator began to descend, and there was a brief sensation of intense heat as they passed the floor where the helicopter had smashed into the side of the hotel, but it passed after a few seconds. In another few minutes, the elevator would likely be unusable without burning its occupants to a crisp.

They reached the bottom, and the doors opened with that same friendly little ding. Burt and Cora stepped out and then walked out of the corridor and into the rain-streaked night.

"Well," Burt finally said, the smell of smoke, aviation fuel, and burning flesh drifting through the night. "Shit."

FIFTEEN
ADVICE FOR THE SOLO PRACTITIONER: GROWING A NEW FIRM FROM SCRATCH

"Correct me if I'm wrong, but we're completely screwed, aren't we?" Cora asked.

"Yup," Burt said.

"I was really hoping you'd correct me."

"Nope. Seems about right to me," Burt said.

Cora ran through everything she knew about the park in her head, but most of what she knew involved patents and trademarks and copyrights. She needed to think like Ryder, with his extensive knowledge of dangerous animals. Or like Nella, and her apparent knowledge about survival situations. Or even like Drake, who apparently always had a nasty little backup plan for how to get out of any situation and still smell like roses.

But they were all extremely dead. And now, Cora felt like she was just waiting to die. All those good grades. All those extracurricular activities. All those practice bar exam questions. And it had landed her on this damn island surrounded by damn genetic abominations without her ever doing a single damn thing she really wanted to do with her damn life. Goddammit.

Cora felt an almost giddy sense of resignation for a moment. There was a certain freedom in the realization that she was a dead woman walking. When another armed rescue team did arrive, they'd identify her by scraping a few shreds of skin and hair out of something's teeth.

Well, she wasn't going to go quietly. She'd fight and she'd claw and she'd scream until she figured out a way off this godforsaken rock. The resignation swerved into equally unhinged defiance.

Cora took a deep breath. Okay. She needed to keep calm. She needed to use what assets she had. Maybe she couldn't think like Ryder or Nella, since they were steeped in a vastly different type of expertise. But she could think like a lawyer.

What was that old saw? If the facts aren't on your side, argue the law. If the law isn't on your side, argue the facts. If neither are on your side, don't take that case.

Well, the law was definitely not on her side. This whole place was built on fraud and questionable contracts. So that left the facts. Did the situation on the ground leave her any sort of opening? She turned out all her mental pockets, hoping there was something she could use.

She still had the satellite phone she'd taken from the BMP. That was something. She could talk to people who weren't stuck on this island with her and call for help. Okay, that was good. She could add that to the plus column.

What else did she have on her side? She still had that kitchen knife from Burt's apartment. That was a potential tool. It was a potential weapon. Not a great weapon against a Piltdown, since they were several hundred pounds of flesh-hungry, nearly unstoppable monkey meat, but it was better than a pointy stick and a can-do attitude alone. It was probably not much help if one of the island's large dinosaurs found her, but at least she could make Big Suzanne's ankles bleed a little before the Carcharodontosaurus chewed her into kibbles and bits. Cora decided to put that in her plus column, too.

And finally, there was Burt. Despite everything, Cora was glad he was with her. Being alone on this awful island was the worst thing she could possibly imagine. But coming in a close second was being alone with someone like Bainbridge.

Burt had his flaws, since he'd been happy enough to do Drake's dirty work. But she had been trying just as hard to worm her way into an equally responsible position. Despite herself, she actually liked Burt. She knew perfectly well that she shouldn't. If the two of them somehow survived until rescue came, he was going to be radioactive from a legal standpoint.

He understood the park's layout and had the access codes to sneak in and out of restricted areas. Even if Cora had her issues with him, she would need to stick with him. His knowledge of Primeval was the third and probably final card Cora had to play. Everything else was against them right now.

Actually, maybe there was something else she could get her hands on. Cora thought for a moment. She wasn't sure how much help it would really be, but she'd feel better if she was actively doing something to improve her situation.

"Come on," Cora said, taking off in a jog around the side of the hotel.

"Where are we going?" Burt asked, catching up behind her. Their wet shoes splashed in puddles as they moved. Even in the storm, the smell of smoke was intensifying. She hoped that the commotion at the top of the hotel would mean that everything on the island would be distracted for a few minutes.

She reached the edge of the hotel and peered around the corner toward the front entrance. She didn't see any Piltdowns milling about, which seemed like a good sign. Looking up, she saw a vast, fiery gash in the side of the hotel. The flames were spreading across several floors, and many of the windows were lit up with internal, flickering light. Charred pieces of the military helicopter lay strewn across the ground near the front entrance, amid a sparkling sea of shattered glass. The field of glass fragments reflected the fire above, creating a shimmering, dancing vision of a beautiful, jagged hell.

She rounded the corner, sticking close to the wall so there was at least one direction where nothing could leap out and start chewing on her face. With each step, she had to avoid stepping on more shards of shattered glass. She still felt extremely exposed, though.

Maybe this was a bad idea. She didn't have a plan for how to use the thing. She didn't even really know how to operate it. It might not even be there anymore.

But then she saw it, right where it had been. Drake's rifle. The giant, German-made M1918 Tankgewehr. The massive rifle was almost comically large, as if the Germans had pressed ogres into service to handle the weapon.

It was still wedged into the door handles at the front entrance, reinforcing the doors. In the end, it wasn't the doors that failed but the shatterproof glass.

The Piltdowns had passed the weapon by without a second glance. Cora had almost expected them to take it. The gun was hefty with a thick wooden stock. It would make a lovely sledgehammer, if the Piltdowns were in the mood to crush some skulls. But in the excitement of chasing Drake up to the roof, they had left it behind.

But Cora knew that they'd be back. Maybe not for the rifle specifically, but they had seen her and Burt disappear in the elevator. In due time, the Piltdowns would make their way back down to search for them and any crisped chunks of meat that might remain among the chopper wreckage. She grabbed the rifle and grunted as the weight of it landed in her arms.

"You ever fired one of these before?" Cora asked, hefting the weapon.

"An anti-tank rifle? No, I can't say I have," Burt said.

"I meant a gun in general," Cora said.

"Not really. I mean, I guess. Some friends took me to a shooting range one time in college and we fired off some pistols. I maybe hit the target once. How are you with a gun?"

"Never fired one before. My family had a convenience store. It was robbed a couple of times. My dad was convinced we'd all get shot if somebody tried holding the store up and saw a flash of gunmetal under the counter. You take it." She handed him the rifle.

He accepted the rifle with considerable reluctance. He pulled a little lever, Cora thought it might have been called a bolt but she wasn't sure, and revealed a single, enormous bullet loaded in the rifle.

"We've got one round. I imagine the rest of the ammo was with Drake," Burt said.

"Better not miss, then," Cora said.

They started walking, putting some distance between themselves and the front of the hotel. Rainwater plastered Cora's hair to her face, but the storm seemed to be easing slightly.

Cora didn't know what lay out in the darkness, but she knew there were a hell of a lot of Piltdowns still in the hotel. There were substantially fewer monsters out in the darkness. They were just a lot bigger. But when they had a giant rifle meant to kill tanks, maybe it was better to have a few big problems rather than a bunch of man-sized problems.

"Listen, I think we're out of options at this point. We need to find a place to hole up and just hide. Another rescue team will come for us eventually."

"Eventually," Cora agreed. "But they'll need to fight their way to our location, assuming we're still alive by the time they get here. So far, the island has a pretty good track record of defending itself against any would-be rescuers. I don't want another team to die trying to save us."

"Papua New Guinea lost their helicopter. I don't know what, if anything, the pilots transmitted before they crashed, but they'll come loaded for bear after that," Burt said.

"That's the problem, though. They need to come loaded for a whole hell of a lot more than bear."

"I didn't mean literal bears," Burt said.

"I know; I know," Cora said. "But I think my point still stands. Every single group that came out here was underprepared for the dangers."

"And you want us to drop a little yellow 'Caution: Floors Wet with Blood, Watch Your Step' sign on the beach?" Burt sounded exasperated now.

Cora's own nerves were frayed to the point of snapping. Then, an idea flashed in Cora's mind. "The cargo tug. It's still moored at the dock. We could take it out on the water. I have one of the satellite phones. Once we're safely off the island, we can call for help."

"That's... not the worst idea. But I think we're better off laying low in a gift shop or something until the next rescue team lands. The last we saw of the docks, it wasn't safe there. Maybe most of the Piltdowns came this way, but there's bound to be a few stragglers at the beach still. I only have the one bullet. And there's a lot of ground between us and the docks. Bad, bad things could happen between here and there."

They moved through the black, wet night, sticking close to the edge of the jungle. The rain roared as it crashed into the canopy, and rivulets of water dripped down on top of their heads as they moved under the partial cover the huge trees provided. The path up ahead forked, with the option to head south toward the docks or stick nearby and wait the night out. They would have to decide.

Cora took a deep breath. "I'm not saying we take undue risks. But we can stick to the jungle and avoid the worst danger. If they can just pick us up from the cargo boat, it'll be safer." Cora could feel the threads of her plan coming together.

"Safer for them," Burt said. He hefted Drake's rifle. "We have a gun and one bullet. The less ground we have to cover now, the less likely it is we need that bullet. Because I don't know if you've noticed or not, but every time we fire a gun on this island, that damn Carcharodontosaurus comes looking for us. It's like ringing the dinner bell. If we get into a scrape, this is the only way we have to defend ourselves, and it'll just get us into worse trouble the second we use it. It's time we turn the biggest risks over to the professionals."

Cora knew there was a certain logic to what Burt was saying, but she'd never been one to sit around and be rescued. She had always pushed, pushed, pushed for her goals. The idea of just holing up and making herself somebody else's problem made her bristle. She became a lawyer to fix problems, not become one.

Then Cora said something she regretted. "Nobody else should die here. Florence wouldn't want that."

Burt winced at Florence's name, and Cora suddenly felt like an ass. She'd wanted to make her point and win the argument. But that was a string she shouldn't have pulled.

"I'm sorry. I didn't mean... I wasn't trying to..."

"No," Burt said, his voice strained like he was lifting something heavy. "You're not wrong. But leave her out of this. You think I don't know I got her killed?"

"You didn't," Cora insisted.

"Not directly. But this park wouldn't be here if I hadn't stolen that data. The corrupted data that took all the security systems offline. She'd still be alive, if not for that."

"Drake is the one who bears the most responsibility."

"Yeah, and I was his stooge the whole time," Burt said. He stood still, his body rigid with barely suppressed emotion. "I had a hand in all the deaths that happened here. I'm willing to take responsibility for that. I am. I'll take everything I deserve after this. But I don't want to join the people who died here. I have unfinished business. I want to do something about this place. I want to blow the lid on everything that happened here. It's the one thing I can still do for Florence. I've got nothing else to offer. I'm one of the very few people left alive who knows what happened here, and I want to make sure it never happens anywhere else." Burt's eyes were far away, looking at ghosts Cora couldn't see.

"I also know what happened here now," Cora said.

"Yeah, and RexNetics is going to beg and plead and threaten you to shut up about it. I'm not saying you would. You've made it pretty clear you want to cut ties with them. But this is my fight, first and foremost."

"Sounds like you might need yourself a lawyer in the future," Cora said.

"Yeah. I just wish I knew any good ones." Burt managed a shallow smile at that.

Cora considered slugging him in the arm again, but she was happy to see some of the haunted, fever-y look fade from his eyes.

"You know, I'm going to be unemployed soon. I could use a client. Maybe some high-profile whistleblower-type. Some do-gooder looking to see justice done, but in need of a good legal defense, too. If you know someone like that, but maybe more handsome and with less attitude, give them my number," Cora said.

"Ugh. Lawyers," Burt muttered.

Cora extended her hand. "Partners?"

Burt took it. His hand was cold and wet, but his grip was firm.

"Partners," he said.

Cora heard a noise from the jungle next to them. The splash of something heavy in a puddle. The parting of bushes. The crack of a big branch.

And then the Suchomimus had Burt in its jaws. The huge, crocodilian head bit down, and there was a massive crunch. Burt lifted up off the ground, his hand wrenched out of hers. The anti-tank rifle clattered to the ground as an enormous dark shape dashed across the pathway, nearly knocking Cora to the ground as it passed.

Cora only caught a brief glimpse of the dinosaur, its predatory eyes glowing in the scant moonlight. The Suchomimus tilted its head back and swallowed a ragged shape before it disappeared into the jungle on the other side of the path as if it had never even been there in the first place.

Cora stood stock-still for a second, and then she realized her hand was still outstretched. She looked down at it and saw a little bit of blood on her palm before the rain washed it away.

And just like that, she was alone on the island.

Cora wanted to scream, but she knew that if she started, she would just keep on screaming until something found her and silenced her. She pulled her hand back and took a couple of steps in the direction the Suchomimus had vanished. She bent down and picked up the anti-tank gun.

She no longer had any doubt. She was going to die on this island.

SIXTEEN
TRUSTS AND ESTATES: HOW TO PREPARE YOUR CLIENTS FOR THE INEVITABLE

Burt couldn't breathe. The dinosaur's throat and gullet muscles were squeezing him. Squeezing, squeezing, squeezing.

And they were forcing him downward. Headfirst he went into the hot, wet depths. Down, down, down.

He couldn't move his arms. He didn't think he had his left arm anymore. His broken right arm was pinned to his side. He felt the splintered bone crack as the muscles encircling him squeezed and squeezed.

Everything was pain. He could taste blood. His feet kicked futilely, but his legs were otherwise immobilized. One of his knees popped, and Burt felt something in his leg shift out of alignment.

He tried to wriggle, but he only slipped deeper into the fetid darkness. And the pressure around him grew and grew.

He groaned, releasing some of the precious little air in his lungs. The sound was lost amid a rhythmic drumming that Burt recognized as the beating of a heart. He felt his ribs compress, on the verge of splintering, and another involuntary groan was pressed out of his lungs.

Florence. He wanted so badly to fix things for Florence, and he just wasn't sure how he was going to do that now. He'd been planning to make things right with Cora, and then he suddenly found himself alone in here. In here… Inside the…

Part of Burt recognized that he was beginning to go into shock. That part of him welcomed the impending oblivion, the freedom from the recognition of what was happening to him.

Yellow and purple spots began to throb behind Burt's eyes. He could see them even in the darkness. He tried to shake his head to clear his vision, but he only smeared foul slime across his face. He slipped another few inches downward, as if he was clinging to the edge of a greased slide and losing his grip. Peristaltic muscles all around him began to squeeze in earnest. Crushing and crushing and crushing him.

The pressure around his head grew and grew as the muscles around him constricted, compacting him, mashing him down. He heard as much as felt a series of pops and snaps. His chest began to collapse one rib at a time, the jagged bits of bone pressing against his organs.

Burt felt his jaw disarticulate from the rest of his face, though it remained attached to the rest of his head by muscle and flesh. He could hear the plates of his skull grinding together like the plates of ice on an unstable glacier. He felt the plates begin to buckle.

Florence, I'm so sorry.

He just wanted to make things right. And now he couldn't.

The lights behind his eyes flared brighter. There was a sensation of warm wetness and a noise like an old tree falling on the rotten roof of an old house.

Then, nothing at all.

SEVENTEEN
SELF-DEFENSE, INSANITY, & OTHER LEGAL STRATEGIES FOR FATAL ENCOUNTERS

Cora couldn't breathe.

She trudged back in the direction of the hotel, the giant rifle cradled in her arms like a precious warm burrito on a cold night before law exams. She could feel blisters forming on her heels. Her damp clothes chafed against her clammy skin. Her hair hung around her face, water dripping from the ends. She walked slow and hunched, like some misshapen thing that had been cast out of the village and doomed to a life of exile.

Burt had just vanished. Part of her felt like she was at fault. If she'd just held onto his hand tighter, maybe she could have somehow pulled him free from the massive, crocodilian jaws. But it would be like hanging onto the hand of a train passenger as the engine left the station, hoping to stop the train.

Growing up in the shadow of Global Fossil Fund's park, she saw plenty of dinosaur merchandise and paraphernalia. Her family's convenience store had even dabbled in selling shirts emblazoned with dino swag and knock-off merchandise. Cora spent endless hours having tea parties with her Mayor Carl stuffie, and she'd spent a significant part of her adult life studying the legal significance of bringing back prehistoric creatures.

But she'd never truly felt the sheer power of these animals. Never fully appreciated them as anything but *big*. It was like the difference between knowing one million was a big number and being punched one million times.

These animals weren't merely big. They were some of the most powerful living things that had ever walked the face of the earth. They pushed up against the very limits of nature's ability to engineer animals.

For all intents and purposes, they were God. Damn. Monsters. As powerful and fast and beastly as anything her imagination could conjure up to live under her bed when she was a little girl. As out of sync with the current state of the natural world that they had no biological niche except as things of nightmare. They came from a different era, effectively a whole different planet, where nature had pushed for ever more teeth and mass.

Yet companies like Global Fossil Fund and RexNetics had cavalierly plopped them down into the modern world. These things came from a time when different gods looked down upon the Earth and smiled as humongous, saurian beasts tore chunks out of each other in a constant war for survival, and now they were used as theme park attractions.

And Cora now walked among them. She had never felt so small. So alone. So thoroughly defeated. If she was lucky, her expectancy on this island was a matter of hours. Maybe minutes.

What options did she have when, at any moment, something could explode out of the trees and gobble her up? She would stay alive for as long as she could, but she did not expect to see the dawn. She walked in the rain and savored the damp and the cold because she knew they were among the last sensations she would ever have.

Cora knew she had missed a turn somewhere and driven south of sanity. There were still road signs for the place, but all the offramps seemed to be closed right now. Her emotions kept ping-ponging between dark, ugly despair and a feral, effervescent mania that came from the freedom to abdicate every responsibility. She knew that the only reason she was keeping it together right now was because the only other option was to sit in the mud and scream herself hoarse.

This was what extinction felt like. She was the last one. No one else was left.

Cora pondered what she wanted to do with what remaining time she had, as casually as she might pick a tune out on a jukebox. The weight of the rifle in her hands gave her an idea that she rather liked.

Was it a good plan? Absolutely not. But did it improve her odds of survival? Also a definite no. She was, to use the technical legal term, fucked six ways from Sunday, and she had decided to embrace it.

Thinking like a lawyer hadn't gotten her anywhere here. It was time to think like Ryder or Nella. And what would they do if they were in her shoes? Well, they wouldn't sit down and wait to die.

As she walked back toward the main plaza, still skirting the edge of the jungle since it partially hid her approach, the sky began to grow lighter. For an instant, she thought that maybe it was the first light of dawn. But no, it was merely the fire that had begun to completely engulf the hotel.

The upper floors of the massive construction project were wholly aflame now, the building standing like some giant warning beacon. The lights inside the hotel had gone out, but a fire alarm kept whooping intermittently. It felt somehow right that this dinosaur-haunted corner of island should be lit only by flame. Cora stood on the precipice of some ungodly intersection of cutting-edge science and a new Stone Age.

Almost-human shapes cavorted in front of the flaming hotel, poking at pieces of the downed helicopter and sometimes finding morsels of Drake and the rescue team to eat. It almost looked like some sort of summer beach party, if they threw those in Hell. The Piltdowns pranced and capered, their bellies likely the fullest they had been for months.

A figure stood atop a bench in the middle of the throng, exulting in the troupe's shared joy. Backlit by the raging flames, Cora couldn't make the figure out very well, but she could tell it was female. And its face was little more than bone and scabs. And it was holding a fire axe like a royal scepter.

The Piltdown matriarch.

Cora clutched the rifle a little tighter.

The matriarch stood in front of her tribe, her arms pumped toward the sky in exultation. Cinders fell around her, swirling and spinning in the violent updrafts like fireflies. The wet concrete around her steamed in the heat, as not even the rain could dampen the fire devouring the hotel floor-by-floor. Standing in front of her tribe, the matriarch looked like some ancient prophet, fresh from communing with gods of the hunt.

What was it that Bainbridge told her? It seemed like eons ago, when she had been standing on that warm, sunny beach. *You've got to go for the jug.*

Bainbridge was dead, but the advice wasn't altogether bad. She had an opportunity here to go for the jugular. She thought that was probably what Ryder would have done, though with his military and government background he probably would have phrased it differently. *Cut off the head of the snake*, maybe. And Nella, well Cora wasn't entirely sure what Nella had done before this, but Cora suspected that the best way to honor Nella's memory was with extreme, targeted violence. Right now, Cora was doing her best to channel Ryder and Nella. Or maybe Beowulf. She'd settle for basically any role model but an exhausted, broken intellectual property lawyer.

Cora positioned herself behind some brush and hefted the giant rifle. Her arms trembled slightly, so she rested the barrel on a tree branch and half-crouched to make the positioning work. She rested the rifle's stock against her collarbone. This was the way they did it in the movies, right? The big, beefy hero sort of tucked the gun into his shoulder and aimed from there? She fought to tuck the weapon snugly into place. Or where she estimated the place to be. The forty-pound weapon seemed to struggle in her grip like an extremely heavy cat that did not want to be held. Where did her hands go? One had to squeeze the trigger. Where did the other go?

She tried to think about every piece of information she knew about firing a gun, gleaned from cheap spy novels purchased in airport concourses and action movies with big stars. You were supposed to hold your breath or something, right? She wasn't entirely sure why. Did it help protect your hearing? The other main thing she knew was you were supposed to squeeze the trigger slowly rather than jerk at it. Otherwise you could throw off your own aim.

She pressed her cheek up close to the gun's wooden stock and tried to look down the sights. She was pretty sure the little ridge pieces on top of the barrel were the sights. Having her face next to the stock was uncomfortable and unnatural, so she pivoted her head up a little bit more where she felt like she could still aim.

Still in the awkward half-crouch, she swiveled the gun barrel around so it was pointing at the Piltdown matriarch. She took a deep breath and squinted down the sights.

Cora knew full well that she couldn't fight off a hundred Piltdowns. But maybe, just maybe, she could cause enough chaos to convince them to leave her alone. Or at least to leave them so disorganized that they had bigger things to worry about than her. She knew that was probably beyond the realm of wishful thinking and into the land of fantasy, but even if the Piltdowns chased her down and bashed her brains in, she'd have the satisfaction of knowing she took down their leader.

Her mind raced. *Okay, you only have this one bullet. Don't miss. Don't you dare miss. This is your one chance to do this right.*

This was for Burt. And Florence. And all the other poor sods who had come here to chase Richard Drake's dream.

Slowly, carefully, she pulled the trigger.

For an instant, Cora thought she had died. There was a flash, and the whole world seemed to end. The noise of the rifle threatened to crack her skull open like an egg. But even over the high-pitched ringing noise that seemed to fill her head like a swarm of mosquitoes, she heard her collarbone break with a meaty crunch. The gun kicked backward like a giant piston, slamming into her clavicle like a battering ram, shattering it. As she lurched backward from the impact, the gun leapt out of her grasp and landed on her foot.

Cora yelped, more in surprise than pain. She automatically tried to bend down and pick the gun back up, and that's when the pain hit her. She felt two jagged edges of bone grind against each other, and she hissed. Her good arm flew up and clamped over her shoulder as if she could just wrench the bones back into place, and that movement too sent pain shooting through her system like bits of broken glass injected into her veins. It felt like a small meteor had fallen directly on her. Despite the pain, she forced herself to look up and focus.

The Piltdown matriarch still stood on the bench in front of the burning hotel. Even backlit by the fire, Cora swore she could see the reflection of flames in the matriarch's eyes. What was left of her face peeled back into what could have been either a smile or a snarl. The matriarch turned so she was seemingly looking through the darkness and straight into Cora's eyes with that terrible, deathly leer.

And then the matriarch pointed her fire axe in Cora's direction in a *bring me her head* gesture that transcended species. The matriarch shrieked, a piercing sound of hunger and unbridled rage. The rest of the Piltdowns took up the scream, their voices rising into the night with the flames. As one, they surged forward, a tidal wave of hairy, stinking flesh, shining teeth, and eyes cursed with too much intelligence and not an ounce of mercy.

Oh Jesus. Oh shit.

Cora felt something inside her turn to jelly as she looked out upon the swarm of creatures charging toward her. Rationally, she'd known this was likely to get her killed, but some part of her still really thought it would work. Some part of her really thought she'd pull it off. Some little part of her brain had absolutely insisted that the clouds would part, and a single ray of sunshine would usher her off to safety somehow. Congratulations. You beat the final boss and win the game. Roll credits.

Reality was less cooperative.

She saw the makeshift clubs that would bash her brains out, raised high in the air and ready to strike. She saw the machetes and knives that would cut the flesh from her bones, their blades dulled and chipped by heavy use. She saw crooked, pointed teeth reflected in the firelight, and Cora knew with absolute certainty that everything she was, everything she ever wanted to be, was about to be chewed to red pulp by those teeth.

In that moment, Cora wanted to kill them all. She wasn't an intellectual property lawyer, perched upon some of the highest boughs of civilization. She was an angry, scared, cornered animal, and she wanted to lash out. She wanted to strike and punch and bite and scratch and claw until her hands were bloody. She *hated* those grotesque, hairy shapes rushing toward her, and it didn't matter that she was exhausted, alone, and injured. She was here to survive, goddammit, and she wouldn't give up the last shreds of her life without one hell of a fight.

She bent down, ignoring the scraping sensation in her shoulder this time, and she scooped up the heavy rifle with her off-hand. Holding it by the barrel, she lifted it like a club. Her arm shook from the weight. All her plans for how to get off this island had fallen apart. The time for planning had ended. Now, it was the law of the jungle. A violent, bloody struggle for life and dominance. She would lose, but she would sell her life as dearly as possible.

The nearest Piltdown was less than twenty yards away when the Carcharodontosaurus burst out of the jungle and onto the main plaza. And then, all hell broke loose.

EIGHTEEN
UNCIVIL PROCEDURE: TIPS FOR MAINTAINING DECORUM IN DIFFICULT PROCEEDINGS

The gunshot. Big Suzanne must have heard the gunshot and come running. It was probably an almost Pavlovian response by now. The noise had become a dinner bell for the huge dinosaur. Because every time she'd heard a gunshot since her mate and offspring were killed, it meant that humans were nearby.

Cora wasn't sure if the Carcharodontosaurus was smart enough to hold a motive like revenge in its saurian brain. But it could sure as hell understand hunger. And that was all the motive she really needed in the end.

The charging Piltdowns froze, skidding to a stop like a medieval militia suddenly confronted with a dragon. They regarded this new threat. The Piltdown nearest to Cora scrunched up its brow, as if contemplating a difficult puzzle.

Big Suzanne also came to a halt, apparently not expecting to see the huge group of Piltdowns gathered here. Surveying the scene in surprise, she seemed to consider her options. She pawed at the ground like a bull about to charge, and she gave a low, rumbling snarl, but she did not attack.

Cora took a step backward. The towering Carcharodontosaurus was an absolutely terrifying presence in the plaza, a gargantuan engine of death that now had a taste for human flesh. Rain streaked down the massive creature's sides in rivulets, running off her back in small waterfalls. Her damp skin and eyes reflected the flames from the burning hotel. Against the dark night sky, she was little more than a giant, deadly shadow wreathed in the impression of smoke and flames.

The Piltdown matriarch hooted. The crowd of Piltdowns shifted a little, as if a shiver had gone through the group.

Then, a spear flew through the darkness and sank into Big Suzanne's hip with a meaty impact. The Carcharodontosaurus roared in surprise and pain. She twisted around and tried to grab onto the spear, which appeared to be a sharpened pool cue shaft, with her teeth. She snapped at the wooden stake but came up short.

More projectiles flew through the air. A few missed outright, and a couple more grazed off the huge dinosaur's hide, but two punched into Big Suzanne's flank. The Piltdowns all shrieked like teenagers at a boy band concert. The noise was drowned out by a full-throated roar from Big Suzanne.

Cora threw her hands over her ears, as the Carcharodontosaurus waded into the mass of Piltdowns. Her gigantic feet came down on top of one unlucky Piltdown, mashing him to bones and red paste. Big Suzanne dipped her head down and came back up with another Piltdown caught in her jaws. She shook her head back and forth, huge neck muscles allowing her to leverage most of the force in her body. The screaming Piltdown in her mouth flew apart, pieces flung off into the plaza in a red hail storm. Big Suzanne tossed her head back and swallowed the remainder before stepping on another Piltdown like a particularly juicy bug.

More Piltdowns rushed forward, heedless of the danger, and began to stab at her ankles with their weapons. Big Suzanne lashed out and sent several Piltdown flying, their bodies crunching against the cold, wet ground half a football field away. But that did not deter the rest of the mob. They were angry now. More screams and shrieks echoed through the night like a chorus of the damned.

Cora knew this was her opportunity to run. This was her big chance to slip away and find someplace to hide. But she couldn't look away. Even the ugly throb of pain from her broken collarbone couldn't get her full attention, not with the spectacle of death playing out in front of her.

Drake had been right. He'd bred them for gladiatorial combat against the dinosaurs, to be a piece of flashy bloodsport for spectators. And something like this would have wowed the whole world. Shocked it. Disgusted it. But everyone would watch. And they would pay for the privilege.

Big Suzanne took another makeshift spear to her shoulder. She snapped at the air, spittle flying from her huge, bloody teeth. The entire tribe of Piltdowns surged toward Big Suzanne like ants attacking a beetle. The Carcharodontosaurus stamped her huge feet, mashing a few Piltdowns into the ground, but others grabbed onto her legs and began climbing. Some of them paused long enough to try to chew bits of flesh directly off Big Suzanne's legs, working the meat off the giant drumsticks with claws and teeth.

Shaking like a dog fresh out of the bathtub, the dinosaur managed to hurl some of the attackers off her body. They lost their grip and went flying, tumbling to the ground or slamming into the nearest trees. One unfortunate Piltdown was flung through a lower window of the hotel and disappeared into the flames that had begun to consume that floor as well.

Other Piltdowns managed to cling on. Some of them were using knives and other sharp tools like climbing pitons, sinking the blades deep into Big Suzanne's thighs and leveraging themselves higher. Big Suzanne's roars took on a different timbre now, not just anger. There was an edge of pain and growing panic now.

Cora saw a familiar figure haul herself up onto Big Suzanne's back, as if this was some sort of bizarre rodeo. The Piltdown matriarch shimmied up to the base of Big Suzanne's neck and then lifted her fire axe high, as if to reach the black, stormy heavens. The axe crashed down.

Big Suzanne wailed now. She thrashed and tried to shake the matriarch off, but more Piltdowns were already summiting. They stabbed and cut and slashed, flaying the skin of Big Suzanne's back with savage efficiency.

The fire axe came down again. The blow would have crushed a human skull into mush. Big Suzanne was simply too large to be felled by such a comparatively tiny weapon, but exposed, bloody bone gleamed in the firelight where the flesh had been cleaved away from the back of the dinosaur's head.

Shaking her head side-to-side, the Carcharodontosaurus had given up on trying to keep the Piltdowns away from her legs, though they continued to hack and chop away at her ankles. Instead, she focused her efforts on dislodging the matriarch. Roaring, Big Suzanne lowered her head and brought her leg up, kicking at the matriarch like she was scratching a particularly troublesome itch.

As Big Suzanne bent and twisted, Cora caught a better glimpse of the damage the matriarch had done. Big Suzanne had been partially scalped. Angry, raw flesh pulsed blood.

The Piltdowns were supposed to be prey animals. Neither Drake nor Burt expected any of them to still be alive by the time this expedition landed. But they had the numbers. And the viciousness. And the utter disregard for personal safety it required to try to take down a prehistoric apex predator with hand tools and kitchen knives. And that was all they needed to rule this island.

The Piltdown matriarch hopped off Big Suzanne's neck to avoid the gigantic claws coming toward her, disappearing into the mob surrounding the dinosaur. Free of her chief tormentor, Big Suzanne tried to turn and flee. But her feet went out from under her, her lower legs whittled down like trees beset by furious beavers.

Big Suzanne tripped and collapsed with an earth-shaking boom. Several Piltdowns had just enough time to shriek before they disappeared under her mass. The downed Carcharodontosaurus kicked and flailed, trying to right herself, but the rest of the Piltdowns swarmed over her, immediately blanketing her.

Knives and tools flashed in the dark as Big Suzanne was reduced to little more than an indistinct shape under the writhing mass of bodies. She continued to buck and squirm, launching hairy bodies into the air, but she didn't rise from the scrum.

Cora could hear the repeated impact of metal and wood on flesh over and over and over again. Piltdowns thrust spears into Big Suzanne's belly like mariners harpooning a whale. They jabbed knives at any exposed patch of skin they saw. They bludgeoned with clubs, pulverizing flesh and muscle.

Cora saw a figure with a fire axe standing at the top of the heap, striking downward like a prospector convinced there was gold in them thar' hills. Big Suzanne's thrashing slowed, becoming convulsive shudders, slowing into sporadic twitches, and then going completely still. Piltdowns tore fistfuls of meat off her body and jammed them into their mouths, chewing even as they tore off more chunks.

Cora stood at the edge of the pavilion, temporarily forgotten. Her shoulder throbbed like the devil's hemorrhoids, but she found she couldn't tear her eyes away from the scene. She'd been hoping Big Suzanne might save her. Maybe the Carcharodontosaurus couldn't kill all the Piltdowns, but Cora thought for sure that her appearance would at least scatter them. But instead, the Piltdowns had taken down the largest carnivore on the island, and now they were eating her before she'd even had a chance to cool.

Damn them. Damn each and every one of them.

The same delirious anger Cora had felt before started to creep back into her system, as she realized that she hated the Piltdowns. Truly *hated* them. They were so close to being human. It wasn't even their fault that they were a twisted, starving parody of evolution. That was Drake's fault. And Burt's, for agreeing to make the things.

And because they seemed so nearly human, it was somehow worse that they were such monsters. Cora didn't exactly begrudge the dinosaurs for trying to eat her. She didn't appreciate it, but she didn't question it, either.

These things, though. These damn things. They were crudely intelligent. They could use tools. They could hunt in groups with some semblance of a social structure.

They were so close to being people. And yet they weren't. They weren't held back by fear or pain. They weren't bound by human morality.

Cora came from a world of conflict. You didn't get to be a major corporate intellectual property lawyer without swatting down claims against your client and pursuing complaints against anyone who tried to move in on your company's turf. But even when she was always engaged in some sort of fight, there were rules. The underlying law. The rules of evidence. The court precedents. And most of those cases ended with negotiations and arbitration.

With these things, there was no negotiation. There was no settlement conference where deals could be ironed out. There was no judge. There was no jury. No appeals process. Just a bottomless hunger.

Cora felt that hysterical fury bubbling inside her, but she now realized it was from knowing that she was playing the game all wrong. She hadn't understood the only rule that mattered. There was only one rule, and that was that there were no rules. She had a moment of clear sightedness. And with that came not calm exactly, but an ugly determination.

She could play ugly. She could toss the rules away. She could fight like a mad bastard. She'd probably still die in the process, but she could play just as mean and dirty as anything on this island.

Cora slipped into the shadows of the jungle, away from the throng of monsters still tearing at Big Suzanne's motionless form. The mad, fevered urge to confront the Piltdowns had broken. But the need to beat them was stronger than ever.

For the first time, Cora truly, truly saw the shape of things on this island. Winners and losers wouldn't be determined by who was guilty or the size of the liability payout. The winners here got to live. The losers would have their bones picked clean.

Cora was a lawyer. She'd been trained in civil procedure and mediation. But she could learn these new rules. She was a quick study. And she intended to win.

NINETEEN
LEADERSHIP IN THE COURTROOM: HOW TO CENTER YOUR PRACTICE AROUND PRINCIPLES AND A GROWTH MINDSET

The Piltdown matriarch forced another gobbet of quivering red flesh down her throat. It had been some time since the troupe made a big kill like this and even longer since her belly had been truly full. She made a show of ignoring the rain matting the fur to her body, though she secretly relished the idea of returning to her favorite nook in the science building and drying out. She chewed with great deliberation, gorging herself. Months of near starvation meant that she wouldn't let any morsel go to waste.

Bits of chewed meat dribbled and squelched out of her mouth where her tattered lips and cheeks failed to keep the material inside her face. A piece of her left cheek had turned black and stank of putrescence. Carefully, she gripped the length of skin and tissue between her fingers and ripped it off. She felt very little beyond a vaguely unpleasant tugging sensation followed by a wet ripping noise. With her finger, she tapped at a newly exposed region of teeth and gums. She tasted blood, but it was her own, and she was too full to find it tantalizing anyway. She briefly examined the squishy, infected scab she'd torn from her face. A couple of maggots wriggled in the blackened, gangrenous meat. She tossed the ragged piece of her face into the darkness, her attention already shifting.

She suspected something was wrong with her, but she would not show weakness. She knew that if she showed weakness, she would be deposed and flung all the way to the bottom of the social ladder. But so long as she remained strong and continued to lead hunts like this, her position was secure.

The return of the not-macaques to the island had been a great boon for her. She did not know what the creatures were. They walked upright like her brethren, but they were hideous and almost hairless. The not-macaques had lived on the island when she was born, though she had never tasted their flesh before this. Then, they had all left for many, many days.

But now, the not-macaques were back, and they were both stupid and delicious. Even better, they had killed a few of her chief rivals for control of the tribe. In fact, they had killed many macaques since their return, but a smaller tribe needed less food. The tribe's food supplies would go much further now, and she would remain at the very pinnacle of the hierarchy. This was good. This was very good.

There was at least one more not-macaque on the island, where before there had been many. She hoped many more not-macaques would come, because the tribe had already grown skilled at hunting them. If more came, the tribe would continue to eat well.

She wanted the last not-macaque for herself. She would keep that one, taking occasional bites whenever she grew hungry. A finger. A toe. An ear. One piece at a time, as needed or desired. Perhaps her most trusted loyalists would also get occasional bits doled out to keep social alliances secure. She was certain she could keep the final not-macaque alive for many days, if needed, eating only one bite at a time.

For now, she was too full to seek out the final survivor, though. She grabbed the shaft of her fire axe with her bloody palms and used it to help leverage herself to her feet. Rainwater dribbled into her mouth through the newly enlarged hole in her face, and she spat it out.

There was no need to track down the last not-macaque right now. Not with all the meat from the dead lizard beast. But she would begin her search in the morning regardless. The not-macaque would help her secure her position at the top of the pecking order, and she did not want anything else to eat the stupid creature before she could be captured.

She briefly thought of the thing the not-macaques had released from the sealed section of the science center. She did not want it to eat her prize. Once she had the not-macaque in hand, she would find a way to kill the monster. With the biggest lizard beasts already dead, her tribe would be able to expand their territory to cover the whole island. Yes, there would be many days of good eating after this, and she would make sure her underlings understood that she deserved the credit and first pick of all the tastiest morsels that would surely come.

Parts of the flaming building had begun to crumble. She decided that, even if carrion eaters managed to steal some of the meat off the carcass of the lizard beast here, it was better to leave. Fire was bad. Fire was unpredictable. Every instinct in her was already uncomfortable being even this close to these flames, though the risk had been worth it to fill her belly unto bursting. She scanned the edge of the jungle, automatically checking for large predators. Even with the largest lizard beasts dead, the jungle still held many dangers. Not seeing any eyes watching, she grunted and signaled to the rest of the troupe that it was time to leave for the night. They would bed down in the science center, as they did every night, and hunt again in the daylight.

Suddenly, a terrible wailing noise pierced the night. The matriarch jerked, her head swiveling around to find the source of the awful sound. The shrill noise cut off before erupting again.

She zeroed in on the sound. It was coming from the science center, their home. Their shelter against the elements. The place where the not-macaques had raised them to maturity before they disappeared from the island.

The last time she heard a noise like that was the night the not-macaques disappeared from the island and the lizard beasts broke loose.

The alarm cried out again like something in pain.

This was the doing of the final not-macaque. The matriarch was sure of that.

Maybe the remaining not-macaque was trying to escape like the others the night the lizard beasts escaped. Maybe she was there to steal food the matriarch's troupe had gathered at the science center. After all, the not-macaques had come straight to the science center before, no doubt hoping to steal what supplies of fruit and meat the macaques had managed to gather there.

This could not be allowed to stand. That food belonged to the matriarch. Distributing it to her followers was a display of her prowess and ability to provide. It was how she controlled the tribe and undercut potential rivals. If the not-macaque stole from the tribe, it would shake the very foundation of the troupe's power structure.

The matriarch howled a rallying cry. The other members of the troupe, already staring at the science center, echoed her scream. They also understood that their home had been invaded.

The matriarch was full. She was tired. She was wet. But she raised her fire axe over her head and gestured toward the science center. A chorus of angry screams filled the night as she began running toward their home.

Perhaps it would be a mistake to keep the remaining not-macaque alive. Yes, on second thought, the strange creature was almost certainly more trouble than she was worth. The matriarch would find her, crush her skull in front of the tribe, and then enjoy a night's rest.

Her troupe had already disposed of so many of the not-macaques today. It would be no bother to kill one more.

TWENTY
STRAIGHT TO THE TOP: HOW TO START FROM NOTHING AND STILL BRING CLIENTS RUNNING IN YOUR LEGAL CAREER

Cora stood over what was left of Perry's scattered remains. She'd found his head first. Then an arm. Then most of his torso wrapped in the remainder of a hunting vest. His tattered remains looked like someone had spilled a cherry pie.

The gene lab was silent except for a low electrical hum as the computers and equipment sat, ready for tasks that would never come. The red light emanating off the central computer terminal was Cora's only illumination as she pawed through what was left of Perry, hoping to find something she could use.

The pain in Cora's shoulder had doubled and then doubled again as the initial shock of breaking her collarbone wore off. She felt like an idiot for trying to assassinate the Piltdown's matriarch. Even if her Lee Harvey Oswald impression had worked, and she hadn't turned her shoulder into a mass of bruised flesh and broken bone, she had no guarantee the Piltdowns would have scattered. And if they had, Big Suzanne likely would have come to investigate the sound of the gunshot and eaten her anyway.

Losing Burt... Maybe she'd lost her mind briefly. Or maybe every problem looked like a nail when you had a hammer, or in her case, an anti-tank rifle. She hadn't played to her strengths and thought things through.

This plan, well, it might not be a lot better. But at least it was on her turf. She'd thought through her end game. A lot had to go right, but this was her best shot.

She looked down at Perry's remains and felt a pang of guilt that she found herself alive while he was stroganoff. The one thing she had been able to salvage was Perry's satellite phone, which now had a distinct bite mark in the plastic casing but was otherwise undamaged. Along with the one she grabbed from the BMP, that gave her two phones. Cora set Perry's number into the BMP phone's contact list and tucked both phones away.

An earlier pitstop at a half-constructed tourist gift shop had earned her the biggest prize. The lighter had been tucked away in a smashed tool chest. Most of the tools had been scattered or snatched up to make weapons, but the Piltdowns hadn't taken the construction worker's lighter.

That gave her the lighter, two phones, a sizable knife, and an extensive knowledge of intellectual property. That was most of what she needed to make a last stand.

From Perry's remains, she moved to one of the gene lab's work desks. The first drawer she opened was full of miscellaneous office supplies. Sticky notes. Scissors. A protein bar wrapper. A stress ball branded with the RexNetics logo.

The second drawer had what she was looking for. File folders and binders with hard copies of company policy, hardware warranties and operating manuals, informational leaflets telling employees to report suspicious emails, and contact sheets with phone extensions for various departments, all of which appeared to have been squirreled away and never looked at again. Cora grabbed as many papers as she could and crumpled them into a big wad.

She glanced around and spotted a smoke detector clinging to the ceiling like a giant limpet. Flicking the lighter, she brought a small flame to life. She held the flame to the ball of paperwork. After a few seconds, it began to smolder and burn. She held the ball directly under the smoke detector and waited.

The papers grew hot in her hand, but still she waited. She was about to drop the ball of flaming paperwork when the fire alarms screamed to life.

Even though she had been expecting it, even though it was exactly what she wanted, Cora still jumped at the painfully loud noise. The movement sent flares of pain through her injured shoulder. The klaxon wail paused and then started up again. Gritting her teeth against the noise and the pain, she dumped the fireball into the open drawer. The fire guttered for a moment and then began to grow again.

Cora took a deep breath before steeling herself. She had to move fast now. They would be coming.

This was where it all started. This was the heart of the island, where Burt's team had first begun crafting the dinosaurs and Piltdowns. It was also the source of the digital corruption that ultimately destroyed the park before its opening. This was where Cora's expedition went off the rails when the Piltdowns ambushed them after they retrieved the data. So it seemed appropriate that this is where Cora would attempt to bring the whole thing crashing down.

One of the phones rang, scaring the bejesus out of her. She looked down at Perry's phone like it was a snake about to bite her. With reluctance, she hit the answer button and lifted it to her ear.

"Oh, thank God. Someone finally picked up. Mr. Crocker? Is that you? Please tell me you have Drake with you," a voice said.

"Who is this?" Cora asked.

"Schraeder. On the boat. I haven't been able to raise anyone on the security team. Who the hell is this? And what is that noise in the background?"

Cora remembered that name. He was the captain of the vessel that brought the expedition to the island. She hadn't interacted with him much, since she had spent most of the trip here in her cabin, avoiding Bainbridge.

"Cora. I'm with the RexNetics legal team. There's a fire alarm going off."

"You must be at the hotel? We can see the fire from here."

"No. I've started a new fire in the science center."

There was a moment of silence at the other end of the line. "Where's Mr. Drake? Please tell me he's with you."

"He's dead," Cora said.

The silence at the other end of the line was louder now. Cora kept moving, not wanting to waste any time "Christ. Alright, how many people are with you?"

"They're all dead. I'm the last one left. Listen, I'm kind of busy at the moment. Can you get in contact with the government of Papua New Guinea? Somebody should tell them that their helicopter is down. The crew didn't make it, unfortunately. I'd like to request that somebody come rescue me, though."

"We're already in contact with them. They've requested assistance from the Australians. Some elite SAS rescue unit is on its way. Special Forces-types. Where are you?"

"I'm at the island's science center."

"I'll tell them to come get you."

"No."

"Pardon?"

"Just tell them to stay on the beach. Don't go in the jungle. Don't go to the island's interior. If I don't come to them, it means I'm dead. They shouldn't come looking for me."

"Hold on. These guys are highly trained. They can take care of themselves. They'll be able to come get you. They expect to be there in a couple of hours."

"No. Tell them to stay on the beach. And tell them that if they see anything that isn't quite human, shoot it."

"What?"

"I need to go," Cora said. She ended the call.

She could hear screams in the distance. The Piltdowns were coming.

The phone rang again in Cora's hand, and she silenced it. She was going to need to be quiet for this. And she was going to need some luck. Maybe a lot of luck. And nobody was going to be able to help her. Not Schraeder on the boat. Not a Papua New Guinea rescue operation. Not Australian Special Forces.

Cora took a deep breath of stale air in the science center. It smelled like sweat and spoiled meat and musky animal funk. She didn't care. She probably only had so many breaths left in her life, and she was going to count each one as a victory.

She took off in a lop-sided run, doing her best to avoid jostling her shattered collarbone. In the distance, the screams of the Piltdowns grew louder now. There were still so many of them, and they were all traveling in one giant group. One of them by itself could probably take her in a brawl, even if she had full use of both her arms. The things were bred to put on a good show battling dinosaurs. She stood zero chance against the entire Piltdown population all swarming over her at once. And they almost certainly knew that.

Cora followed a sign on the wall. She recognized the set of doors where Drake had accidentally led everyone to the Biological Containment unit previously. She went in a different direction.

Her mistake before had been that she tried to think like someone else. She tried to think like Ryder or Nella when she tried to kill the Piltdown matriarch. And all she had to show for that was a broken collarbone.

She had to think like an intellectual property lawyer. An intellectual property lawyer intent on surviving an attack by dozens of genetically altered murder monkeys that all wanted to rend her limb-from-limb.

She could do that.

Cora dashed through a set of doors and into the science center's main atrium. The glass paneled walls and ceiling mostly showed unforgiving darkness outside, though she had a partial view of the park's hotel beginning to collapse in on itself as fire hollowed it out.

When she first saw this giant room, the floor had a few centimeters of standing water from broken glass panels. Now that the storm had struck the island, the water level had risen by several inches. More rainwater trickled in from above in little rivulets and waterfalls. Cora splashed gracelessly through the employee cafeteria, feeling terribly exposed in the wide-open space. The open mezzanines from the upper floors felt like they loomed over her.

When the RexNetics corporate staff and science team had been working here, the mess hall would have been quite pleasant. With the natural light and views from the atrium windows, it was probably a nice place to sit and sip on coffee during off-hours. Now, mold flourished on the walls. Dirt and filth clung to the unwashed windows. Tables and chairs had been knocked over, and the kitchen ransacked. Now that Cora knew what to look for, she even saw a few of the Piltdowns' cave painting-style handprints on the walls, blending in with the rot and ruin.

Cora looked up. Several more floors loomed above the cafeteria, with balconies and conference rooms. Since Primeval was its own little city-state and company town rolled into one, the corporate offices upstairs were the administrative heart of the park.

The auxiliary power system batteries that Cora knew so well were on the uppermost floor, where they could be most easily hooked up to the roof-mounted solar arrays. No doubt the Piltdowns had taken over those floors as well, but it looked like nobody was home up there, either. The entire Piltdown population had mustered out in their quest for food.

Cora gritted her teeth against the pain in her shoulder and placed Perry's phone down on one of the cafeteria tables, setting the first part of her plan into motion. She turned the volume all the way up on the phone.

Splashing through the water, she moved toward the grand stairway leading to the upper floors.

An elevator sat next to the stairs. Its doors had been pried open like a cooked clam, and some sort of ooze was dribbling down from the car's ceiling in long, phlegmy strands.

Cora scrambled up the damp stairs as quickly as she could, sodden carpet squishing under her feet. Her wet clothes clung to her and tried to restrict her movement. Her cold limbs felt as though they weighed four times more than usual. She felt less like she was pushing herself forward and more like a salmon compelled to swim upstream.

Mezzanine level.

Third floor.

Fourth floor.

Fifth floor. This was it. The highest she could go without climbing out onto the roof. She stood near the balcony, overlooking the flooded cafeteria. Brown water churned below her. It looked like the sort of spot where a widowed bride might hurl herself off a sea cliff on some dark and stormy night in a gothic novel. If that scene was somehow set within Cora's undergraduate business school building.

This floor was less opulent and more utilitarian than the others. Unlike most corporate offices, the executive staff stuck to the middle floors instead of the topmost levels. Here, those were for security and practical concerns. From up here, it was possible to see above much of the jungle canopy, giving an unobstructed view of the employee facilities, docking zone, and all the ugly little pragmatic necessities of running the island. From the middle floors, it was still possible to believe the illusion that the building was centered in the middle of an untouched Cretaceous jungle.

There was something ironic about the fact that the better people could see the whole of the island, the less appealing it was. All the important people stayed ensconced in their little dream factory, away from the view of the inaesthetic logistics that undergirded their reality. Out of sight, out of mind. All the better to focus on what really mattered, like market share and licensing opportunities.

This ended here and now. Cora's plan had a few simple steps. That didn't mean there wasn't room for error. She might still very well end up dead. But she had a chance.

Cora pulled out the satellite phone she'd taken from the BMP. She pulled up Perry's number from the contact list, and selected it. After a few seconds, Perry's phone began to loudly ring in the cafeteria below. Each bleat of the fire alarm drowned out the satellite phone, but it could be heard clearly in between the alarm's wails.

Downstairs, the howls and hoots of the Piltdowns grew louder. They'd heard the phone ringing as well. They hadn't realized she was upstairs yet, though they would eventually. If she hadn't wrapped things up by then, they would simply storm up the stairs and kill her.

The first tiny step of her plan already complete, Cora prepared herself for the second step. She immediately spotted the door she wanted, which was marked with a dozen bright yellow warnings. It hung in its frame by a single hinge, busted down long ago by the Piltdowns. Cora looked at the doorway to the auxiliary power room and smiled.

That's when the Tyrannotitan attacked.

TWENTY-ONE
CONFLICT RESOLUTION FOR THE RECENT LAW SCHOOL GRADUATE: HOW TO SURVIVE YOUR MOST DIFFICULT CLIENTS

There was a rumble from the elevator shaft. For a second, Cora thought that perhaps the elevator itself had been signaled somehow and was grinding upward. But no, she'd seen the pried-open elevator already on the ground floor. This was something different.

The closed, stainless-steel doors to the elevator shaft began to open as they were forced apart from the inside. Something meaty began to force its way out. It looked something like a gigantic pile of wet, rotting linen with teeth.

The Tyrannotitan was no longer pale to the point of translucence. Its body had turned a deep red, though Cora could still see dark, opaque lumps denoting its organs. And smaller lumps marking the half-digested bodies it had swallowed. The dark, reddish hue that had spread through the Tyrannotitan like ink was blood and liquified meat from its meals.

The inside of the elevator shaft was thick with mucus-like strands of goop. More slime covered the creature's body.

For the briefest instant, Cora pictured a caterpillar finding a secluded spot and spinning a chrysalis for itself. She didn't know if that was what the Tyrannotitan was doing. God, she hoped that wasn't what it was doing, because she never, ever wanted to know what such a thing would pupate into.

But even if that was what it had been doing in the elevator shaft, wrapping itself up in layers of its own snot like some vile mummy, it wasn't above one final snack. A bit of extra protein before it hatched into its next life stage, perhaps.

Cora took a step backward, toward the broken-down door to the auxiliary power system. She felt the jagged, swollen ache of fractured bone in her shoulder. She felt the cold, damp clothes sticking to her skin. She felt the exhaustion of a night spent fleeing and dodging death. It all felt like she was underwater, swimming toward the surface with more and more weights shackling onto her ankles as she kicked and clawed her way upward toward life.

Down below, she saw the Piltdowns surge into the flooded cafeteria, led by their matriarch. The Piltdowns cast about for a moment, looking for her. Then, the matriarch looked upward with her gruesome, half-rotten face, and she locked eyes with Cora for a split second.

Then, Cora spun on her heels away from the approaching Tyrannotitan and dashed into the backup power supply center.

***

The matriarch charged through the doors to the science center. She snarled at the flashing lights and the wailing siren, but she didn't immediately see any sign of the final not-macaque. She didn't see any threat at all, which only infuriated her further.

This was her den. *She* was in charge here. No one else. Nothing happened here without her express permission.

High up on a wall, a little red box flashed a light every few seconds. The ear-splitting noise seemed to be coming from the strange box. The matriarch grabbed a club from one of her underlings and heaved it with all her considerable might at the screaming box. The club missed, tearing a gaping hole through the drywall instead. The matriarch shrieked her displeasure.

Taking after her example, more Piltdowns tossed objects at the flashing siren box. A flying pipe wrench hit the box dead-on. The box fell silent.

But there were still more sirens deeper inside the facility. The matriarch stormed down a corridor toward the heart of the building, her retinue screaming war cries behind her. They smashed every siren box they came across along the way. At the end of the corridor, the matriarch saw the glow of fire from the room where her troupe had killed the first not-macaque earlier. A desk was fully engulfed in flames, and the fire was beginning to spread across the carpet.

The matriarch screamed. There was rage but also fear in that scream. She had put on a show of courage outside the burning hotel, choosing to feast on the lizard beast relatively near the flames. The fire had frightened her, but by showing indifference to it there, she had gained even more esteem among the tribe.

That was there, though. This was her home. Fire here could drive the whole tribe out into the jungle. It could destroy their meager food stores and their shelter against the lizard beasts.

This was the doing of the final not-macaque. She had snuck in here when the tribe was preoccupied. She had invaded their home and caused this trouble. The matriarch should have killed the not-macaque earlier. She should have sent a group to track her down and drag her in front of the tribe. She should have stood atop the carcass of the slain lizard beast and brought her axe down on the final not-macaque's head in a crushing blow, cementing her ultimate authority over the island. Instead, she looked weak for allowing this to happen.

Suddenly, the matriarch heard a noise. It was similar to the sirens but different. Quieter. More subtle. Another alarm box was smashed, and she heard it more clearly. Her head whipped around, zeroing in on the noise.

It was coming from the atrium and cafeteria. That must be where the not-macaque was hiding. The matriarch bellowed her anger and took off toward the main atrium. She bounded down the half-flight of stairs that separated the atrium from the pathways to other parts of the science center, her feet splashing into several inches of brown water. The rest of her tribe followed her, also shrieking and howling, following her lead.

Rainwater dribbled down onto them from the cracked and broken skylights. Leaves and branches lashed the intact windows as a gust of wind stirred the jungle.

The matriarch did not immediately see the final not-macaque, but she could still hear that strange noise, almost like the chirruping of some large insect. The noise cut out and then started again. After a moment of searching, the matriarch found the source of the noise.

It was a peculiar little plastic box sitting on a table. The box had a series of buttons, each one with a little symbol. The box had a screen that emitted faint light, and a nubby antenna sticking out one end.

The satellite phone rang again.

The matriarch smashed it against the table. Bits of jagged plastic buried themselves in her palm, but she barely even felt the ragged cuts. She simply licked the first gush of blood off her hand.

The phone did not ring again. The matriarch swept its scattered components off the table and into the filthy water.

This was some sort of trick. The not-macaque had made the strange little box ring and brought her and the entire tribe here, ready for blood. But the not-macaque was not here. The matriarch felt hot, simian rage boil inside her. She did not like being tricked. She did not like finding her home disturbed. She did not like looking like a fool in front of the entire tribe.

Suddenly, one of the other Piltdowns hooted and pointed upward. The matriarch followed her tribemate's gaze and saw the not-macaque high above, standing near the balcony on the very highest level of the building. The Piltdowns only rarely bothered to go up there because most of the rooms contained only metal boxes and wires and nothing good to eat.

The matriarch started forward, ready to charge up the stairs to the top level when she saw something else up there with the not-macaque. It was the creature from the sealed room, the beast the not-macaques had released earlier.

The matriarch hissed. The creature smelled wrong. It looked wrong. She instinctually feared it, which made her want to kill it. Its presence here was effectively a direct challenge to her leadership. If she could not drive it away, the building would not be safe to inhabit any longer. But the creature had already eaten several macaques today, ignoring spears and blows.

She started toward the staircase, ready to do battle with the wretched thing, but her feet stopped in the water before she'd made it more than a few steps. The tribe's strength lay in its numbers. Those numbers had been diminished in their battles with the not-macaques and the lizard beasts. Not that the matriarch would have allowed that to stop her. But she realized that there would be no room to fight at the top of the staircase. Only a few Piltdowns would be able to stand on the balcony if the creature chose to turn and confront them. That would leave most of the tribe standing impotently on the stairs, unable to even slash and stab at the thing.

They had taken down the lizard beast near the hotel with their numbers and won. But the idea of facing this thing with only a handful of her troupe at a time was much less appealing.

But perhaps she could still turn the situation to her advantage.

Instead of charging up the staircase and into pitched battle, the matriarch stopped and watched, her eyes glaring from beneath her jutting brow. She paced in the water, unable to contain her agitation, but she proceeded no further.

The other Piltdowns lurched to a stop, and the matriarch forced herself to stand patiently. She heard some chuffs and grumbles, but she stood firm. If she feigned a calm she did not feel, she would look strong to the tribe. The mass of bodies around her shifted and swayed with uneasy, angry energy, but they held their ground.

Let the not-macaque and the creature kill each other. There was no escape from the upper balcony, other than a plunge down to the flooded cafeteria floor. She would allow her opponents to fight, and then she would swoop in with her numbers and slaughter the winner.

She assumed the creature would win, thanks to its mass and its voracious appetite. And then, the stupid not-macaque sealed her own fate. She retreated into one of the rooms that the matriarch knew for a fact had no other exit. The creature would no doubt corner her and devour her.

A pity. The matriarch still would have liked to feast on the final not-macaque's tender flesh. Maybe she could cut the not-macaque's remains out of the creature's foul belly and find some meat that was still edible once her tribe dealt with the remaining threat.

The matriarch sat back and waited for the inevitable.

***

Cora ducked through the doorway to the auxiliary power room. Her plan had worked perfectly. Right up until it hadn't.

Triggering the fire alarms had brought the Piltdowns running back to the science center to see what had caused the commotion. And then, dialing Perry's satellite phone had drawn them to the cafeteria. All according to plan.

But plans, in the battlefield or in the courtroom, never survived first contact with the enemy. If the universe had been trying to teach Cora anything since she arrived on this island, it was to not put too much faith in fragile little things like plans.

Because now, she was all out of plans. She patted down her wet clothes, as if she might magically find a flamethrower on her person that she had somehow forgotten about. Her broken collarbone was stiffening up, rendering her right arm mostly useless. The pain was a constant pulse now, one that emanated out of her shoulder in time with her heartbeat and made her want to curl up and lay very still somewhere. Maybe after throwing up from sheer discomfort, just for good measure.

Her fingers touched something. The handle of the kitchen knife she'd taken from Burt's little kitchenette.

She pulled it free from her belt like she was unsheathing a sword and about to charge headlong into battle. She looked at the blade. It was a few inches long and read "Made in Costa Rica" in tiny print near the handle.

She looked at the Tyrannotitan. The monstrosity was the size of a city bus, engorged with the blood of its victims, had a gaping maw like a combination lamprey jaw and butthole, and it was in the process of squeezing its boneless body through the doorway like melted candle wax through a keyhole.

Cora looked around for something, anything she could use. The room smelled like hot electronics and mildew. Fluorescent lights buzzed overhead like angry insects. And evenly spaced around the room were sixteen roughly refrigerator-sized battery units, each a few feet apart from the others in a grid. The batteries looked a bit like a miniature model of some futuristic downtown district composed of identical skyscrapers. Each one had enough juice to run a whole office building, if the software running their power distribution wasn't hopelessly corrupted.

The fluorescent lights cut out for a second, casting the room into total darkness as the power temporarily failed again. There was a click and a loud hum as the auxiliary power system booted itself up again, and the lights came back on.

She'd built her whole plan around the auxiliary power system because she knew it so well. Cora looked at the knife in her hand. She looked at the monster forcing its way into the room with her, taking up more and more space like a slowly inflating balloon.

Could she somehow kill the thing with a kitchen knife? She didn't think so. That left running away. Could she escape from the power room? Maybe. She'd have to lure the monster to the far side of the room and then dash back through the doorway before it could lurch around and get her. The one advantage she had in here was that she was a lot smaller and nimbler. She felt like a mouse in a terrarium with a snake. She could play keep away for a while, but her time was limited.

Then what? She could run, but there was nowhere to go except downstairs, toward the Piltdowns. There were dozens of them, and she wouldn't stand a chance against even one of them in her current state. Just staying up on the balcony wasn't an option, either. The Tyrannotitan would wriggle its way out again, and with more open space on the balcony, it probably could twist around and snatch her up.

She looked at the Tyrannotitan. It extruded more of itself into the room with a sound like mud flowing down a pipe. Its teeth snapped at her in a spasmodic frenzy. Cora didn't want to be chewed to red rags by those jagged teeth. She didn't want to be hacked to bits by the Piltdown matriarch's fire axe. So what did that leave her?

She could slit her own throat with the kitchen knife, but she wasn't even sure she'd finish bleeding out before the Tyrannotitan forced itself the rest of the way into the power room.

That did give her an idea, though. She looked at the Tyrannotitan. This was the first really good look she'd gotten at the thing.

It didn't have eyes. Not exactly, anyway. It had a set of dark spots near the front of its head, not much more than jelly of a different consistency than the rest of its body. Burt had said it had some photo-sensitive eye spots, able to detect light and movement.

But the Tyrannotitan had emerged from the elevator without being able to see her. Back in the Biological Containment vault, it hadn't immediately realized that people were in there with it. No, this thing wasn't hunting her with its eyesight. It was hunting her through some combination of sound and smell.

She held the knife and drew it across the palm of her right hand. The skin sliced open, and blood instantly welled up. Cora hissed in pain and pressed her palm up against the nearest battery unit, leaving a red handprint like those the Piltdowns had smeared across the walls in so many locations. She smeared her hand around, leaving a pool of blood dribbling down the side of the battery's case.

The Tyrannotitan pushed the widest part of its mass through the door frame with a noise that might be used in a cartoon demonstrating the efficacy of an anti-constipation drug. It immediately began to wriggle its way deeper into the room, unimpeded now, leaving a snail trail of slime behind it. Snapping and gurgling, the miscreated dinosaur zeroed in on Cora's position.

She slid around the back of the huge battery, already working on the next step in her new impromptu plan. She unplugged a thick electrical cable from the wall and gathered up the long length cord from a now inactive control panel. She used the knife and sawed off the thick cable at the base of the panel. The cable was a dense rope of smaller cables, and she had to kneel down and stomp on the knife with her full body weight to cut through. The blade dented, but it managed to slice through with some effort.

Reeling in a long length of cord, she turned around just in time to see the Tyrannotitan fitting its mouth around the blood-smeared battery unit. The battery shuddered, its plastic and metal frame buckling in places. But after a moment of effort, the Tyrannotitan managed to uproot the battery from its mounts on the floor, swallowing it like an eel gulping down a fish.

The batteries were all separate, each one wired into the grid as an individual unit rather than lashed together like a dogsled team. That was so engineers could pop the batteries in and out in case anything went wrong with a single individual unit, meaning they wouldn't bring the whole power system down if a single component fried out. Smart engineering. Placed a premium on park safety. Didn't matter for shit when every operating system in the park was infected with malware from bootleg dinosaur DNA. It was also extremely inconvenient to the plan Cora was now developing.

She took her makeshift rope and scurried to the far end of the room. She tied one end of the cable snuggly around another battery unit, and then smeared blood all over that battery as well. The surface of the battery casing was unpleasantly hot from the park repeatedly stopping and restarting the auxiliary power system again and again. The blood gave off an unpleasant odor, like someone trying and spectacularly failing to cook bratwurst. She banged on the case of the battery with the hilt of the knife.

The Tyrannotitan immediately shifted to face her and moved with surprising swiftness now that it was free from the doorframe. Cora closed her bloody palm into a fist, even though the pain made her squeal just a little, doing her best to decrease the smell of blood coming from her own direction. Then, she looped around the edge of the room, weaving between a couple of the batteries to make it harder for the Tyrannotitan to twist around and grab her in its maw.

The coil of cable started to unspool in her hands as the Tyrannotitan choked down the battery she'd marked with her blood a few moments before. With the cable roped around that battery, it was like watching a fishing reel twitch as a bass swallowed the bait, hook and all. She looped the cable around another of the batteries and then covered that one with as much blood as she could, too.

She cursed that she wasn't bleeding more heavily. She smacked the battery unit with her palm a couple of times. Pain shot up her arm and rattled her broken collarbone. More blood oozed from her cut hand. Cora shouted, a harsh, wordless cry of defiance and desperation and hurt. The Tyrannotitan shifted its attention in her direction.

The lights went out in the science center again, faster than Cora would have otherwise expected. With the Tyrannotitan popping batteries loose, the power system was struggling to compensate for the last power reserves. Not only was the software bugged to hell and gone with malware, but it had fewer resources to pull from.

The darkness lasted longer than the previous blackouts, filled only with the muffled noises of the Tyrannotitan slithering closer. For a moment, Cora didn't think the power would come back on. But then there was a strained hum, and the lights flickered to life with considerable reluctance.

Cora decided that she couldn't mark any more of the batteries without risking plunging the whole system into irreversible power failure. She took her long length of heavy-duty cable and began working her way back toward the door, now clear of the Tyrannotitan's mollusk-like rear half.

The Tyrannotitan latched onto the third battery, its teeth gripping the sides of the frame and pulling it backward so the teeth further back in its throat could latch on and guide the object inward. It was like watching a black hole eat a planet.

Cora looked away from the revolting sight and eyed the length of cable in her hands. The makeshift rope was slowly unspooling in her grip as the Tyrannotitan engulfed the third and final battery she'd marked.

Surely the Tyrannotitan would eventually regurgitate the inedible batteries, but until then, it would no doubt continue to work its way up the cable like someone slurping up the world's longest strand of spaghetti.

Cora looked back in the direction of the elevator. The amount of cable she had to work with wasn't long enough.

She couldn't make the cable any longer, but she didn't need to. Not if she brought the Tyrannotitan to her.

Grimacing, Cora brought her hand up to her face and rubbed her own blood on her cheeks and forehead. It was both warpaint and a way to make herself more enticing. She banged her bent and useless knife on the balcony railing like she was about to announce a toast.

She glanced down and saw the Piltdowns waiting for her. The matriarch bared her long, yellow teeth. The other Piltdowns hooted and snarled. Cora felt like she'd climbed onto a tall building ledge and was looking down at the crowd assembled below. Except this crowd would storm up here and bludgeon her to death if she didn't jump. The Piltdowns were strong. They were vicious. But they weren't dumb. They were waiting to see the results of the battle up here before they attacked.

The Tyrannotitan twisted around, shifting its great, slimy bulk. Without hesitation, it began oozing toward her. The swallowed batteries inside its body distorted its shape, like an overly full tent. But they didn't slow it down.

Cora backed up, holding the end of her cable like a leash. The other end of the cable led into the Tyrannotitan's gaping maw. She took several more steps out onto the balcony, leading the Tyrannotitan forward like she was taking a blind Cocker Spaniel for a walk, if Cocker Spaniels were the length of an amphibious assault vehicle and full of half-digested body parts.

The Tyrannotitan shifted and squeezed and wriggled, managing to haul its bulk back out the doorway, even with the batteries inside its body. Cora knew this was her one chance. She'd been able to outmaneuver the Tyrannotitan inside the battery room, using the battery frames and her blood to confuse and evade it. Here, on the open balcony, she didn't think she could double back again. She couldn't just lead the monster on a strange little parade until the cavalry arrived. She had one chance at this.

The power went out again. Cora cursed. She took a blind step backward. And another, aware that somewhere behind her the open elevator shaft yawned open. She did not want to step out into open air and plunge five stories straight down to the flooded first floor. A few inches of water would not cushion her fall in the least. But she didn't dare stop moving backwards, either. Better the fall than inadvertently ending up caught in the concentric rings of teeth that made up the Tyrannotitan's mouth and throat.

With a groan like a wounded elephant preparing to breathe its last, the power wheezed back on. The Tyrannotitan had three of the park's sixteen batteries inside it, almost a quarter of the total reserve power needed to operate Primeval on an emergency basis. Perhaps that was too much for the other batteries to pick up the slack. Maybe angry red alerts were popping up on a screen somewhere in the park's main control room, announcing an imminent and cascading failure.

But she just needed the power to last for a few more minutes. She was going to use every little advantage she could, all the way to the hilt. And she would squeeze every last drop of juice this place could give her. Just a few more minutes. Just a few more minutes, baby.

She took one more step, and she reached the open elevator shaft where the Tyrannotitan had been nesting. It was full of slime and rancid goop. At the bottom, she saw the elevator itself.

Cora took the sturdy electrical cable in her hands and reached out into the shaft, plunging her hands into some thick, mucus-like slime. She grabbed the elevator cable buried within and seized it. She tied the line she'd been holding to the elevator cable.

Then, she hit the call button.

There was a ding. A little green light popped to life next to the open elevator door. The elevator below began to rise. And as it did so, the cable began to spool through the elevator's pulley mechanism. And that began to reel in the cable attached to the batteries inside the Tyrannotitan. The cable instantly went taut.

The creature immediately and dimly realized that something was wrong as it began to be pulled forward by the batteries in its guts. It struggled, not wanting or maybe unable to disgorge the perceived food in its belly, but the elevator mechanism hauled it steadily forward.

Cora stepped out of the way as the Tyrannotitan slid past her, its whole body scrunched up as it tried to arrest its forward movement. The cables in the shaft groaned against the weight, but they didn't snap. And the elevator didn't cease its upward movement.

The Tyrannotitan came to the edge of the gap and teetered there for a second. For the briefest instant, Cora thought the cable would pull the batteries free from its mouth like some macabre claw machine game.

But then, the Tyrannotitan's front end lurched over the edge and began to rise upward like a fish on a hook being drawn to the surface. It didn't have far to go. They were already on the highest floor. The pulley mechanism was at the top of the elevator shaft.

There was a sound like someone ripping wet denim as the Tyrannotitan met the hydraulic sheave, which gamely tried to pull the monster through the narrow gap. Cora saw chunks of meat and teeth begin to rain down the shaft from below.

Then, something gave way. There was a loud, fleshy noise, and the whole Tyrannotitan tore free from the mechanism and shot downward and smashed into the roof of the elevator. The cable snapped with a horrible twang, and the Tyrannotitan and partially crushed elevator fell down the rest of the shaft in a tangled mass of flesh and metal.

***

For the first time since she had assumed power in the tribe, the matriarch felt unsure about what to do.

To her enormous surprise, the final not-macaque had reemerged from the room high above. And now she was leading the monstrosity from the sealed room behind her. There was still a chance the monster would manage to grab the not-macaque, but the matriarch could tell something was amiss.

The not-macaque had some sort of cord that led to the monster. Led *inside* the monster, to some bulky, geometric shapes inside its body.

Something was wrong. She didn't know what, but the matriarch suddenly knew she should not have waited. Numbers be damned, she should have sent her entire troupe charging up the stairs at the first opportunity, overwhelming everything before them in due course.

High above, the not-macaque reached into the elevator shaft and did something with the cable in her hands. There was a soft ding, and the monster following the not-macaque suddenly reacted violently and began sliding forward.

That was it. The not-macaque had done something. She had some other piece of mischief. It would be her last. The not-macaque had already caused far too many problems. She could not be allowed to escape again.

The matriarch shrieked a battle cry and raised her axe. The other Piltdowns took up the cry as the matriarch began splashing through the shallow water toward the stairs. Her bare feet kicked up explosions of filthy brown water with each loping step.

Up above, she heard a terrible noise. Like overripe fruit falling from a tree and splattering against the ground, except the noise seemed to go on and on. Then, suddenly, mercifully, the sound cut out.

The matriarch sensed rather than saw something heavy moving through the air, and then there was a spectacular, meaty sound from the base of the elevator shaft. And the sound of metal and plastic buckling and fragmenting.

The huge batteries ruptured, as did the Tyrannotitan's body, when they hit the ground five floors down. The enormous amount of stored energy shot out like a lightning bolt, conducting through the water as if someone had dropped the world's biggest toaster into a bathtub. Cora's plan culminated in a brief but spectacular surge that shot through the entirety of the flooded cafeteria and into the bodies of the charging Piltdowns.

There was a huge burst of blue-white light, and then the water was alive with frying, sizzling, arcing pain. The matriarch felt all her muscles go rigid. She felt her jaw clench so tight her teeth fractured to jagged stubs. She felt her organs explode one after the other, splitting open like squashed beetles. She felt arcs of electricity shoot out of her with such force that they blew chunks of meat away with them. And for the first time in her entire life, her deadened nerves felt pain.

She had just enough time to marvel at the sensation before her heart popped like an overlarge tick, and everything faded to black.

***

Cora hissed again as the Australian medic stitched up her palm.

"Sorry," he muttered.

Cora merely grunted in response before turning her attention back to the SAS man and the couple of Papua New Guinea soldiers flanking him.

"Ma'am, we *have* to do a search and rescue operation. It's not an option to leave without confirming that there are no other survivors."

"I'm confirming it for you. No one else made it. Get your men back here. Now." Cora was exhausted, but there was steel in her voice.

The Australian SAS leader scowled at her, but she didn't flinch. She scowled right back at him. Worse things had stared her down in the last twenty-four hours.

Dawn washed over the island, with only a few clouds in the sky to mark that last night's storm had ever happened. At a glance, it looked like there was an additional, single dark storm cloud hovering directly over the island, but it was merely a huge plume of smoke from where the park's hotel had burned to the ground. A smaller fire was still chewing through the science center, though it had never gained the same foothold in the building without helicopter fuel to sustain it.

"Ma'am, we'll debrief you momentarily, but for now I have to ask you to stop impeding an official military operation. We have this under control," the SAS man said.

Somewhere on the island, there was a burst of gunfire followed by the distant roar of a Suchomimus. More gunfire crackled.

The SAS captain's radio crackled.

"It got Martin! Holy shit! Run!"

Cora sighed as the SAS man turned his attention away from her and began firing off orders and questions into his radio. More gunfire crackled from somewhere on the island.

A few hours later, the small military flotilla began steaming away from the island, minus three of the soldiers it set out with. Cora had been allowed to make a single phone call before the debriefing began. She used it to call RexNetics headquarters to announce that she was resigning, effective immediately.

That would give the legal team back home about five minutes of warning that she was no longer bound by the rules of attorney-client privilege. She turned to the shaken Australian military lieutenant standing on the deck of the ship with her. She wouldn't talk to the SAS captain. She wanted to speak to someone who had set foot on the island and seen the creatures still living there. The man's eyes were haunted. Three of his men were still back there, their bodies deemed irrecoverable.

With all her legal duties to RexNetics satisfied, Cora began her first recitation of the facts. She knew there would be many more in the near future, to many different authorities and hostile defense attorneys.

And Cora, who had dedicated her career to protecting trade secrets and securing exclusive patents, would be happy to give them every last detail.

TWENTY-TWO
EVIDENCE 101: DOCUMENTATION, VERIFICATION, AND ADMISSIBILITY

Dear Cora,

We hope this email finds you well. However, we must express grave concerns with your activities since your departure from the RexNetics Family.

We feel it is our obligation to remind you of the rights and duties which are still attached to you from your employment here at RexNetics. You signed a variety of nondisclosure agreements upon accepting employment within our legal department. Please see the attached files showing your signature on these agreements.

Any violation of these agreements will be taken with the utmost seriousness by our legal department. While we can sympathize that you experienced certain hardships in the course of your duties to this company, any previous agreements are BINDING.

Information related to RexNetics and/or Primeval's trade secrets or their intellectual property is privileged. Under no circumstances should this information be shared with anyone outside RexNetics.

Please respond to this email immediately to avoid preemptive legal actions being taken against you. You may be eligible to be rehired by RexNetics at a substantial increase in salary and benefits, pending a review of your post-employment actions.

Sincerely,

Randall Black,

Acting head of RexNetics Legal Dept.

Cora printed the email out, grabbed it off the tray, and walked down the hallway to her boss's office. She knocked on the door to announce her presence.

Assistant Attorney General Beatrice Alvarez looked up from a binder big enough to serve as a desk for Santa's elves. Beatrice was old school and liked to annotate all her trial binders herself. She looked up and then went back to scribbling something on a sticky note, which she then placed on one of the papers in the binder.

"Hey, Cora. What's up?"

"Got another email from RexNetics." Cora held the printout up.

"May I?" Beatrice took the paper and scanned through it. Her eyes marched back and forth for a few seconds. Then she snorted. "Please respond to this email immediately to avoid preemptive legal action being taken against you. You may be eligible to be rehired by RexNetics at a substantial increase in salary and benefits," she read aloud.

"Not very subtle, are they?" Cora asked.

"Might as well threaten to send some guys with a baseball bat over to have a conversation with your kneecaps. Doesn't build on the case itself, but I'd argue it says something about awareness of wrongdoing. Do you need this back?" Beatrice held the paper up.

"Nah, feel free to add it to the folder," Cora said.

Randall Black, the acting head of the RexNetics legal department, did not seem to appreciate that the contracts Cora had signed were void if they regarded criminal activity. Randall Black might not even fully know the depths of the criminal activity RexNetics had been involved with, given that Drake and Bainbridge were dead and couldn't inform him. But once that came out, there was no stopping the rest of the truth from coming tumbling out.

"How's that case with the junior mad scientist team going?"

Cora sighed. "I'm still getting used to the juvenile law aspects. That keeps tripping me up."

"Oh, right. The younger one is only seventeen. Go have a talk with Greg. He's the brains around here when it comes to juvenile prosecution. He'll get you set up."

Cora nodded. This was her first big case since being hired by the Department of Justice's new genetic crimes team. A pair of bullied high school students had planned to wreak revenge upon their tormentors and teachers. Only these two didn't go and try to get their hands on an assault rifle with the intention of going out in a blaze of glory. Instead, they used a simple CRISPR kit to modify a bit of *E. coli* into a super doomsday bacteria and managed to smuggle it into the cafeteria for distribution. In the end, they only succeeded in giving themselves, about fifty other students, and a PE teacher an apocalyptic case of the flying Hershey squirts, but the genetic crimes team was still taking the incident seriously.

The rest of her caseload wasn't as alarming, but it was still an emerging area of the law. A Montana sheep rancher who was going broke selling wool and lamb chops, so he used a bit of genetic material to impregnate all his ewes with hybridized Uralic Mountain Bighorns, which he then released and charged hunters to shoot on his property. Hundreds of hybridized sheep were now loose in the area and wreaking absolute havoc on the local environment by consuming vast swaths of native flora. Cora was still trying to figure out what, if any, wildlife laws that violated. There was the fellow who had genetically manipulated poppies to create a defoliant-resistant breed, which he had then sold to a criminal syndicate in Central Asia planning to use them to grow a buttload of opium.

And then there was RexNetics. Cora wasn't personally prosecuting them, since she would also be a witness when the case was finally brought. But the next few years of Beatrice Alvarez's life were going to be consumed pursuing various civil and criminal penalties against Cora's former employer.

Cora left Beatrice to her work and went back to her office to archive the email RexNetics had sent her. It would need to be preserved.

She sat down at her desk, and her chair gave a little groan. The DOJ office wasn't much. Compared to her previous office at RexNetics, it was downright shabby. Her pay was a lot less, too. And every time they spoke, Cora's mom all but begged her to find a new corporate law job with an appropriately flashy title.

But Cora was staying right here. The genetic crime team needed attorneys who understood the science behind such complex cases. Finding attorneys who could grasp the problem and then translate it into laymen's terms for judges and juries was essential.

DOJ already had teams for complex computer crimes and financial crimes. It was painful enough getting a nearly retired judge to understand cutting edge technical issues without a defense attorney trying to muddy the waters. It was equally difficult to find a jury that could sit through six hundred pages of spreadsheets in a financial fraud case and glean any bit of information from the numbers. Those attorneys did as much teaching as they did persuading.

But the genetics crime division was still painfully understaffed. It was hard to find people with both the scientific and legal background required for the job. So the Department of Justice had jumped at the chance when Cora applied, even if they had to set up some safeguards to make sure she wouldn't be inappropriately involved with the RexNetics case that was already brewing.

Please respond to this email immediately to avoid preemptive legal actions being taken against you. You may be eligible to be rehired by RexNetics at a substantial increase in salary and benefits, pending a review of your post-employment actions.

Cora thought about the email RexNetics had sent her and smiled. She'd known Randall Black, if only vaguely. He'd sent her a few emails trying to either buy her silence or lure her back.

But he'd made a critical mistake each time. He'd sent those emails to the wrong person. He'd sent them to the old Cora, the junior associate he'd known back at the office. But it was the new Cora who had received those emails. A different Cora who had studied an entirely different type of law in the time since she last saw Randall.

Cora sat alone in her office and gave a predatory smile as she logged and archived the email so it could be used as evidence later. Yes, gone was the old Cora. Gone was the timidity. Gone was the hesitation. She was in charge of her own life now, maybe for the first time.

Because since she went to that island, Cora had learned a new type of law. Not criminal law, which she and Randall would have both sat through in law school. No, this was something Randall had never experienced or practiced before: the law of the jungle.

For Burt. For Florence. For everyone else who lost their lives on that miserable island. For herself, and the nightmares that sent her bolt upright in sweat-soaked sheets. She would fight tooth and claw, she would gut the company she once worked for, and she would win.

Cora added the email to the growing binder of evidence on her desk and got to work.

ABOUT THE AUTHOR

Jonah Buck wanted to study eldritch tomes and commune with pale, semi-human creatures that flit across the sunless landscape to terrorize the living, so he became an attorney in Oregon. His personal interests include history, professional stage magic, paleontology, and exotic poultry. Despite these personal flaws, he is happily married. He is the author of several novels, including *Carrion Safari* and *Substratum*.

CHECK OUT OTHER GREAT DINOSAUR BOOKS

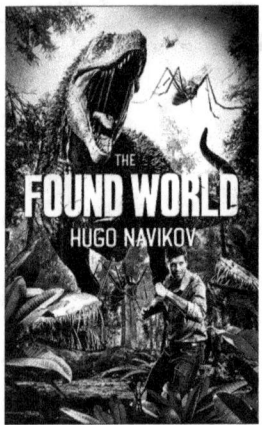

THE FOUND WORLD
by Hugo Navikov

A powerful global cabal wants adventurer Brett Russell to retrieve a superweapon stolen by the scientist who built it. To entice him to travel underneath one of the most dangerous volcanoes on Earth to find the scientist, this shadowy organization will pay him the only thing he cares about: information that will allow him to avenge his family's murder.

But before he can get paid, he and his team must enter an underground hellscape of killer plants, giant insects, terrifying dinosaurs, and an army of other predators never previously seen by man.

At the end of this journey awaits a revelation that could alter the fate of mankind ... if they can make it back from this horrifying found world.

HOUSE OF THE GODS
by Davide Mana

High above the steamy jungle of the Amazon basin, rise the flat plateaus known as the Tepui, the House of the Gods. Lost worlds of unknown beauty, a naturalistic wonder, each an ecology onto itself, shunned by the local tribes for centuries. The House of the Gods was not made for men.

But now, the crew and passengers of a small charter plane are about to find what was hidden for sixty million years.

Lost on an island in the clouds 10.000 feet above the jungle, surrounded by dinosaurs, hunted by mysterious mercenaries, the survivors of Sligo Air flight 001 will quickly learn the only rule of life on Earth: Extinction.

SEVEREDPRESS

CHECK OUT OTHER GREAT DINOSAUR BOOKS

PRIMORDIA
by **Greig Beck**

Ben Cartwright, former soldier, home to mourn the loss of his father stumbles upon cryptic letters from the past between the author, Arthur Conan Doyle and his great, great grandfather who vanished while exploring the Amazon jungle in 1908.

Amazingly, these letters lead Ben to believe that his ancestor's expedition was the basis for Doyle's fantastical tale of a lost world inhabited by long extinct creatures. As Ben digs some more he finds clues to the whereabouts of a lost notebook that might contain a map to a place that is home to creatures that would rewrite everything known about history, biology and evolution.

But other parties now know about the notebook, and will do anything to obtain it. For Ben and his friends, it becomes a race against time and against ruthless rivals.

In the remotest corners of Venezuela, along winding river trails known only to lost tribes, and through near impenetrable jungle, Ben and his novice team find a forbidden place more terrifying and dangerous than anything they could ever have imagined.

PANGAEA EXILES
by **Jeff Brackett**

Tried and convicted for his crimes, Sean Barrow is sent into temporal exile—banished to a time so far before recorded history that there is no chance that he, or any other criminal sent back, has any chance of altering history.

Now Sean must find a way to survive more than 200 million years in the past, in a world populated by monstrous creatures that would rend him limb from limb if they got the chance. And that's just his fellow prisoners.

The dinosaurs are almost as bad.

Check out other great

Dinosaur Thrillers!

Rick Poldark

PRIMORDIAL ISLAND

During a violent storm Flight 207 crash-lands in the South China Sea. Poseidon Tech tracks the wreckage to an uncharted island and dispatches a curious salvage team—two paleontologists, a biologist specializing in animal behavior, a botanist, and a nefarious big game hunter. Escorted by a heavily-armed security team, they cut through the jungle and quickly find themselves in a terrifying fight for survival, running a deadly gauntlet of prehistoric predators. In their quest for the flight recorder, they uncover the mystery of the island's existence and discover an arcane force that will tip the balance of power on the primordial island. Things are not as they seem as they race against time to survive the island's man-eating dinosaurs and make it back home in one piece.

P.K. Hawkins

SUBTERRANEA

Fall, 1985. The small town of Kettle Hollow barely shows up on any maps, and four young friends are used to taking their BMX's outside of town in an effort to find anything interesting to do. But tonight their tendency to go off by themselves may have saved them, and also forced them into the adventure of a lifetime. While they were away, Kettle Hollow has been locked down by the government, and a portal to another world has opened on Main Street. It's a world deep below the ground, a world where dinosaurs roam free, where giant plants and mutant insects hunt for prey. It's also a world where all their family and friends have been kidnapped for sinister purposes. Now, with time running out before the portal closes, the four friends must brave the unknown to save their loved ones. Time is running out, and in the darkened tunnels of Subterranea, something is hunting them.

www.ingramcontent.com/pod-product-compliance
Lightning Source LLC
Chambersburg PA
CBHW071512170626
46811CB00007B/2827